The Butterfly Effect Series book #2

THE CURSE

New York Times Bestseller of Ugly & Mistrust

Margaret McHeyzer

THE CURSE

ISBN-13: 978-0-9946460-6-4

Cover Design: Book Cover by Design
Editor: Debi Orton
Interior Formatting by Tami Norman, Integrity Formatting

www.facebook.com/authormargaretmcheyzer
email: hit_149@yahoo.com

The Butterfly Effect Series book #2

THE CURSE

New York Times Bestseller of Ugly & Mistrust

Margaret McHeyzer

CHAPTER 1

Jude

WITH MY PHONE in my hand, I pace the floor of my office. I stop every few steps and look down, waiting for *the* phone call to come.

"Where the hell is she?" I say aloud to no one.

Swallowing my anger, I run my hand through my hair, then down the back of my neck to squeeze the tense muscles. She's been gone for nearly two weeks, and no one knows what's happened to her.

Everyone I pay at the police department to keep me informed is failing miserably. I've called on every contact I have, and no one knows anything. It's like she's vanished.

The raid on my house was a damned ruse. It was orchestrated to get Lexi out and take her away from me. But I still have no idea who did this. One department is saying it's another department, and no one seems to know anything for sure.

Stopping in front of the desk, I swing my laptop around and play the security footage taken just before they took Lexi from me.

I watch as they come into my house, I watch how the men I paid to look after her froze and dropped to the floor instead of grabbing Alexa and hiding her in the safe room. They've all been fired, replaced with men I know will do exactly what they're supposed to do. Some are even mercenaries, hired for their comfort with extreme brute force.

Placing my phone on the desk, I flex my right hand and rub my bruised knuckles. Don, the guard at the door who let them enter my home, copped the worst from me. He let those animals inside my house. He let them take my girl without even questioning their fake credentials.

He had to be held responsible. He deserved what he got. Everyone knows what happens when you cross me.

I stretch my hand once more; the ache is a welcome. If I could, I'd go back and bludgeon his skull in again. But he's been disposed of, like the trash he is.

My eyes keep watching the screen, how they're handling my girl. They're careful not to touch her. They know. They have to know. They wouldn't go to all this trouble to get her if they didn't.

My head of security, Ronan, was with me when it all happened. He was remotely watching over the house, and the moment he saw it unfold and informed me, I left my meeting with the Sorrell family and took the jet straight back here. Hell, I even had the pilot put it down on the landing strip here, instead of at the hangar.

But we were six hours too late. Lexi was gone. Frank was beaten nearly to death, and most of my men were dumped in the middle of nowhere.

The van that took Lexi disappeared.

We can't find it, and we have no idea who has her.

Ronan's been searching and hacking into every security system he can to find her. I haven't slept since she's been gone. I'm on the very edge of losing my shit and about to start breaking down doors until I get the answers I need.

Ronan appears at my door, with his laptop in his hand. His eyes tell me I'm not going to like what he's found. She'd better be alive, or I'll find and torture every person who's been part of her death. Every person who's profited from, touched, or hurt her, *will die.*

"Ronan." I gesture for him to come into my office. "What have you got?"

He doesn't speak. He's usually the quiet type, the guy who gets things done and doesn't say much. I like him because he takes instruction well. He's been my right-hand man for as long as I've been in this business.

"I've found her." He types furiously on the screen, bringing up multiple images.

The one in the top left hand corner is of the van. Destroyed and crumpled. The front of the van is completely destroyed. It doesn't look like the driver could have survived the wreck.

"Who has her?" My eyes furiously search all the images on the screen.

Ronan is quiet.

Fury overtakes me.

Something inside me snaps. Ronan's silence is alarming and I'm ready to murder every fucker who's put their hands on her.

"Who has her?" I shout at Ronan.

"You're not going to like this . . ."

CHAPTER 2

Lexi

SITTING IN THIS room is driving me crazy. It's nothing like the room I had at Jude's. This is more like a cell. It's a small, dark room with a mattress on the floor and a bathroom with only a toilet, a shower, and a sink.

I get fed twice a day, and usually it's just thrown into the room in a brown paper bag. I'm treated worse than an animal.

I haven't met whoever instigated this yet. Apparently, I'm going to meet 'the boss' tomorrow. It's been seven days, and truthfully, I'm terrified.

The men who took me come in and watch me shower. One of them even started masturbating while I was washing myself. He made my stomach curdle with sickness. My skin crawls and my heart hasn't slowed from its frantic beating since I was brought here.

Every time I hear the locks being opened, my anxiety peaks to a point where I think I'm going to pass out. Dressed all in black, they usually enter, and look down at me before either throwing food on my mattress or ordering me around.

One guy's eyes – I'm sure he's the one who took me from the van – always roam all over me. They search me up and down, and he licks his lips like he wants to taste me. He scares me the most. His eyes are dark and beady, and his nose is crooked, like it's been broken many times before. He always comes in here holding a gun in his hand, leering at me.

Seriously, what does he think I'm going to do? Run away? I have no idea where I am, or even what state or city I'm in.

He's truly terrifying, the stuff my nightmares are made of.

As I sit on the mattress, I look down at my dirty clothes. I haven't changed them since they brought me here, because they haven't given me anything to change into. I don't dare ask for anything, because I really don't want to hear their voices. *They frighten me.*

The main guy, the scary one, has a deep, crackly voice. I can't help but imagine years of yelling and chain smoking contributed to the harshness of his voice.

While my eyes take in my surroundings, my heart breaks. Loneliness and sadness constrict my soul. A few short months ago I was a normal teenage girl, who had a best friend and a family.

Now I've been kidnapped, *twice,* and I'm sitting in a room where I'm sure many people have died before me. This place is nothing like Jude's. At least he allowed me some type of freedom. I had clean clothes, and food. And even though the experience was frightening at least I was able to sleep at night.

Here, I'm too scared to close my eyes, because I don't want to wake and find someone on top of me, taking something that doesn't belong to them.

The ache inside my body keeps reminding me of how good I had it with Jude. He may have stolen me, but he treated me well. Yes, I know he's a monster. But with me, he wasn't. And he didn't let anyone else handle me badly, either.

The door rattles, and I hear what sounds like chains, unlocking deadbolts, or whatever else they use to secure me in this dingy room. I crawl up to the top of the mattress, and when my back finds the wall, I know I can't go any further.

My throat constricts and my hands begin to shake. Praying, I keep my eyes toward the door.

When all the locks and bolts are unlatched, my eyes widen and terror washes over me. Is today the day I'm going to die? Or maybe today is the day that whomever comes into this room will do unspeakable, cruel things to me.

Either way, I'm frozen with fear. Panic shoots through my veins in the form of burning terror.

I feel myself stop breathing, holding it because I'm unsure of who's coming or what's going to happen.

The door opens slowly.

Saliva collects in my mouth, and my breathing is labored.

The door hits the wall behind it, coming to a complete stop.

Tears well in my eyes, and a sudden wave of bile quickly rises.

A man steps into the room.

My heart constricts with dread.

It's the man who scares me most.

Trembling, I try to move even further back. Everything inside me wants to scream, but I know it's not going to do any good. There's no one here who cares, or even wants to hear me. It would probably lead to my death.

But maybe death is my only way out. If I try to run, he'll shoot me. He holds his gun on me every time he enters the room, obviously to threaten me. He wants to intimidate me. *Guess what, asshat? It's working.* The gun is a warning that if I try to run, he'll kill me. Maybe, just maybe, it's worth trying.

Crazy ideas flood my brain. I can sacrifice myself. If they kill me, I'll no longer be stuck in this hellhole.

"Princess," he says while checking me out.

Vomit threatens to appear. His eyes are so scary and his dark features even more terrifying. "Wha-what do you want?" I manage to respond. My voice is tight with stress and worry. I try and curl into myself more, hoping the wall swallows me whole.

"The boss wants to meet you."

"I thought I was meeting him tomorrow?" I ask and quickly clamp my hand over my mouth. Terror spikes inside me, warning me.

"You are." The scary guy looks me over again, his eyes landing obviously on my breasts. My stomach roils with anticipated worry.

Stop looking at me like that.

"And what do you want me to do?" I look away from him, afraid of the answer.

Although I'm not looking directly at him, I notice the side of his mouth pull up into a smirk. He moves his free hand and grabs his crotch, scratching himself. "I have a few ideas." I gag on the bile. "Don't worry, princess, we're not allowed to touch you." Why should I believe him? Relief isn't instant. As a matter of fact, all that happens is the terror intensifies and manifests further. *"Yet,"* he adds in a cold tone. "You need to clean yourself up."

I feel like yelling at him and telling him I have nothing to change into. But I have a distinct feeling he isn't the type of guy to mouth off too. He's definitely not Jude. Instead I look down at my clothes, and struggle with what to do. I'll need to wash them and hang them over the shower head, hoping they'll dry by tomorrow.

"Don't worry, princess." God, I hate how he calls me princess. "I'll have some clothes delivered to you later on." He smirks again, the smile evil and malicious. "I'm sure you'll like what I bought for you."

My skin prickles and my palms sweat with panic and worry.

I opt to say nothing. He *does* have a gun.

He looks me over again, licking his lips. I know what that means, I'm not an idiot. He's going to enjoy himself with me when his 'boss' gives him the go-ahead. Tears pool in my eyes, but I hold them back.

He turns and exits the room, leaving me with the darkness of my own mind, in my own private nightmare.

When I hear the door locking, I finally breathe easy. It's stupid, because I'm locked in here on my own, but I feel as safe as I can be because of the locks on the door. I know it'll take them at least a minute to enter the room. And in that minute, I'm still safe. I'm safe from whatever horrors await me.

For now.

CHAPTER 3

I SLEPT WITH one eye open. With every creak, I jump up and prepare myself for whatever is about to happen.

Each time, my poor heart hammers so hard I think I'm going to die. Actually, I wish I would.

It's morning, or at least I assume it's the morning. The lack of windows or any other way to tell time has me confused. But, I'm hoping my instincts aren't completely off.

I sit on the mattress cross-legged and wait for whatever will happen. I'm meeting 'the boss' today, and I'm so scared of what that means for me.

The door begins to unlock, and I shuffle back away from it until my back hits the wall. It's a stupid reaction, because truthfully, this room isn't very big, and there are no windows. I can't try to run away. All I can do is wait.

Wait for them to open the door.

Wait for them to feed me.

Wait for them to decide what my future holds.

Wait.

My eyes are glued to the door. It opens and the scary guy walks in, holding his stupid gun and a paper bag. He throws the bag toward me, but it lands at the foot of the mattress. "There's food in there, and the clothes you have to wear for the boss."

I swallow hard, my throat feels like it's lined with sandpaper.

"Okay," I respond, still staring at him.

"You have an hour to eat and get ready."

How am I supposed to know how long an hour is? I have no clock. "Okay," is the safest answer I can muster. Anything else may result in my death.

Sighing as he closes and locks the door I entertain the alternative. *Death.* It could be a welcome change from what I'm going through now.

Dragging myself forward, I snatch the paper bag and open it. My stomach gurgles with hunger. They don't really feed me a lot, and even though I've only been here for just over a week, my pelvic bones have started sticking out more than normal.

Sitting on top of the clothes in the bag, is a wrapped muffin. My stomach rumbles with hunger again. Unwrapping it from the cling wrap, the sweetness of the aroma invades my nose. "Oh, my God," I breathe before inhaling the muffin in a matter of seconds.

Because I'm ravenous, the muffin doesn't even touch my hunger. "I needed that," I say to myself. I pick at the crumbs that have fallen on the bed. I know the bed's filthy, but I'm so damn hungry. Licking my finger, I try and stick the crumbs to the end of it then eat them. When there's nothing left, I stand and head into the bathroom. I figure I may as well wash myself and get ready to meet 'the boss.'

Once out of the shower and wrapped in the scratchy towel, I head over to look at what's in the brown paper bag. Balking, I lift the article of clothing with my pinkie. "You have *got* to be kidding me," I sigh. The clothing is quite intimate, and completely see-through.

It didn't cross my mind how small the brown paper bag was, or the fact that there was a black lacey object under the muffin. Shaking my head, I look back in the bag, and find the panties to match the lacey, transparent, baby-doll negligee. They can barely be called underwear.

It's a thong, a teeny-tiny thong that hides nothing. "I'm not wearing this," I say as I look at it with disgust. The problem is, I have nothing else to wear, because I only have the underwear I've been wearing, and I washed them in the sink last night.

"I'm not wearing this," I say again as I slump down on the bed, with only the towel protecting my exposed body.

Sneering at the stupid 'attire' I shake my head with contempt and revulsion. I cannot believe this is where I've ended up, in a small room with no window, being forced to perform for some guy known as 'the boss.' And I've ended up here not because of anything I did, but simply because of what I'm capable of.

Taking myself into the bathroom, I lean my hands on the sink and look down into the small basin. "This is bullshit. I need to get out of here," I say to myself. Looking up, I stare at myself in the mirror.

My left eye is half blue and half green. I still have no idea why it's changing color, or even if it's going to affect my right eye too.

"You have to do this, Lexi." Trying to convince myself sounds dumb. What's the worst thing to happen? They'll kill me and my life will be over. I don't think that's a bad alternative at all. At least I'll be free. And I won't have to dress up and parade myself in front of a group of sleazy men. I may not have seen them, but judging by the scary guy who comes in, and the lewd, insulting scraps of material I'm being made to wear, I can only imagine the horny men I'll be paraded before.

My own underwear hanging over the curtain rod of the shower catches my eye in the mirror. I turn and grab it, wringing it out the best I can. My panties are still wet, but at least they cover all my bits up. It's bad enough they'll see my breasts through the sheer material of the baby-doll lingerie. I refuse to allow them to see everything else too.

I take my towel off, completely aware of how likely it is there's a camera in here. Placing my undies in the towel, I try and wring them out more. The towel will hopefully help by absorbing some of the moisture out of them. I keep doing this until I know there's only a few minutes before the scary guy comes in to get me.

Unravelling the towel, I check my undies and find they're still damp, but at least they have dried out enough for me to wear.

Sliding my undies up my legs, I put on the stupid negligee. Looking at myself in the mirror I roll my eyes at my reflection. I look like I'm ready to have sex. Thankfully, my undies are black and match this stupid lingerie, and fortunately all my bits are covered up.

As I stand in the room, waiting for the door to unlock and open, I can't help but wonder what kind of lion's den I'm going to be led into. Or should I say, forced into.

My stomach knots in anticipation as I reluctantly wait for the scary guy to collect me.

My hands sweat and I rub them down the cheap, lacey material of the baby-doll.

My heart hammers inside my chest, while my breathing quickens until I'm sure it's quite audible.

"You can do this," I give myself a pep talk, encouraging myself to get on with it.

The unlocking of the first lock is deafening. It seems so loud it's piercing my ear drums. Not literally, but the tension in my body has ramped up to something I've never felt before. My shoulders are so tense it's painful, and my entire body responds by shaking.

The door finally opens, and the scary guy walks in, carrying his stupid gun. His beady, cold-blooded eyes take in my appearance. He arches a brow and bites on his bottom lip. "You look good," he says with his husky and scary-as-shit voice. His gaze lands on my breasts, and I want to cover myself up with my hands, but I know he's not the type of man who'd let me get away with it.

Swallowing hard, I try to lower the strain beating on my body.

His ogling travels further down to my underwear. He knots his brows together while his jaw jumps with obvious tension. "You're not wearing what I provided for you."

Shit, I knew this was going to happen. What do I say? What do I do? "They don't fit," I automatically respond. "They're too small."

His mouth twists into a smug smirk. He knows I'm lying, I can see it in his face. "Too small you say?" He scratches his chin with the nozzle of his gun.

God damn it. Why didn't I just wear the stupid scrap of material? But I pull my shoulders back and stand tall. If he's going to kill me, I'm going to die with dignity, not as a stupid show girl in even stupider skimpy underwear. "Yeah, they're too small." *Stop talking, Lexi!* Stop it.

"I'll make sure the next ones fit better."

Shit, what does he mean by that? How should I respond? What should I say or do?

Instead of commenting with something sassy, I elect to remain quiet and berate myself for even speaking to begin with.

He taps on the door, earning my attention. He's standing in the doorway, waiting for me. "Hurry up," he spits toward me.

In this case, I hurry up. Following behind him, he leads me down a long, well-lit corridor. My bare feet scramble to keep up with him, but I manage it.

We reach a set of stairs that lead up, and at the top of them is a heavy metal door. "Hmm," I mumble quietly to myself. Figures, I've been kept in a basement dungeon like a chained-up animal.

He opens the door, and steps through it, revealing a gaudy, over-decorated foyer, primarily in gold and dark wood. Can this place be any tackier? I hold in the eye roll I'm so tempted to give to this gross place. It's obvious to me that whoever owns it has the worst taste ever, because everything is so garish.

"Hurry up," the scary guy barks as he holds the door open.

My gaze finds his and I see the anger bubbling away behind his darkened eyes. "Sorry," I mumble, hurrying my steps.

As I approach him, he grabs onto my upper arm and squeezes tightly. I don't need to look at where he's squeezing to know he's wearing gloves. I can feel the cool leather against my skin.

He pulls me in close into his body. His stale breath makes me gag. He has an odor about him of sour sweat and strong cigarettes. I hold my breath, and hold in the vomit.

"I'm going to enjoy playing with you when the Boss tells me he's done." He leans in closer. Sweat rolls down my back, and the vomit I'm holding back creeps further up my throat. He licks my face, and I gag before the vision takes me over.

Standing in a room, I turn my head to look at my surroundings. The music is loud, and the room is decorated in black and red. The scary guy is sitting on a deep red lounge chair, completely relaxed into the high back. He's nursing a glass of dark liquid. In front of him is a table where a scantily-dressed woman is on her knees sniffing a white powder through a rolled-up bill.

The scary guy is watching someone behind me, and when I turn to see, it's a girl, no older than me, dancing . . . and stripping . . . and grinding against a pole. "Oh man," I sigh as a lump of disgust sits in my stomach. I'm not judging her, but her cold and distant appearance tells me she's here because she has to be. The track marks running up her arms confirm it. She's here, in this vile and dirty place, to feed her habit. Loathing washes over me, and I want to get out of here. But I'm in the scary guy's vision. He'll be coming to this club tonight, and I need to see everything. It may be the only way for me to get out.

Turning my attention back to him, I watch as he watches the girl on the pole. His concentration is on the girl, his own hand on his crotch, and he doesn't see the man who enters the room. He's dressed all in black as he creeps in behind the scary guy.

He looks around him, checks the door, and then turns to the two women in the room. Neither see him. One's high on drugs, and the other is dancing for her drugs with her eyes closed. He places his hand in his pocket, and takes out a long, thin piece of steel wire. He lifts it over the scary guy's head and . . .

I'm back to the present, staring at the smug face of the scary guy who's just licked me. It brings me happiness to know that after tonight, he'll no longer be scary.

Hell, what's happening to me?

Am I turning into something I'm not? Am I becoming bloodthirsty?

He pulls away with a stupid proud smirk, as if he's telling me that when he's given permission, he's going to do whatever he wants to me. I feel like laughing in his face and telling him, he won't be around for too much longer.

But I want him dead.

It's a public service *not* to tell him, to let him discover his future on his own.

"S'pose you saw something?" he condescendingly asks as he pushes me toward a black van.

"I did," I reply as I step into the van.

"Come on, princess, tell me what you saw." He chuckles at me. His laugh is demeaning, like he doesn't believe in my ability.

Well screw him.

"You're going to have a great time tonight at the strip club. Although, judging by the women you hang around, you don't care if they're comatose or even of legal age."

He laughs as he sits opposite me. "You're right about one thing, princess. The younger the better."

His words make my stomach twist with disgust, and a shiver runs up my spine. "You're revolting."

He winks at me, and smiles, showing me his rotten teeth. "You're on the higher end of the age I like, but don't worry, I'll break you in."

Ugh. What a vile man. I've never known a person as loathsome and vulgar.

Looking away from his smirking face, I choose to stare at the inside of the black van. I'd rather look at nothing than this disgraceful, pitiful excuse for a man.

CHAPTER 4

WE ARRIVE AT what looks like an industrial park. There are rows and rows of factories, all looking quiet and abandoned.

I can imagine this is a place where bodies are tortured and screams aren't heard.

The van slows to a stop outside one of the cookie-cutter doors. The scary guy rolls the side door open, jumps out and points his gun at me. With a flick of his head, I know I need to get out too.

Great, this is where I'm going to die.

He takes a card out of his pocket, and waves it in front of a small black box, then presses his thumb print into a scanner.

Yep, there's no way out for me.

If there are so many obstacles to get into the building, it's designed to keep whatever is inside, *inside.*

My heart feels like it's been beating a mile a minute since the day I was kidnapped. I've been living on the edge of sanity, waiting to fall over into an abyss.

"This way," the scary guy says and pushes the barrel of the gun into my lower back. It's freezing cold. *Just like him.* The gun is an extension of him. He'd likely feel naked without it. Wherever he is, his stupid gun is too.

I wonder if he gets off from inflicting fear on people? Probably, which is why it's always attached to his hand.

"Up the stairs." He pushes the gun into my lower back again.

I try and take in my surroundings. Maybe I'll be able to make a run for it. I doubt it though. There are men with compact machine guns everywhere.

This really looks like your stereotypical bad guy movie setting.

Dingy, dark, and scary as hell.

Making my way up the metal staircase, there's a man with a gun eyeing me up and down. "She's a cute one," he says to the scary guy behind me.

"She is," he replies. I can hear the sleaziness in his voice. I know he's checking out my butt as I walk up the stairs, and knowing his eyes are on me makes me cringe inside.

"This way," the guy at the top says when I reach the platform. He points to an open door that leads to a waiting area.

This is it for me.

This is where my role will finally become apparent.

A thin layer of sweat coats my palms and my skin pebbles with fear and uncertainty.

The room I'm pushed into has a musky type of smell. It reminds me of stale water and sweat mixed together. God, this is putrid.

Adjoining the room is another, with yet an extra armed guy standing by the door leering at me. They all resemble savage beasts who haven't eaten in days. I can't imagine they'd be the type to respect females. They'd be the type to happily hurt us, and then discard us like an inferior product.

Slowly, I drag my feet into the room and see a man sitting behind a desk. He's looking over some papers lying flat on the desk in front of him. He's rubbing his temple with one hand, and the other is tapping a pen on the paper.

"Come in," he says in a thick accent and directs me to sit opposite him, all while still looking down at the paper.

I get pushed again, and I nearly fall into the seat. Looking around, I notice the number of men crammed in here. They all have machine guns and they're all staring at me.

God, I feel so sick. My stomach is churning and my hands are shaking. My leg bounces up and down as I wait for this guy to look at me and tell me what he wants.

The atmosphere in the room is thick with tension. My body is stressing out as the sweat gathers at the nape of my neck and rolls down my spine.

"So," the man behind the desk says. He lifts his chin to stare at me. His left eye is . . . missing. Gasping, I try not to stare at his missing eye. "Do you know who I am?"

I shake my head. "No," I whisper still trying not to look at the blank spot where his eyeball should be. But I can't help it, it's right there, and disgusting.

"Do you know how this happened?" He points to where I'm staring.

Considering I don't know who you are, how am I supposed to know how you lost it? "No," I reply with the safest answer.

"In my youth," he starts reminiscing, "a boy in my village bet me to see if I could climb the highest tree. He was trying to steal a girl I liked." He chuckles and shakes his head. "I climbed that tree."

His heavy accent draws me into his storytelling. His confidence is somewhat admirable, though I don't make the mistake of being swept up in the story. He waits for me to respond, but I have nothing to say.

"I climbed to the top, and yelled that I was going to be coming after him. My girl laughed and punched the boy in the arm."

I want to pull the smile back, but so far, I like this story. It's not scary, though I know the frightening part must be coming.

"On the way down, I saw him punch my girl back. This made me so mad, I began to swing, like Tarzan from branch to branch." His accent grows thicker, and I struggle to understand him. "I got to the bottom, I picked up a fallen branch and I cracked his head. Right here." He shows me a line starting at his forehead above his missing eye, and runs his finger down toward his ear.

I can't help but scrunch my brows together, shocked not that he'd beat someone, but there was so much violence in him as a boy.

"He lost his eye because the branch had smaller spikes sticking out, and poked his eyeball out."

I lift my hand to my mouth, completely engrossed, though turned off by what he's saying.

"He recovered, and came after me. Told me, 'an eye for an eye.'" He really doesn't need to tell me anymore, because I'm getting a crystal-clear picture of what happened.

"Oh," I reply, hoping he stops talking.

He stands from behind his desk, and straightens to his full height. Man, he's tall, like basketball player tall. How the hell did he fold himself beneath the desk? And he's old. He has to be pushing sixty, if not older. He walks around, and leans back against his desk. Crossing his arms in front of him, he takes in my appearance. He then flicks his eyes up to someone standing behind me. "She's to be dressed properly, not like this. Not like a whore."

I swallow hard. I want to turn around and look at who he's talking to, but the moment he answers with, "Yes, Boss," I don't need to look to know it's the scary guy.

He looks around the room, and flicks his head to all the men in here.

Crap. Is this where I'm going to die? Is this the end of my life? Dressed in lingerie in an office with an old guy who only has one eye? Or will he make me perform sexual acts on him? Oh, my God, I'm going to hurl.

The door closes with a resounding bang, and I jump in my seat. Everything inside my body is speeding at a million miles an hour. My heart is about to thump out of my chest, and my pulse is running so fast, I can feel the vibration inside my veins.

"You don't know who I am?"

"No," I respond without making eye contact.

"I saw you the night of the charity event. You were with Jude

Caley, yes?"

"Yes," I say then swallow.

"You have something I want, Lexi."

Oh God, I hate how he knows what to call me. "Which is?"

"You're a witch."

Witch? It's the same word Jude used. Exactly the same. "Your accent?"

"I am from France. I'm sorry, let me introduce myself." He holds his hand out to me. "Enzo LeRoy," he says and moves his hand closer to me. He wants me to take it, to get a glimpse into his future.

Hesitating, I extend my hand, then pull it back when I'm nearly touching him. I don't want to see what's in his future. I don't want to see it at all.

But my hesitation angers him, and he pushes off the desk, grabs hold of my hand and wraps it in his.

I'm standing on the deck of a yacht, the water gently tilting the vessel from side to side. I seem to be here alone; I can't see anyone. I look down the side and see no one, so I concentrate and move to stand on the opposite side.

Enzo is at the rear of the boat, with one of the other guards beside him. He smokes a cigar as he talks to the guard.

The guard's back is to me. I can't see him, but I know it's not the scary guy. His build is different. I walk toward them, making sure they can't hear me. I know I'm in the future, but I've had visions where I'm convinced they can hear me. The wooden deck makes a creaking sound beneath my bare foot, and Enzo looks over the guy's shoulder toward me.

He can't see me, but I halt my footsteps and hold my breath—*just in case.*

He turns his attention back to the guy, who now heaves a black duffel bag over the edge of the boat. The guy looks down, and I follow his line of sight where there's several more laying by his feet.

"You exceeded my expectations," Enzo says to the guy.

"Thank you." He grabs another duffel and throws it over the edge of the boat. I step closer to try to see what's in the bag. The floor creaks again, and Enzo puts a hand to the guy's shoulder, stopping him as he looks in my direction. "What is it?" he asks and turns toward me.

It's then I recognize him. It's the guy from the strip club with the long piece of wire.

"Shit," I murmur to myself. The guy . . . and the duffel bags . . . and the strip club. It doesn't take a genius to figure out what or who he's throwing overboard. The blood seeping out of one of the bags confirms my thoughts.

I'm back in the office, and Enzo crosses his arms in front of him.

With my heart erratically beating, I sit back in the chair and stare at one-eyed Enzo. "What did you see?" he asks, amused. He knows I know.

"Exactly what's going to happen. But, why?"

His lips pull up into a smirk and he runs his hand through his thinning hair. "Because he slept with my granddaughter."

I shiver in revulsion. I know he likes them young, and knowing he slept with his boss's granddaughter almost makes me want to avoid asking anything else. But I do anyway. "How old is she?" I wince at the expected number.

"She's eighteen."

I let out a sigh of relief. Fortunately, he didn't say anything younger. I'm not sure I'd be able to stop myself from vomiting. Crinkling my forehead, I exhale a thankful breath again. "But you're wondering why he's going to die? Yes?"

No, don't tell me. Yes, I want to know. "No need to tell me your business."

"He slept with my granddaughter."

"You already told me that."

"And that is the only reason."

Huh, how weird. "Are you trying to tell me you're going to kill everyone who sleeps with your granddaughter?" I find this conversation, peculiar.

"I will if they give her drugs too."

But, he just said . . . man, this is too much for my brain to comprehend. "Look, what do you want from me?"

"I'm going to use you for your talent."

Now we're getting down to why I'm here. "My talent?" I play dumb, even though we both know what it is.

Enzo tilts his head and winks with his one eye. He shakes his head and chuckles. "Really? You're going to play these games? I shook your hand, you saw what I'm going to do, and you want to insist you have no talent?"

"What exactly is it you want from me?" We may as well get to the bottom of this.

"To use your talent. You'll be by my side, and when I tell you to touch someone, you will. You'll report to me every detail you see."

"I don't know how this thing works. I wasn't given an instruction manual with it, it just kind of . . . happens. What if you want it to work for you, but it doesn't?"

"Then I'll give you some motivation to make sure it works." He pauses for a moment, then calls out, "Jimmy."

The door opens and the scary guy walks in, dragging someone behind him. *Dallas.*

"Dallas!" I jump up out of my chair and head straight for her. Without thinking, I hug her tightly. It transports me to her vision. She's kept in a cage, it's dark and dirty, and she's frightened. She's cowering in the corner of this cage, she's hugging her knees and rocking back and forth, crying.

A door creaks open and I hear heavy footsteps coming toward us. Dallas holds her breath and looks to where the footsteps are approaching. "Please no," she begs. Tears fall down my cheeks as I watch the cage door open, a hand reach in, latch onto her hair and yank her out. She tries to gain traction, but her feet slip from beneath her. "Please, no, no!" she continues to plead.

I'm back in the office, with tears streaming down my face. I look at Dallas's distressed face, and I take in her disheveled appearance. There's no spark in her eyes. Her lip is fat and her clothes are dirty and torn.

I turn to look at Enzo, and straighten my shoulders. "I have one condition." I know this is a risk. He could easily kill me and hurt Dallas. "If you're a businessman, which I know you are, then you'll understand that this is a good deal I'm about to offer you."

"You're most certainly not in a position to make me any type of offer." He draws his lips up into a smirk, as if he's got something over me.

Ultimately, I'm the one with the power here, and if he wants me to work for him, he'll have to agree to what I want. "If you don't take my deal, I won't help you. If you kill or hurt her, I won't help you. If you torture me, I won't help you. And if you kill me, I *can't* help you."

His sneer slowly disappears as he considers my words.

I pull my shoulders back further and hold my head high.

"What do you propose?" he asks, his face dark with anger.

"You move her in with me. If Dallas . . ." I think about my wording before I add, "or my parents are harmed, I'll stop using my gift for whatever it is you want."

His mouth turns up into a snarl, and he moves forward toward me. I shelter Dallas with my body, and brace myself for whatever he's about to do.

The back of his hand connects with the side of my face. Burning pain flares through my cheek, I've never felt such intense pain on my face before. He comes back for another strike, and I brace myself for it.

"You don't call the shots here, Alexa," he roars with anger, his hand connecting for a third time.

When the strikes end, I keep my head down and cup my stinging cheek. Dallas is crying behind me, but I manage to hold the tears in. I won't let him break me. Dropping my hand beside me, I straighten my shoulders again and stand tall to Enzo. "My conditions are . . ." Enzo crinkles his forehead, drawing his brows together. He lifts his hand to hit me again, but I push past the world of hurt he's about to inflict and stare at him. "My conditions are: if Dallas or my parents are harmed, I'll stop using my power for you."

He hits me, again.

I straighten, *again.*

The fierceness etched on his face tells me to stay down, my stubborn nature and need to protect the ones I love tells me to get back up and fight for what's important.

My family.

"My conditions are: if Dallas or my parents are harmed, I'll stop using my power for you," I repeat again, this time through gritted teeth and the blazing pain which keeps getting worse with every blow.

"Stay down," he yells as he lifts his arm above his head.

"My conditions are: if Dallas or my parents are harmed, I'll stop using my power for you!" I'm nearly yelling now, but I will not back down.

He hits me on the other side.

My cheek explodes with the all to familiar intense burn. He'll have to either kill me or agree with my terms. Either one. "My conditions are: if Dallas or my parents are harmed, I'll stop using my power for you."

He lifts his hand again. Blood trickles from my lip, my skin's inflamed and the swelling starts to set in.

"You won't stay down," he says as he steps back.

"My conditions are: if Dallas or my parents are harmed, I'll stop using my power for you." I sound like a broken record, but I don't care. "Kill me or agree. If you kill me, I'm useless to everyone, including whatever master plan you have. Or agree, and I'll comply with whatever you want me to do."

He swallows hard, and looks me up and down. He runs his tongue over his teeth and clenches his jaw tightly together.

His eye looks over to Dallas, then back to me. "Get 'em clothes, and get 'em out of here."

We're pushed out the door together.

Dallas's crying can be heard a mile away. I'm not sure if he's agreed to my 'working conditions' or if he's going to kill us. Either way, Dallas and I will get a resolution. If we die, then at least we'll die with our dignity.

"What's happening, Lexi?" Dallas asks through her sobs.

"I can't explain right now."

She reaches for my hand and links our fingers.

I'm in a room. It's slightly brighter than the one I've been kept in, and it has a proper bed. There's a bathroom attached to the room. It's not huge, or beautiful, but it's much better than what either Dallas or I had before. We're both sitting crossed-legged, facing each other on the bed, Dallas is crying and holding my hands through my t-shirt.

I'm back into the now, and Dallas looks over to me. "I promise, I'll explain everything," I say.

Dallas nods her head, and reaches for my hand again.

But this time, I don't take it. Instead, I think about the vision I just had.

I had it while I'm in motion. Which means my power is increasing.

A small smile tugs at my lips and my arms pebble with goosebumps.

CHAPTER 5

ALTHOUGH I HATE Dallas being here with me, it's made the last two days bearable. We've been locked in this room the entire time, only having the door opened when they throw something in here for us to eat.

They treat us better than they initially did. But I know it's because of what I can do for Enzo. I'm also not under the misguided impression that Enzo won't kill us both when he's finished with me. Until then, I have to make myself useful to him.

As Dallas and I lay on the bed, my mind keeps going to my parents. They're first and foremost in my thoughts. I hope they're safe.

"Lexi," Dallas says in a small voice.

"Yeah," I sigh, looking up at the ceiling and noticing the patches of discoloration.

"This thing you have . . ."

I told her about my gift the night I made the deal with Enzo. "It's so complicated, Dallas. I have no idea what I'm doing, all I know is I have to protect you and my parents."

"I've been thinking about it. It only happens when you touch people?"

"Yeah, skin on skin contact."

"The first time you noticed it was when you woke after you

had your appendix taken out?"

"Yeah."

"So, obviously, someone did something to you in the hospital."

"That's what Jude thinks too."

"Jude Caley, the first guy who kidnapped you?"

We've been over this a million times, and it's likely we'll go over it a million more. This is new to her, but I've lived with it since . . . since . . . God, it feels like forever. "Yeah, but it's not like that with him." I try to justify his actions, and I suppose in comparison to Enzo, Jude is a saint.

"Hey, he's evil too. He took you away from your parents, from me, in order to use you. Don't forget that incredibly important fact."

She's right, he did. But . . ."Here's the thing, Dallas. Look at the risk I'm putting on you and my parents. I don't belong in the normal world anymore. I don't even know how many people know about this thing I can do, and the more who know, the more will want me. And having the knowledge that people like Enzo and Jude exist, it's scary stuff for me."

"I want to hug you, but I know I can't," her voice trembles with worry. I take a deep breath. "It's going to be lonely if you'll never be able to touch anyone again."

"I'm getting better at controlling it. I'm able to do more than when I first got the . . . I don't know what to call it. Jude's called it a gift, but to me, it's more like a curse."

"What's it like? When you get these visions." She sits up in bed, and leans her back on the wall. "Is it as real as you and I are right now?"

"The first time it happened, I was in the hospital, and I thought I was hallucinating from the drugs, you know?" I smile weakly, because in all honesty, I wish I could go back and warn Hayley. I wish I knew what this was much earlier. I could've saved her life. "I saw a girl get shot." Dallas gasps and brings her hand to cover her mouth. I too sit up in bed, pick a spot on the blanket and stare at it. I can't look at her; the disappointment will hurt me too much.

"What do you mean?" she asks. Man, even her voice is soft. This makes me sadder, because I know I could've saved Hayley, but I didn't.

"I was in recovery when I woke up, and she was a nurse there. She touched me to take my vital signs, and I was transported to the train station parking lot . . ."

"The woman you saw get shot?"

I'm almost too lost in the memory, but I really don't want to relive it. "Yes. Hayley, the nurse from recovery."

"Hang on, the first person you had a vision for was a nurse at the hospital?" I nod my head and wipe at the tear which has spilled over. I hate this vision. I hate how I didn't save her. "Whoa," she huffs. "Heavy."

"Hayley touched me to take my vital signs, and I was immediately in a vision. I thought it was a hallucination. I thought people would think I was losing my mind if I said anything. Then I assumed no one would believe me." I take a deep breath and gather my thoughts. I need to push through this. I can't be the weak girl who's stuck in a room with only her feelings to drive her insane. I need to accept the choices I've made.

"What happened when you went into the vision?"

"I was standing right there. Hayley was only a few feet ahead of me. She had her bag on her shoulder, and I could see her walking toward the train. A man called to her, and we both turned to look at him. I heard the shot before I saw him. It happened so quickly."

Out of the corner of my eye, I notice Dallas reaching for me, before she swiftly pulls back. Turning to face her, I question her rapid withdrawal. "I don't want to make this thing you have, any harder."

Nodding, I turn from her. "That vision nearly made me lose my mind. I had no idea what was going on, what to say, or even who to say it to. Then over the days, every time someone touched me, I had a vision. The only people I didn't get visions from were Mom and Dad."

"I wonder why?"

Shrugging my shoulders, I can't answer the question. "I don't know. I don't know how or why I got this."

"You can't have just woken up with it. I mean, it makes sense that someone put it in you while you were sedated during the operation."

"Who?" I question. If only I knew, I could have it reversed and my life would be back to the way it was.

But, would it?

"I don't know. Think back, did anything peculiar happen in the hospital?"

"Seriously, Dallas? This whole thing is strange. But there was a doctor and his nurse who came in to see me."

"What was weird about them?"

"Well, first, she had high heeled shoes on, and when he touched me, I saw him driving a car, but everything around him was blank. The best way I can describe it is like a green screen in an action movie. He and his nurse were in the car, neither of them were talking, and there were no noises or scenery. Almost every vision I've had, I've been able to identify where I am. With Jude, it was at the docks. With you, we were at the mall."

"Wait up a second, you had a vision of me?"

"Yeah, we were walking in the mall, as Jude was walking toward us. And I had another of you, but that one didn't eventuate." Please don't ask me what the second vision was.

"What happened?" She leans forward, listening more intently.

No! "Dallas . . ." I swallow hard and take a deep breath. "I can't tell you."

Her hand covers her gaping mouth, and tears spring to her eyes. "It was bad, right?"

"Can we not talk about what could've happened? I already feel guilty with you being dragged into this. Somehow, I have to learn to live with the danger I've forced on you and my parents, and if you make me say what I saw, I'm not sure I'll be able to handle it. So, please, can we just . . ."

"I'm sorry, Lexi. I was thinking of myself and not how this must be for you. It's got to be hard, seeing things happen before they do, and having the chance to be able to change the future."

"It's so difficult and I hate how the people closest to me are being punished because of me and this." I tap my head.

Dallas pulls back, leaning her head against the wall. She tilts her chin down and runs her hand through her long hair. "People aren't being punished because of you. They're being punished because of what was done to you."

Huh?

"What do you mean?"

"You didn't choose this. All your choices were taken away when they put this thing inside of you. And I know plenty of people who have routine operations, like you did, who woke up with no special gifts. You're more of a victim than me or your parents because you have to live with it for the rest of your life."

"What if whoever put this in me has a way to take it out?"

"Lexi, look at your eye. It's already half blue. I'm no genius, but I'm smart enough to figure out, the more your eye changes color, the more ingrained this thing is in you."

"And I'm getting stronger."

"Like you can lift a car over your head, stronger? 'Cause if you can turn into the Incredible Hulk, or Iron Man, why the hell are we still sitting here?" she says with a giggle.

"I'm not a Marvel character." I chuckle and roll my eyes.

"Just saying . . ." She offers me a smile, and it's the first one I've seen from her since she's been here. "But tell me how you're getting stronger. As in, what way?"

"In my visions, I'm able to move around and when I speak, the person can hear something. I want to be able to choose when

I go in a vision, but it's not like I have a lot of opportunity to practice."

"Practice on me." Dallas moves forward and offers me her hand.

"What do you mean?"

"Touch me, and try to not go into the vision."

"What if I can't?" I ask, suddenly nervous about what I'm doing.

"You have to keep trying to control it. I don't know how it works either. But I dare say, it's like anything else. The more you practice, the better you'll get at it. Consider me your practice partner." She thrusts her hand out to me.

I lift my hand and reach out to touch her, but pull back almost immediately. "What if . . . ?"

"There are no 'what ifs.' You just have to keep going until you master the skills you need."

"I don't know how long it'll take me to do this."

"Look around, Lexi, we're not going anywhere." She chuckles and gestures to the room we're locked in. "Just keep going until you've got it."

She holds her hand out and urges me to take it.

"Okay," I say. "I'm going to close my eyes and I need you to move your hand until your palm is touching my finger. But give me a few seconds to center myself. And remember, I don't know what I'm doing."

"You've got this. *We've* got this."

I get myself into a comfortable position, and close my eyes. My heart is going crazy, because this time, I'm trying something new. Something I've never been able to do before. "Calm down," I chant to myself.

My mind begins to blank. A beautiful scenario of an open field with tall grass and brightly colored wildflowers appears in my mind. I'm transported to a place of peace and serenity. The warm sun beams her angelic rays upon my face. Her gift of light makes my heart happy. "Beautiful," I murmur as I tilt my head up to soak in her vitamin D.

As if I'm in a time machine, I'm rushed into a room. I stand in the corner, and watch as Dallas and I sit on the bed, me trying to control my gift, and Dallas helping me. "I can't do it," I cry in frustration.

And just as quickly as I'm in the vision, I'm out of it and sitting on the bed. Opening my eyes, I look at Dallas. Her eyes eagerly look at me. "So?" she asks.

"It didn't work, I can't do it."

"Bullshit, Lexi. Make it work. Try it again." She holds her hand up to me. "Again."

"Same, okay?" I ask. She nods her head.

Closing my eyes, I'm easily transported back to the field. "That was easy," I murmur, surprising even myself. While I walk through the field, the palms of my hands touching the tall grass and wild flowers, I'm sucked out of it and thrown into our room. I stand and watch us. I try to take myself out of this vision.

Closing my eyes in the vision, I relax and take myself back to the field. "It worked," I tell myself as I take a step in the field.

I'm drawn back into the present. Dallas smiles at me. "How did it go? Did it work?"

"Kind of, but not exactly. I have to practice more."

She leans forward and peers into my eyes. "You're still pretty bruised up, but I think your eye is bluer, if that's even possible."

I jump up off the bed, and go into the bathroom, where there's a tiny mirror above the old pedestal sink. Leaning in, I look at my eye. She's right. The blue hasn't covered more area, but it's become brighter than it's ever been before.

Heading back out to the bedroom, I try and wrap my head around everything that's happened.

"You okay?" Dallas asks.

I nod. "I need to try again. Just once more for today, because I'm feeling really tired."

"Are you sure? We can wait until later."

"We need to keep going." I sit opposite her, close my eyes, and begin to center myself again. Lifting my hand, I wait for her touch.

I'm in my field. My field of peace. I'm walking along skimming the grass with my hands, soaking up the rays of the sun. Suddenly, I'm standing in our room. Dallas and I are on the bed, practicing. This time, I'm not frustrated or angry. I'm in a vision of me being in a vision. "Fascinating," I say as I walk around the bed looking at myself.

"Lexi, are you here?" Dallas is holding my hand on the bed, but she looks up to where I'm standing.

"Dallas, can you hear me?" I ask and move closer to her.

"Lexi?"

Damn it. Obviously, she can hear something, but it's not clear enough for her to make out what I'm saying. I take several deep breaths, and really focus on communicating with Dallas. "Dallas," I say again.

She startles and swings her head around, it's almost as if she's staring straight at me. "Lexi, I can only just make you out."

Focusing with everything I have in this strange moment, I say, "I'm here, next to you."

Her eyes stare straight through me, like she can see me. "I heard you." She looks at me sitting on the bed opposite her, then back to where I'm standing. "This is so weird. Can you see yourself?"

"Yes," I respond.

Weird doesn't even cut it. Surreal and unnatural. It's kind of freaky and magical all in one. My wildest imagination couldn't make this stuff up.

"I don't know what to say or do. Should I break the connection?" Dallas asks.

"No! Let me try to get out of it on my own. Whatever you do, don't let go of my hand."

"Okay." She looks around the room, her shoulders visibly shuddering. This must be even weirder for her than it is for me.

Standing back, I watch us in the room. I have no idea how to get out of the vision without her breaking it off first, but I need to learn so I can gain further control of this ability.

I don't know where to start, but I have to do something.

Watching Dallas and myself, I first try to control my breathing. I count the Mississippi's for every breath I take. Concentrating on where our hands are touching. With every breath I take, I fall further and further into a relaxed state. My mind clears, my heartbeat evens out and my eyes become heavier.

I will myself to break the connection.

Opening my eyes, I'm back in the room staring at a shocked and surprised Dallas. "You're here," she says and looks to our joined hands.

"I'm here," I squeal with excitement.

Which is short lived because I'm back in the vision.

"Damn it," I nearly shout.

"You had it for a few seconds, Lexi. We need more practice and you'll be able to control it."

And just like that, I'm sitting on the bed. Dallas's hands are in her lap. I'm so mad at myself, I nearly had it. "Ugh," I grumble. I stand and angrily pace back and forth on the rug. "I almost had it."

"You did have it. You just need more practice. This whole thing is weird. Did I look okay? Did I say or do anything?" She too jumps off the bed and leans against the wall. "This is like beyond Disney weird, man."

I turn and look at her. "Disney weird? How is Disney weird?"

"Seriously? A chick eats an apple and falls asleep. Another chick goes to live with a bunch of short guys who don't look like they shower. A chick has such long hair she can drop it from the top of the Trump Tower and people can use it as a ladder. A ladder, Lexi! And not to mention, a chick falls in love with an animal. And you're telling me none of those are weird?"

When you put it that way . . .

"What did it feel like to you?" I ask.

"What did what feel like? Because as I said, this whole thing is weird as anything. Spooky strange." She wiggles her fingers beside her head and widens her eyes.

"Ugh, I have to remember when I'm in a vision, it's a future vision. Your present self has no idea your future self and I talked."

Dallas looks at me, and shakes her head. "You know what's even stranger than you being able to have visions of the future?"

"What?"

"What you said actually makes sense to me." She chuckles, even in this bizarre and stressful situation. "Lexi?" Her happiness is short lived. The sound of my name coming from her is stressed.

"Yeah?" We both sit on the floor, our backs against the bed. Right now, in this moment in time, we're two teenage girls who've been thrust into a horrible situation.

"Are we going to live?"

Man, what a loaded question. I want to say yes and give her a hug, but I have no idea at all. Enzo is a man who'll use me until he no longer needs me, which means my days are numbered. And if my days are numbered here, Dallas's are even fewer, because she has no ability and is of no use to him at all.

"Lexi?" She shoulders me. There's hope in her voice, but the undertone conveys that she already knows the answer.

I give her all the optimism I can. "I hope so. I haven't seen an end for either of us."

But in this situation, I highly doubt it.

CHAPTER 6

WE'VE BEEN PRACTICING like crazy for the past week. I keep trying to break the connection so I can achieve control over what I have. I'm getting better, and I think in the next few days I'll be able to control it when I go into a vision. The thing that spins us both out, is when I have a vision and I talk to Dallas, she can hear me talking to her hours later. We're not sure how it works, but somehow, it does.

The past two days have been intense, and by the time we're finished practicing, I'm spent. It really takes it out of me, I end up so drained I collapse on the bed and sleep.

"Hey, you awake?" Dallas asks as she nudges me over the blanket we share.

"Yeah, kinda. You okay?" My voice is sleep-heavy, as is my body. I don't want to wake, but I know I have to. We need to practice.

"I've been thinking of something."

"Could be dangerous."

"Shut up, loser." She playfully slaps me. We may not be in the healthiest or best environments, but at least we make the most of a shit situation.

Chuckling, I turn over to look at her. "What are you thinking?"

"I wonder, if I touch you while you're sleeping, if you'd get a vision?"

I blink a few times to wake up, then rub my hands over my eyes. My face is still a bit sore when I touch it, but nothing like it has been. "You woke me to ask me if I get visions if I'm touched while I'm sleeping. Seriously?"

"Well, yeah."

I kick her under the blanket and then turn over. "I'm going back to sleep."

She pokes my lower back. "No sleep for you! We need to practice."

"I-"

The door is unlocked and an armed guy walks in. He sees both Dallas and I in the bed and smiles sleazily at us. "Having a party and I didn't get an invite?" he asks.

What an ass. "What do you want?" Dallas bites toward him.

His smile quickly disappears, and mine stretches across my face. *Sassy Dallas.*

"Boss wants you ready. You have work." He slams the door shut, giving us no more information.

My heart jumps and I suddenly become nervous. "Great guy," Dallas says after a few seconds. "Full of personality."

"Yeah," I reply. The strain of the severity kicks in. "What if I screw up and do something wrong?"

"Just do what he asks, and you'll be okay."

"What if I can't get a vision from whomever I'm supposed to read?" I turn to look at her. "It means they'll kill you, Dallas." Her mouth closes sharply, and tears spring to her eyes. "This is a huge responsibility and I don't want to screw it up."

Dallas tries to hide her tension, but she can't. She's my best friend in the entire world, and I know her so well. I can see the obvious signs of her stress. She's not yet on the hysterical side, but I imagine it'll only be a matter of time before she gets there. And that'll put more pressure on me.

For my sake, she manages to hide the fear that's lurking deep in her eyes. "Do what you can do, Lexi, and don't worry about me. Whatever happens, I'll know you did the best you could."

"I can't not worry about you."

"Listen . . ." She sits up in bed and crosses her legs, forcing me to do the same. "I'm here as leverage to force you to do what he wants. They're not going to hurt me now, knowing you'll stop working. Relax, take deep breaths, and let this gift of yours shine through. You've got this. I have faith in you."

How can she stay so calm when her life depends on my ability to perform on demand?

But her confidence in me is strangely calming. There's something about the way she's looking at me, telling me I'm going to be okay, that I believe.

"I can do this," I say as I exhale deeply.

"Yes, you can." She looks around the room and turns back with a questioning expression. "Did Mr. Personality bring in clothes?"

"Nope, he just said Enzo wants me."

A few moments pass, and the door unlocks again. The same guy enters holding a brown paper bag, and two bottles of water. He tosses the bag on the bed then drops the water by the door. "Breakfast. Boss said he's getting you clothes, doesn't want you looking like that." He gestures toward me in disgust. His mouth turns into a snicker, while his eyes wander over my body. What is it with these men? Are they all sex-crazed? "But I wouldn't mind taking a bite of you right now."

Shaking my head, I gag on my own saliva. This guy is disgusting. When neither Dallas nor I respond to his lewd remark, he leaves the room.

"Why do they all have to be so revolting?" Dallas asks my unspoken question, almost as if she can read my mind.

"I was thinking the exact same thing."

"Well, sex is the oldest form of currency in the world. Sex can be traded for favors."

I turn to Dallas and scrunch my nose at her. "How do you

know these things?"

"It makes sense. Sex was around before drugs were, and I'm sure drugs closely follow the sex trade."

"How did we get on this conversation?" I reach over and grab the brown paper bag, as Dallas stands and walks over to retrieve the two bottles of water.

"It's all about power, Lexi. Why do you think we're in this position to start with? Power. You were taken because they want more power, and you can help them get it. I was taken because your love for me gives them power over you. It's about what you can do for them and how far you can propel them."

"Yeah, I know. I also know once Enzo gets where he wants to be, he'll kill us both."

Dallas's entire body shudders, and her shoulders slump. We both know, with Enzo, our lives can end at any moment. Jude may have initially scared me, but toward the end of my time with him, I didn't feel threatened. I felt . . . safe.

"Crap, sorry," I apologize. Regret stains my voice. I said aloud what we both are already well aware of.

The new security guard is sleazy, but not as bad as the other one. He came into the room in the early afternoon, threw two bags on the floor and told Dallas and me to get dressed.

Neither Dallas nor I knew why she had to come along, but I suppose it's best she stays close to me wherever I am. That way, if they hurt her, I'll stop working.

Now, we're both sweating bullets and waiting for the door to open. I'm wearing jeans and a long-sleeved t-shirt with the ugliest gloves ever created. These are even worse than those awful ones Jude made me wear. Where do they buy these things? Is there an 'Ugly Gloves 'R' Us' store?

Dallas wears an incredibly short jumpsuit, showing off her legs.

It doesn't take a genius to figure out I'm wearing what I'm wearing so no one can touch me, and she's wearing what she's wearing so Enzo can ogle her long, toned legs. *Pervert scumbag.*

We've both been quiet, anticipating the activities we're going to be lead into.

As we sit on the bed, Dallas turns to me. "If we die tonight, just know, this isn't your fault." She gestures with a loop of her finger, around the room.

"How can it not be?" The one thing to stay with me until my last breath will be guilt.

Innocent people have been dragged into my nightmare, and innocent people have been hurt. *Guilt* is the only thing I can feel, aside from constant fear. I wish I was never given this stupid curse.

The door opens and two security guards walk in. Both are armed, and both intimidate me. Dallas inches closer when they enter the room. She must be feeling it too.

"Get up," one says in a deadpan voice.

Dallas and I are on our feet within seconds. Neither of us want to test the hardware they're holding.

"Boss is waiting," the other utters.

I swallow hard, and reach for Dallas's hand. Grabbing hold of it, the scratchy material of the ugly gloves stops me feeling her clammy hands. But the fact they're shaking, tells me she's nervous.

The two of them wait until we're near the door. One goes ahead, the other behind us. *Herding us to our slaughter. Driving us to our slaying.*

The thickness of the air and the pounding of my heart inside my chest tells me tonight may be the end of us.

The logical part of my brain tries to reason with the fear, but the fear is winning out.

He won't kill you or Dallas; he needs you.

Yeah right, he's a psychotic guy who had his own man killed.

He needs you.

The more my brain argues with itself, the more worked up I become.

We both get to the gaudy foyer dripping in gold, and we're hurried out the front door where there's a limousine with black windows waiting for us. The back door opens, and Enzo steps out.

"Ladies, you both look beautiful." His words come across as wrong and super creepy. Like a pedophile trying to lure us into his car. The problem is, we have to go with him, because if we don't, we die.

I squeeze Dallas's hand, and climb into the back of the limousine. Dallas follows quickly behind me. We sit on the bench seat, with me in the middle and Dallas closest to the opposite door. She quietly tries the handle, only to find it's locked.

Enzo is in the car within seconds, just in time to catch Dallas trying the lock. "Don't bother trying, my dear. I'll put a bullet in your brain after I torture you," he says with his stupid accent. His one ugly eye glares at Dallas.

"I . . ."

"She didn't mean to," I interrupt whatever Dallas was going to say.

The car begins down the long driveway and the air is thick with tension. Enzo stares at Dallas's legs, then pulls himself together before he starts drooling like the dirty old man he is.

"Where are we going?" I ask when I notice he's composed himself.

"A last-minute business meeting."

"What's my role?" I ask.

"I'll introduce you to everyone. I want you to see if anyone is undercover police. DEA, FBI, any arm of the law."

Great. I imagine that if I rat someone out, they're not going to go home to their family. And I'll be responsible for their death.

On the other hand, if I don't tell Enzo what I see, and he figures out I've kept the information from him, then Dallas and

I will die.

My stomach knots as pain envelops my heart. Either way, someone will die.

The choice is mine.

And mine alone.

"And if there *are* police?" I ask, afraid I already know what'll happen.

A sly smile tugs at his lips, sending a shiver up my spine as bile gathers at the base of my throat.

"Then I'll deal with them." This remark makes me feel even sicker. How can someone be so callous when it comes to human life?

Especially considering the person he'll 'deal with' has probably woken up today like it's any other day, kissed his family goodbye and left for work.

Now I'm torn even more. Whose life do I sacrifice?

Whose life means more?

Who am I to decide?

The rest of the car ride is spent in silence. In my head though, there's so much turmoil happening. A cyclonic wave of devastation fills every inch of my mind. Either way, someone will die, and it all comes down to me who that someone will be.

The best possible scenario is that no one is police, and I'll be able to report my findings to Enzo. But considering his business, it's likely someone *is* police. And I'll have to make a decision based on what I know.

My parents would be ashamed to know I gave up an officer of the law to Enzo. But then they'd be horrified to find me or Dallas dead, dumped in a ditch.

So many thoughts are running through my mind. I'm trying to keep my body steady and not freak out, but I'm not doing a very good job of it. The sweat coating my palms is making the gloves I'm wearing sticky. And the sweat rolling down my back sends a cool shiver through my body.

Who on earth would want to have what I have? No one. No one in their sane and logical mind would want this.

We arrive at a building that is quite isolated. It's more like a large shed than anything else, maybe fifteen feet long and ten feet wide. Man, I have an uneasy feeling in my stomach. It's churning and gurgling, and all I want to do is grab Dallas and run as fast and far as we can.

Even though the shed is isolated, there are a few fancy black cars parked outside. Dallas releases my hand, and grabs my thigh, squeezing it tightly.

I turn to look at her, fear coursing through me. "Are you okay?" I ask.

"I'm okay." Her shaky voice belies her words. She's nowhere near *okay*.

"When we enter the room, you're not to make eye contact with anyone," Enzo instructs me.

I nod my head, too afraid to reply in case the tears start.

"I'll introduce you to who I want you to get a read on."

I nod my head again.

The driver opens Enzo's door, then runs around to open the other side. "Wait, isn't Dallas coming with us?" I ask. The fear inside me intensifies, and my body becomes weak with dread.

"She'll be waiting for us." He nods toward the driver, who pulls a gun out of his holster, pointing it toward Dallas.

Tears spring to my eyes, and Dallas's face drops when she sees the gun.

"Can I hug her?" I ask Enzo. I need to say goodbye, in case neither of us make it out.

"Just don't touch her," he orders.

I throw my arms around her, and hug her. Her cheek brushes mine.

And I'm in a vision. This one is located where we are. It's the most immediate vision I've ever had.

Dallas is standing outside while Enzo's driver is lewdly

gawking at her. She's leaning up against the car, and he's standing on the other side in his defensive position, ready to shoot her.

I leave her here, because I know there's distance between the driver and Dallas, even though he's staring at her like he wants to feast on her. I leap up the few steps and Enzo and I enter the shed. There's a round table in the middle, and on the table, there are bricks of a white powder wrapped in clear plastic. Heroin or cocaine, I'm not sure which one. There are three chairs around the table, all occupied by men in suits. Enzo and I are standing beside the table. He takes a small tool kit out, and a clear plastic pouch.

"It's pure," one of the men opposite me says. I flick him a quick glance, and notice he's staring at me.

"I'll determine its purity," Enzo replies.

Another man cuts into another brick with a thin scalpel, licks his finger, dips it into the small amount he's lifted with the tip of the knife and rubs it into his gums.

I grimace and try to look away. Whatever he's doing is gross.

He nods his head to Enzo, indicating it's pure. "How much have you got?" The guy who rubbed the drugs into his gum asks.

Enzo touches my shoulder, and points toward the gum guy. "We haven't had proper introductions, this is my business advisor, Alexa," Enzo introduces me.

All the men burst into laughter, while their eyes travel the length of my body.

Feeling intimidated is one thing, feeling like I've been cornered is something else. "Business advisor? If you said she was a sweet piece of ass, I'd believe that. But 'business advisor'?" the guy says.

"Alexa?" Enzo gestures for me to shake his hand.

I take off the gloves to grasp his hand, and I watch myself. I must be having a vision, because the moment he drops out of our handshake, I turn to Enzo and whisper something to him.

Shit, what will I see? What have I said?

Enzo turns, and nods his head toward one of his men, the man from the boat who killed the scary guy. He pulls out a gun, and shoots him in the head. I scream and back away. And suddenly there's chaos unfolding around me. People are shooting, and even the driver of the car is in here shooting.

My mind goes directly to Dallas.

I break the connection, grab onto her shoulders and smile.

"You're going to hear gunshots. Run and stay low. Try to use trees to hide behind. Don't go to the police; they're not who they pretend to be. Go to the sunglass store on Leonard Street downtown, and look for a woman named Stevie. She has a daughter named Bella. Tell her to call Jude, and when he gets there, tell him everything," I whisper everything in one continuous breath hoping no one heard.

"No skin contact," Enzo yells.

"My hands are on her shoulders," I shoot back at him.

"Time to go," he says. Turning, he walks toward the shed and looks over his shoulder at me.

I have no idea how the outcome of this meeting will turn out. All I know is what I've seen. This might be Dallas's only chance to get away, and if it means I sacrifice myself to do so, then I'm okay with it as long as I know Dallas has a fighting chance.

I head inside. I already know the layout and have seen the faces of everyone in here.

Enzo leans over and whispers to me, "This is your test. It's up to you if you live or if you and your friend die."

Scrunching my brows, I instantly become worried. He said if I live or if my friend and I die. Does this mean one of us will die either way? Or am I reading too much into what he's said? Either way, I doubt his word holds any merit. The one thing I know for sure is he won't hesitate to kill me, or Dallas.

I have to find a way to make this work.

"Gentlemen," Enzo announces once we're inside the shed.

A few turn to look at him. The guy who Enzo eventually

shoots looks over his shoulder at us. His eyes go directly to me. Bringing his brows together, his gaze wanders over my body. Not in a sleazy way though, more like, he knows me from somewhere and is trying to place where the 'somewhere' is.

"Enzo," a few men chorus in unison.

It's odd being in here. I have no idea who any of these people are, all I can gather is most of them are in the same type of business as Enzo. None are questioning my presence, and no one makes any kind of remark about me.

I'm the only woman in this shed, and could easily be pinned down and raped or tortured. But no one is looking at me like they want to do anything to me.

This somewhat settles my frazzled nerves. It calms me enough to allow me to work knowing I'm not prey to these monsters.

Observing the room, I see the guy who took out Enzo's right hand man, the one in the strip club and on the boat. He's standing over in the corner, hands behind his back, chin lifted and eyes dead set ahead. The look in his eyes is savage; every inch of him is lethal. I saw the way he took out Enzo's guy, he had no remorse, no consideration, no feeling for him. And they had probably worked together for years. Which makes him possibly borderline insane, and much scarier than I could ever imagine.

Enzo makes his way closer to the table. I follow.

He takes a small kit out of his jacket pocket and places it on the table. A couple of bricks wrapped in clear plastic get thrown on the table by one of the men sitting in a chair.

And so it starts.

The beginning of the end, or the beginning of Dallas's salvation. I take a deep breath and wait for the conversation to commence.

I know what's going to happen. I've seen it. The only thing I can hope for is for Dallas to get away and get to Jude. He'll be able to protect her from Enzo.

"What's the cut?" one of the men standing around the table asks the guy suppling the drugs.

"It's pure," the supplier, sitting opposite me, says. I flick him a quick glance, and notice he's staring at me.

"I'll determine its purity," Enzo replies.

Another man cuts into another brick with a thin scalpel, licks his finger, dips it into the small amount he's lifted with the knife and rubs it into his gums.

I grimace and try to look away. Whatever he's doing is gross.

Déjà vu.

He nods his head to Enzo, confirming it's pure. "How much have you got?" asks the guy who rubbed the drugs into his gum.

Enzo touches my shoulder, and points toward the gum guy. "We haven't had proper introductions. This is my business advisor. Alexa," Enzo introduces me.

All the men burst into laughter while their eyes travel the length of my body.

"Business advisor? If you said she was a sweet piece of ass, I'd believe that. But 'business advisor'?" says the gum guy.

"Alexa?" Enzo gestures for me to shake his hand.

My heart jumps as I take a step closer to the guy. Man, this is hard. So difficult.

As I take my gloves off, my palms are coated in sweat. I want to rub them down the front of my pants, but that's going to look bad. I can feel my breathing become labored as I try to concentrate on the job at hand.

I have to work.

I also have to sacrifice myself to make sure Dallas gets away. I know this is the opportunity, because I've already seen in it in a vision.

I extend my hand to the guy. He looks at it as if I'm contagious.

Take my damn hand!

He reaches over, and grasps my hand.

I'm in his future. Looking around, I notice the similarities in the room. It's a place I know too well.

It's my home.

I'm standing in the hallway but I can hear my parents in the dining room. Running in there I see them on their knees. The guy has a gun pointed to my Dad's head, my Mom is crying.

"It's okay, sweetheart," Dad says to Mom. "We'll be with Lexi soon."

A shot is fired and my father falls forward onto the hardwood floor. I can't scream, I can't move, I can't do anything. Stunned, I stare at his lifeless body, my mother's sobs intense in the background.

"Dad," I whisper while tears fall from my eyes.

"Lexi?" Mom asks, lifting her chin to look around the room.

The next shot is fired and Mom falls beside Dad. The way she falls forward, it looks like her head is leaning on his shoulder.

There's blood sprayed everywhere. The scene looks like a horror movie. The man who pulled the trigger walks over and nudges my Mom with his foot. With a satisfied smirk on his face, he looks around the room, then turns to leave.

Walking behind him, just before his hand lands on the door handle, I lean in and blow air on his ear.

He swipes at me, and whips his head around to see who's there.

"You won't lay a hand on them," I say.

"Who's there?" he angrily shouts drawing on his weapon again. "Who is it?" His head turns from side to side.

Anger pulsates through my blood. I need for him to pay for what he's going to do.

It's then opportunity presents itself.

I'll tell Enzo he's a cop. Enzo will kill him, sparing my parents, and Dallas will be able to run.

"You had your chance," I say before I break the connection and am snapped back into the present.

I stand looking at him for a split second. This is the easiest choice I've ever had to make. It's him or my parents. It's him or Dallas.

Easy.

Him.

Turning to Enzo, I reach up on my tiptoes and whisper in his ear, "DEA."

Enzo doesn't even question me. He turns, stares at his henchman and gives a slight nod.

The assassin steps forward out of the background and shoots the guy in the head.

I've managed to save my parents and my best friend, all because I made a choice. A decision I'll have to live with for the rest of my life.

It's a decision I'll never regret.

Suddenly Enzo pushes me out of the way, and there are so many people shooting I have no idea where all the gunshots are coming from. The driver runs into the shed, his gun aimed and ready.

In a state of fear, I slump down behind an overturned chair and cover my ears while I watch the bloodshed transpire. Enzo looks like he's bulletproof. Nothing is touching him. His henchman and driver are both standing in front of him, protecting him while bullets are being fired from everywhere.

It seems to go on for hours, though in reality it's probably only seconds.

There's shouting coming from every direction. A few car doors are being slammed outside and tires screech as they quickly drive away.

My hands might be over my ears, muffling all the sounds, but the shots being fired are loud and clear, scaring me even more.

I can't look at any more blood. I've seen too much. But at least my parents are safe now. And so is Dallas. She would've heard what I told her to do, even though I whispered, and hopefully she'll be gone by now. I don't know if she's going to find Jude, but I hope she gets to him before Enzo gets to her.

Someone kicks my shoes, and I open my eyes to see Enzo's henchman standing over me. Slowly I lower my hands, and try not to look at the bloody and gruesome scene inside the shed. Turning my head to the side, I try and focus on wherever there's no blood. But that's impossible.

"Get up," the guy says to me in a steady, even voice. How can he remain calm when there are so many dead people around?

My eyes dart back and forth, the images of death burned into my memory. Something I'll never be able to forget, or unsee.

There are at least four bodies lying dead on the floor, one of whom is the driver of the car.

Blood is sprayed everywhere, running down the walls, dripping from the ceiling. *Everywhere.*

Slowly I stand, my stomach churning with a nauseating knot of doom. Running out of the shed, the fresh air hits me and collides with the gorge rising up my throat. I make it out just in time to throw up. The vomiting hits me hard. Holding onto the side of the shed, I double over, and a shooting pain charges through my body.

"Oh, my God. I did this," I mumble to myself.

"You did your job," Enzo replies stoically.

So many people have died. It's all on me.

The one who was going to kill my parents, I don't even think about. But the others . . . *shit.*

"Get in the car," the henchman demands of me.

With saliva dripping off my chin, and my body frozen with fear, I manage to shuffle toward the car.

Before I make it to the car, Enzo backhands me. My cheek erupts in pain, and tears spring to my eyes. "What did I do?" I ask between sobs. I can't control the stupid tears. Today's bloodshed has been too much for me.

"Your friend, she ran away. Now I have to waste my time to find her and kill her."

"Please don't." *Yes,* she got away. I'm so damn proud of her. She must've heard my whispers and now, hopefully she's on the way to find Jude. God, I hope this all works.

"Great friend she is to you. She abandons you the moment life gets slightly difficult."

Slightly? Gunshots are not '*slightly.*' Being kidnapped is not '*slightly.*' I don't say anything, I remain quiet. I'm happy she got away. Now, I'm praying she makes it to Jude.

Enzo backhands me again, this time the force of it slams me into the side of the car. He grabs a fistful of my hair, and pushes me into the car before he slides in behind me and slams the door shut. "Go," he angrily spits toward the the henchman, who's now driving the limousine.

"Boss," he replies. Seconds later I feel the car in motion.

"You did this," Enzo says and smashes my head into the window.

"No, I didn't." *Yes, I did.* I warned her. Finally, I've used my ability to save Dallas and my parents. This thing that's inside me has at last come in useful.

"Somehow, you did this. You warned her. You saw what was going to happen and you warned her."

Smash.

Warmth trickles over my eyes, down my cheek and drips onto my jeans. Looking down, I see deep red drops forming a circle on my thigh.

"For that, I'll have my men have their fun with her when she's found."

Please Dallas, find Jude first.

"I didn't do anything. She probably ran away because she was scared of everything that was happening."

Slam.

"Now she'll pay the price."

This blow was harder than the ones before. His tone is angrier, and he tightens his fist to the point it's pulling on the strands of hair enough to make me cry out in pain.

Blackness quickly begins to draw me into its oblivion.

I know I'm not dying. I'm becoming unconscious because of the blows. I wish I was dying, because another moment with Enzo is a lifetime too long.

CHAPTER 7

ONE EYE OPENS, and then the second one does. I lift my hand to move my hair from my face, and I wince as my fingers find the gash above my eye. "Shit," I grumble as I sit up in bed.

My head defies my body, and vertigo quickly overtakes me. The room spins, and my head feels as if it contains a whirlpool spinning around. Licking my chapped lips, I try and focus on one point, hoping to stop the spinning.

Standing, I slowly make my way into the bathroom and look at myself in the mirror over the pedestal sink. "Oh man," I say regarding the purple bruising around my face. "You look like shit." I try to turn my head to get the full impact of the variations of colors on my face. Most of the bruises are brilliant with purple coloring. Some are darker and some have even started healing.

I hear the door open and something gets thrown to land with a soft thud on the bed.

I pee then head out to see what's been hurled on the bed.

Another brown paper bag is sitting on the bed, along with a bottle of water. It's like I'm on rations, and I have to wait for whatever scraps of food they want to give me. Opening the bag, there's an apple, a muesli bar and small muffin.

"Seriously? Muffins?" I mumble. "I need food, and this isn't food."

I take the bag and water, and sit on the floor ready to eat when I hear the door unlocking. It flies open with so much force, the handle bashes up against the wall. Startling at the force and the noise, I jump to my feet within seconds.

The henchman enters, closely followed by a raging Enzo. His one eye is wide open, the hole where his other eye is supposed to be is veiny and ugly. His body is vibrating with anger, his hands clenched tightly at his sides.

I watch as he gets to me in a few quick strides.

"You'll fucking pay for her," he yells. Spittle flies out of his mouth and lands on my cheek. Enzo nods at his henchman.

"What did I do?" Shit, does he know I saved Dallas? How does he know? What gave it away?

His henchman lunges toward me, his right hand coming up and grabbing me around the throat. He throws me back toward the wall, another jab of pain sears through my body.

But I'm transported into a vision.

I'm standing in my living room, *at home*. Mom and Dad are sitting at the dining table, eating dinner. They look so sad. Mom's lost so much weight, and Dad's pushing whatever's in his bowl around.

There's no talking, or laughing, or even living.

I know what's about to happen. Enzo knows my power, and by having his henchman grab me by the throat, he's showing me what my parents are about to endure.

"RUN!" I yell at the top of my voice.

They both drop their cutlery and stand in haste. The chairs topple over, they stand so quickly. "Did you hear that? It sounded like Lexi," Dad says with hope in his voice.

"Run! Run out the back door! they're coming for you!" I scream again.

But they stand still, looking at each other. Why aren't they running? "It was Lexi, where's it coming from?" Mom asks.

"Mom, Dad, please run. They're going to kill you. Go, leave. Trust me, run!"

"Sweetheart, where are you?" Dad asks.

There's a knock at the front door. They both look, they're

faces break out into ecstatic smiles. "Lexi," Dad calls as they both run to the door.

"No! Don't open it," I plead.

They open the door.

And within a second of them opening the door, they're both dead.

They fall backward, collapsing on the floor.

"NO!" I cry as I run and throw myself on them. I can't feel them, I can't touch them. But I don't need to, because I love them with all my heart.

The henchmen steps inside. His black gun has a long silencer on the end. Enzo enters behind him. A smug and satisfied flash appears on his face. "You bastard," I yell as I lie on the floor with my parents. "You killed them."

His lips drag up into a conceited smirk. "No, *you* did this, Alexa. You brought this on them."

Crying, I try to hug my parents.

I wish I could feel them.

Suddenly, I'm back in the room. Struggling to breathe, I gasp for air as I slide down the wall. Smiling, the henchman steps back from me.

There are a few feet between us.

"You're going to kill them," I say once I've regained my breath.

"Don't betray me again," Enzo says in a low, poisonous voice.

My throat closes as my head falls into my hands and I cry. I hear the door slam shut, and I'm left alone.

Alone is exactly what I am.

I may be getting fed, I may even have a bed to sleep on, but I'm so alone.

When Dallas was here, it made it easier to survive. But this isn't a life I'd want anyone to live. I don't want it for myself either. I can't merely exist. I was given this gift for a reason, and I'm sure it's not to help a vile criminal further himself in the underworld community.

It's in this moment I really feel like I've lost everything. My parents will die in a few hours. My best friend is gone, escaped, for which I'm grateful.

But as long as I live, there'll always be a target on her back, and I'll always be someone's property. I'll always be a possession. A trophy for the next asshole to obtain because he wants more power.

A living, breathing trophy.

My sobs ease as I consider what my options are, *realistically.*

In my head, I'm hoping Jude will find me and rescue me. But I have to face the truth. In order for him to do this, he'll have to go to war with Enzo.

Enzo has no moral compass, and I'm positive he'll destroy Jude if it comes to a fight. And no one in their right mind would sacrifice everything they've built to rescue a girl who means nothing to them. So, I do the only thing I can. I push that ridiculous thought out of my mind.

There really is only one other feasible option.

My heart beats quicker as I think about my future.

I feel sick. I know what I need to do to get out of this situation. It's the only way I can control my own destiny. Granted, it's not ideal. But it's my only choice.

I need to come to terms with my actions, and decide how I'm going to end my life.

It really is the only way for me to be guaranteed of death.

I have to wait for the opportunity, and run. Run so Enzo sees me running, and gives the order to kill. It's the only way to stop this nightmare.

Crawling up on the bed, I cry myself to sleep. I don't want to eat or drink. My parents' lives will be over shortly, and if I'm lucky, my life will end soon too.

I can't stay here, and be a potential threat to Dallas and her family.

There is no other way out.

In order for Dallas to be free, I must die.

CHAPTER 8

OPENING MY EYES, there's a heaviness in the pit of my stomach. Last night my parents were killed by the madman who's keeping me here.

He came into my room, and proudly announced how surprise took them, and how his henchman shot bullets into their heads. He also told me it was because of me he killed them.

I cried myself to sleep.

I wanted to die.

I still want to die.

Turning over in bed, more tears leak from my eyes. *I killed them.* I thought I was doing the right thing, but it turns out I did everything wrong.

All I can wish for is that Dallas made it to the sunglass store, and got in contact with Jude. He'll protect her. I hope.

The door opens, and one of the guards comes into the room. He looks at me lying in bed, crying, and he smiles smugly at me. He throws a brown paper bag and a bottle of water on the bed, then leaves, slamming the door shut behind him.

I have no will to eat, or to even drink.

Curling up into myself, I hug the corner of the blanket. I wish I could've seen my parents one more time, held them and told them how much I love them. More tears fall as I wrap my head around what I have to do.

The crying eases as I fall back to sleep. I have no energy to go on. Maybe my heart will stop beating because it's broken. Maybe I'll never open my eyes again. Maybe, just maybe, this will be the end for me.

If not, I'm prepared to sacrifice myself to make sure no one else is hurt.

"Get up. Boss wants you."

My face is showered with something wet. Startling awake, I wipe at my forehead and eyes. "What did you do?" I angrily yell at the guy standing beside the bed.

"Boss said not to touch you." His mouth draws up in a wicked smile. "Told us he don't want you seeing what he's got planned. Considering I'm gonna be there to watch, didn't want you seeing nothing."

What an idiot. He can't even string a sentence together. "Whatever," I reply and lay back down on my wet pillow.

"Get up," he says again.

"Go away."

I try to cover myself, but he rips the blanket off my body. Grabbing me by the hair, he pulls me off the bed. I land with a sickening thud, before he kicks me in the back. The pain is instant and deepens when I try to breathe in.

And the worst part of all this is, I don't even care what they do to me anymore.

In a flat and lifeless voice, I say to him, "Go away."

He grabs the neck of my t-shirt, and brings his hand up to give me a backhand. I stare at him with no emotion. There's nothing they can do to me that will hurt as much as the ache tearing through my broken heart.

Not a God damn thing.

"Boss wants you," Enzo's henchman says as he enters the room.

"I already told this stupid bitch, but she ain't getting up." He lifts his hand higher.

I don't even brace for the impact of his hand. I have no reason to live. I don't care.

"He wants you." The henchman grabs his hand before he has a chance to bring it down across my cheek.

He releases the grip around the t-shirt and steps back. An evil smile tugs on his lips, though I can see the frustration behind his eyes. He wanted to rough me up; he was hungry to hit me. And he was going to take great pleasure in delivering me to Enzo with a bloody lip and a swollen eye.

"Next time," he spits toward me as he backs out of the room.

And again, I don't care.

The henchman stands at the foot of the bed. He's wearing one of those holster things, and has two guns flopping against his chest. He waits for the other guy to leave before he approaches me and offers his hand to help me up.

I don't want to see his future.

Standing without his aid, I sit on the edge of the bed. "How long do I have to get ready?"

He drops his hand, and backs a step away from me. "A few minutes. Boss wants to see you now."

I feel like screaming at him to get out of the room, but I doubt it'll work. Standing, I head into the bathroom, clean myself up and make my way back out to the bedroom. "I'm ready," I announce with an emotionless tone.

He juts his chin toward the door. Dragging my feet, I head out of the room and down the hall. When we get to the foyer, I notice there's an entire cleaning crew here. A few of them swing around to check me out, others are too focused on what they're doing.

"That way," the henchman indicates.

I head toward where he's pointing, and I come to double doors. He knocks on them once, then steps back and waits.

"Come in," I hear Enzo's voice from the other side.

The henchman turns the handle and opens one side of the double doors. As I step in behind him, I can't help but feel the sickness swiftly rise to the back of my throat.

This is Enzo's bedroom. The enormous, round bed in the middle of the room, the ceiling of mirrors, the gaudy, over-the-top murals on the walls, all scream bad taste. Enzo comes out of his bathroom, drying his hands. He's wearing briefs, and nothing else.

The sickness in my stomach churns and causes goosebumps to form on my skin. I know why he's called me here; he's going to rape me.

"Alexa," he says as he approaches me.

His body is all old man saggy skin. There's no elasticity in the skin around his stomach, so it just droops. God, he looks so old.

Turning my head to the side, I attempt not to throw up. "What do you want?" My tone is curt. I have no time for his shit. Just get it over and done with.

"I'm throwing a party tonight."

Ugh, great. "So?" I still refuse to make eye contact. Not because I'm scared of him, more because I'm revolted by him.

"I need you there."

"Whatever," I reply.

"Look at me," he demands.

Slowly, I turn my head to look at his one eye. Gritting my teeth together, I stop myself from attempting to scratch his other eye out. I want him to die, but I know he's too well protected for me to get to him.

Thoughts travel in my mind while his eye inspects me. "This won't do." He points to my choice of clothes. My t-shirt and sweat pants. "You need to be appropriately dressed for this party."

The henchman laughs, and I force myself not to turn my head and flip him the bird.

They want to break me. They won't. They'll have to kill me before they break me.

"Whatever," I say again.

Enzo steps forward, and I stand my ground. He has nothing to hold over me anymore. He grabs my hair, and yanks my head down so my body is distorted and bending from the waist. "You'll do what I want you to, Alexa, because if you don't, you'll wish you were dead."

"Too late," I laugh bitterly. "Too fucking late." I glare at him. I let him know wanting to die is high on my agenda.

He moves his face closer to me, his bad breath coating my nostrils, his wild eye warning me. His jaw jumps, and he tightens his grip in my hair. "If you want me to show you pain, I'll happily accommodate." He jerks his hand down, ripping a good chunk of my hair out.

I cry out in pain, an involuntary reaction. I don't want to show him any weakness or emotion, but my head is pulsating with a blistering sting. I grab onto the spot that's hurting most, trying to cradle it in my hand.

Enzo throws the clump of hair at my feet and steps back. "I'll fuck you over. Watch yourself." He points to me before he turns to leave. "Get her out of here."

His henchman taps me on the shoulder, and flicks his head to the side. I leave Enzo's bedroom, and make my way back to my room. Before he closes the door, he steps toward me. "Trust me, make this easier on yourself and do whatever he wants."

"Why? Don't you want to kill me?" I sarcastically add with a roll of my eyes.

"If he gives me the order, I'll kill you. Without hesitation. I don't want to, but mark my words, I will."

"Great, a heavy with a conscience." I flop on the bed, still nursing the pain on my scalp.

He chuckles and backs away. "And that's the biggest mistake you'll ever make, if you really think I have a conscience. I'll be back soon with the clothes Enzo wants you to wear." He slams the door and leaves me alone.

Exactly how I like it.

My pillow is still wet from the water incident, so I turn it over, lay down, and close my eyes.

I have no will to live at all.

I want to be with my parents.

"I love you so much," I say to my parents. "I'm sorry you died because of me."

The tears spill again as I remember the last time I saw my parents.

CHAPTER 9

THE DOOR OPENS, and Enzo's main guy enters. My eyes are stinging from crying so much, but I know I need to go to work.

"Get up, the guests will be arriving soon."

Throwing back the cover, I stand and walk over to him. He's holding a bag in his hands, and I know it's what I'm supposed to wear for this stupid party. The bag is tiny, which means, whatever is inside is tiny.

I extend my hand and take the bag. Looking inside there's a very see-through bra and panties so small, everyone will be able to see everything. And a pair of gloves, of course.

"No shoes?" I ask sarcastically. Enzo is dressing me like a whore you'd find in a cheap brothel.

"No shoes. But, there's make-up in the bag the boss wants you to wear."

In the bottom of the bag are blue eye shadow and red lipstick. That's it. "Seriously?" I mutter too loudly.

"Seriously," he responds with mirth in his voice. Yep, he's probably going to give me to someone as a reward. Or he'll sell me to someone for the night. There's no way Enzo will get rid of me, I'm far too valuable to him. "This is what you're to wear."

"Fine." I start stripping right in front of him, showing no modesty at all. This 'outfit' leaves nothing to anyone's imagination. I'll basically be paraded around the house naked.

There's nothing more they can do to me to make me feel any worse than I already do.

But I'd take being shown off in these degrading clothes over having my parents killed. That choice is long gone now.

He backs up and leans against the wall as I stand, chest exposed, sliding on the stupid, useless bra. "Nice," he says, greedily ogling my breasts.

I glide the sweatpants over my hips, hooking my thumbs into the underwear I'm wearing and drag them down with the sweatpants.

He clears his throat, gawking at me.

Kicking them off, I grab the disgusting itsy-bitsy panties, and pull them up over my legs and hips. They really hide nothing. And by nothing, I mean *nothing.*

"You've got a hot little body," he says as he pushes off the wall and stalks toward me.

Pulling myself together, I stand tall and face him. He has a predatory gleam in his eyes. They sparkle with need; a desire so strong I know me saying 'no' will make no difference in the equation. I doubt he's a man who'd respect a woman if she refused, so I hold no hopes he'd control himself around me. Especially considering the way he's looking at me while he walks toward me.

He reaches me, lifts his hand to run it through my hair but stops himself short just as he's about to make contact. I stand, perfectly still, watching him . . . waiting. I shoot him a look of disgust.

"Damn it," he grumbles and steps back. He lowers his head, and stands as far away from me as he can. "Get ready." He lifts his chin and stares up at the ceiling while he leans against the wall and crosses his arms in front of his chest. "Get ready now." The strain in his voice is obvious. The struggle for him is real. For me, there's no struggle at all, because I know at some point tonight, someone will ruin the last living part of me.

I've lost my family, and soon I'll lose everything else.

Grabbing the ridiculous make-up, I head into the bathroom. I don't bother looking at myself, because it'll tear my heart out even more than it already is. I focus on getting the blue eyeshadow on my eyes, and red lipstick on my lips.

Enzo wants me to look like a clown.

I pack the eyeshadow right up to my eyebrows, and smudge the red lipstick with the back of my hand across my face. Flipping my head over, I shake out my hair, roughing it up so it's wavy and messy at the same time.

Staring at myself in the mirror I can't help but look forward to death. I'll welcome it, and embrace it when the time comes. And hopefully, death will make an appearance tonight.

Pulling my shoulders back, I strut my stuff out to the bedroom.

The henchman looks at me, his eyes roaming the length of my body slowly. He takes in every single part of me; his eyes stare down my body, and slowly return up to my face.

I feel nothing at all.

I'm not irritated by his animalistic stare. Not even remotely aroused by the bulge growing in his pants. I'm dead on the inside, and soon I'll be dead on the outside.

"I like the make-up. You look even sluttier. Just the way I like my girls."

I give him another look of disgust, but show him no other emotion. "Take me to Enzo," I say in an emotionless voice.

"I'll gladly take you anywhere you want, sexy."

He gestures for me to leave the room. I hear his heavy footsteps following me out and down the hall. By this time, the cleaning crew has left, and there are more security guards standing around in the foyer.

I feel all their eyes burning into my body as Enzo's right-hand man indicates the direction I should take.

We enter a huge ballroom, and I can hear Enzo's bellowing laugh the moment I'm inside.

There are many men in here. They range in ages, sizes and

what they're wearing. There are also a lot of young women, around my age – some even younger – dressed very similarly to me, lining the walls. Some are performing explicit sexual acts while others look frightened and huddle together.

This entire scene makes my stomach churn. The women are half, if not a quarter of the age of these men. But these men don't give a shit that these girls don't want to be here.

Enzo's roaring laughter makes me want to strangle him. If I can take him out with me when I die, I will.

"What do you want me to do?" I ask, interrupting him talking to other men. Most of whom are shamelessly staring at me.

"Who's this?" one asks as he sidles up closer to me.

His body is nearly touching mine, but Enzo steps between us. "This one is for me and me alone," Enzo warns while he shields me from the old guy eyeballing me.

"Oh, come on, Enzo. You've never been one to begrudge us a little taste. Is she sweet? I bet she tastes delicious." He makes my stomach stir with revulsion.

I peer around Enzo's shoulders and look him straight in the eyes. "I taste so good I'd bring you to your knees. But you're way too old to handle me."

Enzo turns and hits me across the face, the men laugh at the slap.

My face is on fire, but I'm not going to allow these monsters to get the better of me. I straighten myself, look past Enzo's fury and smile at the old guy. "I'd be surprised if you could still get it up without drugs."

This earns me another slap across the face.

"You shut up. Stop disrespecting my friends."

With each hit, I get angrier. But then I realize I'm not having visions when Enzo's hand touches my face.

I breathe in, straighten again, and shake out my hair. "I bet all you have left between your legs is shriveled-up skin."

And again, I'm hit, this time with a closed fist. A sickening crack echoes in my ears.

A stinging pain shoots ice throughout my body, starting at my nose.

I'm in so much pain, but I don't care. Tonight, I *will* die. But I'll die on my terms, not anyone else's.

The pain is incredible, agonizing and intense. My eyes water and my throat is closing. My nose is definitely broken. I can already feel my face swelling. I breathe through the pain and lift my shoulders.

"Do you have shares in Viagra?"

A punch, this time to my stomach.

"Damn, this bitch has balls. I want to break her, Enzo. I'll give you five hundred thousand for her."

"She's not for sale," Enzo yells at the old guy I'm taunting. "And you . . ." He grabs me around the upper arm, dragging me out of the ballroom. But I have no visions. I can't see anything. We get to the entrance, and he pushes me, making me fall forward to land on my knees. "Stay here until I need you." He strides back into the ballroom, leaving me alone.

I take a few deep breaths, then push off the floor to stand.

Blood is dripping out of my nose, droplets forming a small puddle on the floor. "Man, that hurts," I mumble to myself.

I drag my beaten body over to the staircase, and sit on the edge of the bottom step. I'm so tired.

Tired of living, and tired of having this damn gift which is turning out to be nothing but a nightmare. *A curse.*

When the fog of the pain lifts, I try to understand why I had no visions when Enzo was beating me. Have they left me forever? If so, I'll go announce it to him right now. Hopefully he'll put a bullet in my head.

But what if the catastrophic events of losing my parents, and the pain he was inflicting on me, somehow only temporarily stopped the visions?

I need to calm down enough to touch someone and see if I get another vision.

Breathing through my nose is impossible, considering it's

broken, so I close my eyes and take long, languid breaths through my mouth. When the adrenaline has calmed down, and I can feel my heart returning to a normal beat, I know I'm ready to test it.

Opening my eyes, I stand and notice one of the extra security men staring at me. "Are you okay?" he asks.

This intrigues me, because I'm sure they'd all have orders not to touch or talk to me. And he's not looking at me like he's a man starving for sex and wanting to consume me. He's staring at me like he's genuinely worried.

"I'll be okay," I reply and stand from the step.

I pretend to wobble, and it forces him to reach out and grab hold of me. The moment his hands touch my bare skin, I'm in a vision.

He's sitting on the floor in a family room, and he's changing the diaper of a little baby. "What's your mommy been feeding you, champ?" The baby looks at him and tries to eat his toes. "Seriously, kid, you stink."

I can't help but smile. Here's a big tough guy who's changing a baby's diaper.

As he wipes the baby, I look around the room. There's a cabinet near the TV that has a framed photo atop it. It's a picture of this guy in a tuxedo, with his arms around a woman in white. She's holding the camera up taking this selfie.

I smile, because this is obviously a wedding photo. It's clear to me from this picture that there's so much love and affection between them. How can he be armed and dangerous, working for an ass like Enzo, and then revert back to a family man? But then again, I've seen what Jude is capable of and he's never been angry with me. Actually, he's always protected me.

As crazy as it sounds, I miss him.

Turning back to look at the guy, he's sliding a little pair of jeans up the baby's legs. "You smell so much better, little man. No more of that awful stench." The baby smiles at him as if he knows what his dad is saying. The man lifts him in his arms and blows a raspberry on the baby's stomach.

His wife enters the room. Her brows are drawn in and her lips are pressed together. "Your boss is here," she says as she looks over her shoulder to someone who's behind her.

Jude follows with a small black briefcase.

"What the . . . ?" And I'm out of the vision.

The guy steps back, and assesses me. "Are you okay?" he asks. "You looked like you were going to fall."

"Who are you?" I ask, now more concerned than ever. Does Jude know I'm here? Did Dallas get to him? Is she alive? Is she safe?

"I'm no one," he responds by looking over his shoulder. "The boss wants you to stay here, so stay." He points to the first step leading up the staircase. "Sit down." He clenches his jaw in anger, and points again.

But I can tell this is just an act. He's putting on a show for everyone else who's here. "Okay," I respond and back away. When I feel the back of my leg hit the step, I squat down and sit.

He walks away, and I wait. I'm not sure what I'm waiting for, but something is going to happen. I'm more aware of my surroundings now.

Watching, I take particular note of the house, seeing where all the guards are positioned. Who's on their phone, who's got their eyes closed, and who I should keep clear of.

I may have my chance to get away from here, to finally escape or die trying.

Breathing deeply, I calm myself and try to gather my strength. I need today to define me. I can't live a life chained to a man who treats me like a punching bag. I have to try and get away.

I have to attempt to make a difference.

The music from the ballroom is loud. There's laughter and talking. I cringe at what could be going on in there. Some of the girls looked so frightened, but some of them looked too high to care.

This isn't a life worth living. Not being someone's caged animal.

The guy by the front door is watching something on his phone. He looks completely distracted. Enzo would kill him if he saw him. A couple more men walk toward the ballroom, they're talking about the girls, and telling each other what they want to do to them.

The hairs on my arms stand. *Sick bastards.*

But I have to keep my wits about me. I have to stay sane, because if I'm going to get away, I need to focus on me, and not on the disgusting things they're saying or doing.

Standing, I back away from the staircase, and slowly, carefully make my way toward the door. I have no idea how anything is going to happen. The guy at the door may be watching something on his phone, but he'll sure as shit see a five-foot-eight, hundred and twenty-pound girl trying to run away. But judging by the lack of food Enzo's provided me, I dare say I'm a lot less than a hundred and twenty pounds now.

The guy at the door places his phone in his pocket, and straightens his shoulders. He presses a finger to his ear, and nods his head. He's obviously receiving instructions.

The outside of this place has got to have more security, and the worst part is, I have no idea where the hell I am.

It doesn't matter, it's now or never.

"You can do this," I mutter to myself. "You have to do this."

I sneak a few steps behind the guy manning the door. My heart beats wildly as my hearing becomes more acute. I can hear so many sounds, but most are relevant to what's happening in that ballroom. But I do pick up on one sound, a heavy popping coming from just beyond the front door. A few men run toward me, but stop short and aim their guns at the door.

Unsure of what's happening, I seize the opportunity and prepare to run.

Hiding behind a pillar, I squat down and watch what's unfolding. Whatever's about to happen, it's going to occur through the front door. This is it. My chance. My only chance to *run.*

I crawl over behind a small table with an ugly bowl housing a goldfish. Ducking down, I stick my head out to see what's happening. I try to contain my noisy breathing so no one will hear me.

The men are all communicating, giving instructions to each other. The one I touched and had a vision of is behind all the others. He keeps gazing around the room, trying to look for something, or someone. Maybe me.

He can't see me, but I can see him.

The popping sounds increase in frequency and in duration, coming closer all the time. And now there are loud voices added to the popping sounds coming from the other side of the door.

Clearly something's going down. I can only assume it's an attack on Enzo.

It makes sense. The men he has here are all influential people in the underworld. Why not wipe them all out when they're in the one place together?

A logistical nightmare, though to me, it's an opportunity to get out. I have nowhere to go, but at least I'd be away from this hellhole.

The men in the foyer inch closer to the door. I try to stay hidden so they don't see me. But I think, in this moment, they have no idea I'm even here. I'm of no concern to them. They need to protect all the men in the ballroom, who by now, I suspect, know about the danger approaching.

My hands shake from nerves. My anticipation of the next few minutes is ringing with excitement and sheer terror.

Whatever happens, I'll be free, one way or another.

A giant explosion throws the men closest to the door back. My ears ring from the deafening blast.

Holding my hands over my ears, I let the ringing calm down for a few seconds before I make a run for it. This ringing will make it hard to get my bearings and run in the right direction. I want to get away from the danger, not run into it.

Where will I go?

I'm going to have to start my life over again. I have no money, and no family left. And anyone I'd trust with my secret would be in danger. I refuse to put anyone else in harm's way.

The adrenalin is pumping hard through my body as I watch what's unfolding. Men dressed in bullet proof vests and holding machine guns, enter the house, and push past the foyer toward the ballroom.

Gunshots sound continuously. People are being shot, people are yelling, and people are dying.

I push up off the floor with my eyes glued to the front door. Watching, I time my escape.

The ringing in my ears has settled, but the pounding in my head has taken over.

This is it.

Escape or die.

Lines of men come into the house, they've all got their guns aimed toward the back of the house, toward the ballroom. None of them have seen me.

When the line dwindles down, I look around the room. There are bodies everywhere. The guy I had a vision of is nowhere to be seen.

I make my run for it. I tear out the front door, jumping over a body laying across the threshold. He's murmuring and begging for help. But if I stop, I might not make it out alive. And I want to live, *if I can.*

I hit the pristine white pebbles on the driveway and they tear at the soles of my feet, which protest in pain, but I don't care. I need to get away. Looking over my shoulder, I'm surprised to see no one is after me.

I thought Enzo would attempt to spirit me away. Maybe he's dead. I can only wish.

I keep running, but have no clear idea where I'm going. I know I have to get away.

A black town car rolls to a stop a few hundred feet from me. My heart leaps into my throat and I stop running. My feet won't make it any further. They refuse to move.

Crap, someone's seen me. Is it Enzo? Did he get away? Is he here to collect his prize?

The back door opens, and I desperately look for an escape route. Even I know I can't outrun a bullet.

I start to run backward across the lawn, unable to think of the consequences of being taken again. I have to die. I can't go back into captivity.

"Alexa!" The voice is familiar. It's someone I know.

Jude.

Turning, I see him step toward me. His hands are up in surrender as he steps closer.

He's here.

"Alexa," he says in a much gentler tone. My feet have a mind of their own, and they take me to him. My heart calms and tears well in my eyes.

When I get to him, he takes in my appearance. Frowning, he steps back toward the car, leans in, and emerges seconds later with his coat. He walks toward me, and drapes the coat around my shoulders, sheltering me.

"Thank you," I whisper as I return my gaze to the ground.

"Alexa." He clears his throat. "Show me your face." I don't want him to see me like this. A tear falls from my eyes and a sob escapes my lips. I look up at him, showing him all my bruises. "Who did this to you?" He points toward my face.

"Enzo . . ."

I don't say another word. I don't need to. He steps closer, engulfs me in his arms, smashing me to his body. Our skin isn't touching, so I don't get a vision from him. Guilt floods me. Every part of me wants to get away from all this shit, all these bastards who think they can own me. But a small part of me likes it in his arms. For the first time in a long time, I feel protected.

"You're safe now," he mumbles. "I won't let anyone hurt you

again."

"He killed my parents," I sob into his chest.

"I know. I was too late. He killed my men who were protecting your parents."

His hands slide up my shoulders and lace into my hair. He kisses my forehead, and for a split second I'm lost in the comfort of Jude and his arms before being thrown into a vision.

"You went after the wrong person, my friend," Jude says to Enzo who's handcuffed to a chair. Jude smashes him in the mouth. Enzo's head brutally jerks to the side, before he turns his head forward. His mouth is bloody, and he spits out a couple of teeth.

"You're declaring war over a stupid bitch?" Enzo smirks.

Jude steps back and smiles at Enzo. "I'm not talking about Alexa. You went after her parents."

Enzo's smirk quickly fades. "They were collateral damage. She needed to be taught a lesson. You'd do the same thing," he says dismissively.

Jude turns to one of his men and gives him a small nod. The guy hands Jude a gun that he takes and aims at Enzo's head.

"Now you're collateral damage."

Before I see anything, I'm torn away from the vision. "Get her to the car," Jude says to one of his men. "Get her in there, and look after her. Anything happens to her, and you die." The guy steps forward and tries to guide me toward the car. I run after Jude and grab hold of his arm. "What?" he asks angrily before turning to see it's me and not one of his men. "What do you need, Alexa?" he asks in a much softer tone.

I stand looking at him, not sure what it is I want to say. I should tell him to not kill Enzo, but I *want* Enzo to stop breathing. "I . . ." My heart beats crazily as tears threaten again. A whirlpool of emotions bounce around inside me. I know he's going to kill Enzo and it's wrong, *and* right, and I have no idea how to resolve what's happening inside my mind.

So much devastation has and will continue to occur because

of me.

Jude watches me, but I'm struggling with what I want to say. "It's okay, Lexi. I've got this." He leans down and presses a gentle kiss to my forehead again. This time, I have no vision.

I don't know why.

"Take her back to the car, now," Jude orders.

Without contest, I allow his guy to lead me to the car and have trust in Jude. Trust him enough to know he'll take care of everything.

Regret soon overwhelms me, and I can't help my reaction. I should stop Jude before he kills Enzo. But then I know if Jude doesn't kill him, Enzo will—without hesitation—kill Jude and then me.

As I sit in the back of the car, emotional turmoil surrounds me.

Who did this to me? Someone put this stupid thing inside me, and now people are dying because of it.

My mind ticks away with old unanswered questions. But a new need arises quickly. I need to know who did this to me, but most importantly, I need to know, *why*.

As I sit in the back of the car, I'm lost in my own thoughts. Whatever horror is happening inside Enzo's mansion is now forgotten as I'm drawn into a world of intrigue, and anger. The longer I sit here, the angrier I get.

Rage overtakes everything else. I no longer feel remorseful because Enzo's going to die. I don't care about him. Instead, the anger inside me keeps building to the point that I want to scream and yell.

My hands vibrate from the sheer fury captured inside my body. Tightening them into fists, I try and relax them. But I can't.

The more time I have, the madder I am.

Someone did this to me.

And I need to find who that 'someone' is, and get some damned answers.

The back door opens, and Jude slides into the car. He looks me over and crinkles his forehead. "Are you okay?" he asks.

Shaking my head, I grind my teeth together. "I need to know who did this to me, Jude. I want . . . no, I *deserve* to know why."

He nods his head then rakes his hand through his hair. The car turns around and takes off down the long driveway. "If you want to know, then I'll find them."

I look at him, and can see he understands my overwhelming thirst to know. "I do. I need to know who's done this, because I want them to take it out of me. Too many people have died. I can't be responsible for more death. I'll go insane. And I want to know *why* they did it, and why *me*."

He lets out a deep breath, and nods his head again.

As we drive down some road, in some city, in some state, the reality of everything that's happened cloaks me with sadness.

I've gone through so many emotions since I woke from having my appendix removed. But the most overwhelming of all is sadness.

I've caused so much pain and hurt to the ones I love, and this breaks my heart.

Closing my eyes, I hold in the tears. But suddenly, my body reacts to the internal chaos screaming at me. I break down and sob. It's not just tears I'm releasing, it's so much more.

Jude pulls me into his arms, and I lean my head on his shoulder. "It'll be okay," he says as his arms tighten around me.

We spend a good chunk of the drive silent. My crying eventually subsides, and my eyes become heavy. The whir of the tires on the road, the gentle movement of the car, and the warmth of the air eventually makes me sleepy.

I bend my legs up toward my chest, cradling them, and lie down on the bench seat. With my head on Jude's lap, and him running his fingers through my hair, I close my eyes and fall asleep.

There's a weightless feeling. I can sense myself moving, but I know I'm not walking. I open my eyes and look around; it's like

I'm floating through the foyer of Jude's house.

"Is she okay?" I hear someone ask. *Frank.*

"She'll be okay. You'll have to get her something to eat as soon as she wakes."

"She looks like shit. It doesn't look like she's eaten since she was taken from us." This makes me smile, because I can recognize Frank's caring voice anywhere.

"She's lost too many pounds. Make sure you've stocked everything she likes to eat."

"I will. Do you need help getting her to bed?"

"No, I've got it. Go back to the kitchen."

"Yes, sir," Frank responds.

When I hear him walk away, I open my eyes and look at Jude. "I can walk," I say to him as he carries me through the house.

"I know you can walk." He smiles at me and tightens his grip.

"You can put me down."

"Not a chance."

I hold onto him, and allow him to take me into my room. He places me on the chair near the bed, then drags the covers back. Without saying a word to me, he walks into the closet, and comes out with pajamas. "I'll have a shower first," I say as he lays them on the bed.

"Would you like a bath? I can get it ready for you." He starts walking away, but I stand and grab hold of his elbow.

"I just want to have a quick shower."

"But a bath will help you relax. Let me draw you one," he insists.

"Jude," I say as I shake my head. "I'm having a shower."

He steps back and rubs his hand over his forehead. "I'll leave you to it then. Frank's preparing you something to eat, so when you're finished . . ."

"Thank you," I say before he adds anything else. "For everything."

"I'll be in my office. I'll return when you're done." He walks toward the door, but stops. I hold onto hope that he'll come back and hug me again. God knows, I need some human contact after all the crap I've been through.

He doesn't turn back and give me a hug, instead he continues out the door.

Relaxing my shoulders, I head into the bathroom, and turn on the shower. Stripping out of this revolting bra and panties, I throw them straight in the trash and get into the hot, pelting water.

Leaning my forehead against the cool tile, I let the hot water work its magic on me.

When I exit the bathroom, I find Jude with a stranger in the suite's living room.

"Alexa, this is Dr. Morrison. I called him here to look you over," Jude says.

The doctor approaches me, offering his hand, but I bury both of mine in the pockets of my robe. I don't think I can handle any more visions right now. Using the techniques Dallas and I worked on, I'm able to take myself out of the vision I experience when the doctor touches my face. When he finishes examining me, he confirms that aside from some deep bruises and a few lacerations, all that's wrong with me is a broken nose. He manipulates my nose for a few moments, and suddenly, I'm able to breathe normally.

Jude shows the doctor out, while I sit on the couch and wait for him to return. After all the pain and fear of the last weeks, I feel empty, numb. I'm tempted to relax in the apparent safety Jude offers, but I know that's a bad idea. Jude is no saint, and he originally kidnapped me so he could use me for his own gain, just like Enzo.

I wonder, not for the first time, if my life will ever be my own again.

CHAPTER 10

"I'm glad to see you're back, Miss Lexi!" Frank makes his way over to me when I enter the kitchen, and moves to hug me. He stops and looks at me. I throw myself into his arms, but I'm careful not to touch his skin. "I'm so happy you've returned. Mr. Jude has been in a bad mood since you were . . ." He pulls back and looks at me. "Well, since you've been gone."

"How are you? Did they hurt you after I left?"

He rubs a spot on his head. "Nothing this old man can't deal with. But you, did they feed you at all? You look like you've lost twenty pounds."

I shake my head and lower my gaze. "I wasn't getting much." Sadness overtakes me. "When he took Dallas . . ." I stop talking and look around. Happiness quickly replaces the misery. "Wait, is Dallas here?" I look around the kitchen, hoping for a happy reunion.

"Miss Dallas was here, but she's home now."

My broad, hopeful smile instantly disappears. As much as I want to see her again, I know it's not safe for her. "She's home?" I ask, full of a perverse hope that Frank is going to say 'no' and bring her out to join me. But this isn't a life for her.

"Mr. Jude took her home himself. He made sure she was inside her house safely before he left."

"Oh," I say. My mood flat-lines, but I'm happy she's home.

I wish I could see my parents again.

"Sit down, I'll make you something to eat. Are you hungry? Thirsty? I can make you anything you like. Pancakes? French toast? Eggs?" He looks at me, hopeful for an answer. But I give him nothing. "How about I make everything and you can have some or all of it?" He ushers me to a chair at the table, and gets to work in the kitchen.

"Frank, it's too late for any of those, they're breakfast foods. How about something simple?"

He lifts a frypan from a lower cupboard and places it on the counter. "And who says they're breakfast foods? I'll make you some pancakes."

He doesn't even bother waiting for my answer; he just starts whipping up the batter. "Okay." What more can I say? Nothing.

Frank is talking as he's preparing the batter, but I've switched off. Instead I sit and watch the rolling green lawn, now lit by the full, bright moon outside, beyond the glass wall and pool. I'm lost in my own mind, when someone touches my shoulder.

Looking up, I'm expecting to see Frank, but it's not. It's Jude. I offer him a small smile then my eyes glance back outside. "How are you feeling?" He sits on the chair opposite me.

"Better. The shower helped, and now Frank's making me pancakes."

"Best damn pancakes this side of America," Frank chimes in happily from the kitchen.

Jude smirks at Frank's words. "I'll have some too, Frank."

"Yes, Mr. Jude."

Silence falls over us. As I watch the beautiful view, Jude watches me. "Tell me what happened while he had you."

A lump rapidly forms in my throat, and tears develop in my eyes. "He wasn't as accommodating as you."

"I can imagine. Tell me everything." He extends his fingers toward my hand, but I move it and slide it under my butt. I don't want a vision tonight, and I don't have the energy left to fight one. I don't want to see into anyone's future.

Jude creases his brows together and lets out a sigh. "Judging by your face, I take it he hit you." I don't reply, I simply nod. "Did he do anything else to you?" The question is leading, he's waiting for me to answer honestly. I know what he means, but neither he nor I are willing to say it aloud. So, I shake my head.

He takes in a sharp, relieved breath.

"He killed my parents, Jude."

"I know."

"He assassinated them in cold blood. They didn't even stand a chance. Because of me, my parents are dead. Because of me, Dallas was kidnapped."

"It's not because of you. It's because of what was done to you."

A tear falls as sorrow fills every drop of blood, every nerve, every single part of me. "Jude . . ." I mumble through my tears. "I can't go on like this. If I stay alive, this will only keep happening. You have to kill me."

Jude abruptly stands from the chair, and paces in front of the table. "What are you talking about? Absolutely not. No fucking way, Alexa." His shoulders are high, and his jaw is tightly clenched. He's angry I've even asked. "I can't do that. Don't ask me."

"Then someone will come after you, and Frank, and Dallas again," I state matter-of-factly. "It's the only way any of you can escape the danger."

"Danger? Do you know who I am?" Jude asks with a cheeky smile.

"How about Dallas? As long as I'm alive, she'll always be a target. They can get to me through her."

Jude sits back down and sighs once more. He sees the logic in what I'm saying, to sacrifice me for the sake of everyone else. "No," he says. "But . . ."

"There's no 'but.' There's no other way."

"There is."

"The only way around this, Jude, is if we find who put it in me, and get them to reverse it and get it out of me."

He stares at me, emotionless. Shit, he's actually considering it. "That's exactly what I was going to propose. We find who, we get answers, and then we evaluate what the next step is. If someone gave you this, then they'll have a way to take it away."

"What if . . . ?"

"Don't question the unknown, Lexi."

Frank places a plate of huge, fluffy pancakes down in front of me. He smiles, sets a bottle of maple syrup beside it, and waits. "Thank you, Frank," I say looking down at the pancakes I no longer feel like eating.

"Miss Lexi, let Mr. Jude help you. He'll always have your back, and I'll always be here for you." He leans down and wraps his arm around my shoulders, giving me a reassuring squeeze.

"But . . ." I try to say.

Frank shakes his head at me. "Take one day at a time, and let him help." He looks at me, then to Jude. "I'll get your pancakes, Mr. Jude." He backs away and smiles.

As I'm lost in thought, staring at my pancakes, Frank places an identical plate with pancakes in front of Jude. He starts eating, and when he's consumed nearly half he says, "You'll hurt Frank's feelings if you don't eat."

Absentmindedly I turn to look over my shoulder toward the kitchen, but Frank has now disappeared. "I don't want to make him feel bad." Picking up my fork I nibble on one of the pancakes.

"Lexi?"

"Yeah?"

"Turn your head, look at me." Facing Jude, I turn my head to the side. "Tell me what you can do with your gift."

I scoff at the word 'gift.' "You mean the bane of my existence?"

"Yes, that. Tell me what more you can do with it."

"Dallas and I were practicing me being able to avoid or leave a vision, like I did with Dr, Morrison while he was examining me. But I didn't get to practice very much because she got away."

"Is that all?"

"I can walk around in my visions, and I can talk to the person, although Dallas said it was faint and weird. Um . . . I think that's it. What do you need me to do?"

"I'm not going to use what you have. But your eye," he says, pointing to my left eye, "is nearly entirely blue. There's less than a third that's green. The rest is bright blue."

In the daze of the last few days, I haven't really examined my eye to see how blue it's turned. "Huh," I mumble to myself. "I know the more I practice, the stronger I get in my visions. But until whatever this thing is can get taken out of me, I want to learn to control them totally. For me. I want to learn how to touch and not get thrown into a vision. If I have to live with it for whatever duration, then I want to learn how to use it for *my* benefit. I need to control it."

"I'll start digging around and see what my people can find. But you have to tell me everything you know."

Nodding my head, I agree to give this a try. "Can you tell me how Dallas is?"

The corner of his mouth picks up in a smirk. "She found the sunglass store, and Stevie, and insisted she call me. Of course, I knew who she was, and we had already found who had you."

"People will always want me if they know what I'm capable of."

"Which is why I had already given the go-ahead to find whoever did this to you."

I should be surprised, but I'm not. It should surprise me that he's started the process to find whoever did this to me, but it doesn't. Maybe, this way I'll get some answers and be able to live normally again. "Thank you," I say quietly.

"You're welcome." He inhales the rest of his pancakes.

"How was Dallas?" I pause for a second thinking about the

time we were together at Enzo's. Then I add, "I miss her."

"She's very spirited." He chuckles. "Frank!" He calls loudly. Frank reenters the kitchen and waits for Jude. "Coffee."

"Yes, Mr. Jude," Frank replies and starts making Jude a coffee.

"You could always say 'please,'" I bite toward Jude.

"Why? He gets paid to work for me." Jude dismisses me, but this pisses me off.

"Kindness costs nothing, Jude. You don't have to be a jackass to the guy who cooks your meals. You never know, he may spit in your pancakes the next time he makes them."

Frank chuckles from behind me, and Jude shoots him a silent frown. It makes me laugh, because Frank clears his throat and pretends not to notice Jude's expression.

"He won't spit in my pancakes," Jude says surely.

"Well, I know he won't spit in mine. Yours, on the other hand . . . let's just say I'm never eating from your plate."

Jude runs his hand over his face, then around the back of his neck. "I swear you give me a headache." He looks up just in time to see Frank placing a coffee in front of him. "Thank you," he mumbles in such a small voice it's barely audible.

"What was that?" I push.

Frank smiles, and Jude nearly bares his teeth to me. "I said, 'thank you.'" He lifts the corner of his mouth, scowling at me.

"You're welcome, Mr. Jude," Frank replies with humor in his voice.

I stand and walk over to the fridge, grabbing a juice, and join Jude back at the table. Frank's left and we're alone again. "Was Dallas angry at me for getting her kidnapped?" My stomach tightens in anticipation of his answer.

Why wouldn't she be mad?

"Not at all. She was worried. She tried to make me get you right away. But, I know Enzo, and I know what he's capable of. I had to wait for an opportunity."

"What do you mean?" I sit back in the chair and cross my arms defensively in front of my chest.

"Don't get angry."

"I'm not angry, but I want to know what you mean. I want to understand."

"Ronan was working on finding out what happened."

My face must reflect what I'm thinking. *Who the hell is Ronan?* "Who?"

"Ronan. He's the head of my security."

"Do I know who he is?"

"I'll introduce you. Anyway, he was working on finding who took you. The people who raided the house were pretending to be government."

"So, who are they?" What is going on?

"We're not sure yet. But, I think it has something to do with what you can do."

"Huh?" What?

"And Enzo took you from them."

"Then it only makes sense that Enzo has more power than they did."

"It doesn't. I think they were ambushed. They weren't expecting another player to enter the game."

Pushing the plate with the pancakes to the side, I lean my elbows on the table and drop my head into them. "What?" I say into the palms of my hands.

"Ronan and I think whoever raided us orchestrated it to make it look like it was a raid by the police against me. But in fact, it had nothing to do with me. They just wanted to separate us."

"Then why didn't they find you and kill you?"

"Because then we'd know for sure it wasn't FBI or CIA or any government department."

"You mean any government department that goes on record. It could be some agency so far underground even the President doesn't know about it."

Jude smiles at me. "Looks like you're becoming quite cynical, Miss Murphy."

"Look at the company I keep," I quip quickly.

"Touché." He smirks. "Ronan is working on finding out who they were. But, they have firewalls like we've never seen before. They have gone to great lengths to hide who they are."

"It doesn't make sense, Jude. Why would someone give me this thing," I point to my brain, meaning the visions I get, "and then go into hiding without trying to make contact with me? It doesn't make sense."

"Maybe they're watching from afar to see how you handle it, what you do with it. Maybe they're waiting for something."

"It doesn't make sense at all. If they're waiting for something, why try to take me a couple of weeks ago? Why not try again? They got in here successfully once, they could do it again. Who knows, maybe they're listening and watching us right now. Maybe they know what we're saying."

"Impossible. I have this place swept every day."

"Every day? Why? No one comes here, and you're like a recluse."

"There's only a handful of people I trust. I have no idea when anyone might turn on me, so I have Ronan sweep for bugs."

"And what if Ronan isn't who he says he is?"

Jude throws his head back and laughs whole-heartedly. "Now you're a comedian."

"There's only one truth I know, Jude. And that is, I have no idea what's happening. I need to question everything, and everyone."

"I can appreciate your way of thinking. You came from a world where you were only a spectator. Now that's all changed." I nod my head. Jude takes a moment, drinking from his coffee cup. "Ronan and I are working on possible theories of who it is. I'm exhausting every connection I have to find these people."

"What if, what if . . ." Man, I don't think he's going to like what I have to say.

"No," he says before I even get to finish.

"You don't know what I'm thinking."

"I know, alright. I can tell by that look on your face. You're ready to walk out of here and head into a situation in which you know they'll be waiting for you. Like going to find Dallas. They'll be watching Dallas."

"If they were watching her, why didn't they stop Enzo's men from taking her?"

"Perhaps they were hoping for Dallas to lead them to you. Or maybe they knew Dallas was just a pawn. Someone they're willing to sacrifice to get to the king, the major prize."

"Ha," I chuckle aloud. "It's the queen who holds all the power. Without the queen, all the king can do is run around the board, his enemy always chasing him." Shit, is that what I'm doing? Merely running, just waiting to be caught. "I have to find them, Jude."

"We will. I promise you, Lexi, we'll find them."

"Either way, I have to make sure Dallas is no longer in danger. Either we find them, or . . ."

"There is no 'or.' We'll find them." He takes a deep breath, and I get lost in the 'or.' "Eat. You need to put some weight back on."

I flip my head to the side to look at him. "Don't you know you should never tell a woman she's too fat or too thin? And yes, her ass always looks good in it. And no, you never say 'you look good for your age.'" Jude laughs and holds his hands up in surrender. "And is this why there's no Mrs. Jude around here?"

"There's no Mrs. Jude, because no one's ever kept my interest." He then mumbles something under his breath I don't quite catch.

"What was that?" I ask.

"I didn't say nothing." He stands from the table. "I have to talk to Ronan; will you be okay here?"

"Sure thing. I can always call Frank. Actually, why is he here so late? Shouldn't he be home?"

"I've moved him in here permanently."

What? "Why?"

He shrugs and looks out the back-glass doors. "Makes sense to have him here. And I can keep an eye on him."

It's obvious to me that Jude cares about Frank, although he'll never admit it. "Okay," I reply, not pushing on for more. He doesn't need to say anything; I can tell.

"I'll be back soon. If you need anything, call Frank to get it for you."

He walks away, but I hear his footsteps reenter the kitchen. As I turn to see if he's forgotten anything, he kisses my head, then leaves again.

"Miss Lexi, may I join you?" Frank asks suddenly appearing.

"Of course." I push the plate away, now no longer hungry at all. I've picked at my food, but I'm not really hungry.

"Didn't you like it?" He looks at the uneaten pancakes.

"I'm not really hungry. I am tired though."

"You should go to bed. You've had a few very trying weeks."

"If only you knew what's been happening." He gives me a half-smile, and it speaks volumes. He knows; he knows everything. He may only be the chef, but he's the chef who hears everything and knows what's going on.

Finishing off my juice, I stand and grab my plate. "I'll do that." Frank takes it from my hands and walks over to the sink. "You look tired, Miss Lexi. It's best you rest."

"Good night," I say as I walk out of the kitchen.

When I get to my room, I brush my teeth, then climb into the bed. Turning the TV on, I flick through the channels until I find a chick flick. Lost in the world of the movie, I'm quickly brought back to reality when Jude enters my bedroom.

My eyes go to what he's holding. It's a briefcase.

The same briefcase I saw in the vision earlier.

"I-"

I hold my hand up to him. "Tell him thank you from me."

Jude looks down at the briefcase, then back to me. "I will." He pauses, watching me. "I won't be long."

I nod my head and smile. "I know," I respond.

Once Jude leaves, I close my eyes and relax into the bed. The TV's noise is on in the background, and my heart instantly cracks. I miss my Mom and Dad so much.

And now, they're gone and I'll never see them again.

CHAPTER 11

THE BED DIPS behind me, and someone gently runs their hand up and down my thigh. Turning, I see Jude, dressed in a suit, sitting on the bed. "Good morning," he says, tilting his head to look at me.

"What time is it?" I sit up in bed and scrub my hands over my face then run them through my hair.

"I like your hair like that." He points, and has a small chuckle to himself.

"Does it look bad?" trying to run my fingers through it, I'm met with definite knot resistance. "Don't answer that question."

"Your bruises are healing." He reaches forward and is about to run his hand down my cheek, but pulls back.

"You don't want me to see what you're doing later?" Truthfully, I'm a little hurt. I've been back at Jude's for three days, and he keeps kissing my head and hugging me.

Human touch is important. In this case, it keeps me sane. "Guilty. But for now, I'd like you to get up and get ready."

I sigh and look down at the fluffy blanket on the bed. "I don't really feel like doing anything. I'm kind of missing my parents." I grab hold of the pillow next to me, hug it and sink back into the bed.

"You've been fairly miserable since you've been back. Not coming out to eat, lying in bed virtually all day. So I'm taking you out." He stands from the bed and in one swoop, he rips the covers off me. "Get up, have a shower, and get ready. Frank's making bacon and eggs for you."

"Have you eaten?" I ask, still defiantly lying in the bed. I try to pull the covers up again, but I lose the battle when Jude rips them clean off the bed and throws them toward the chair in the room.

"Nope, I'm waiting for you."

Exhaling a deep breath, I curl up further into my pillow. "I'll be there soon." *No, I won't.*

"No, you won't."

Damn him for being able to read me. "Yeah, I will. I promise. Go away, let me get dressed in peace." *I mean, let me go back to sleep.*

The bed dips again, and I roll my eyes. "Not going anywhere, sweetheart. Get up. I'm waiting here until you're ready."

"Just . . . go away."

"Nope. And if I have to pick you up and strip you to get you in the shower, then I'll have no problem doing that."

"Why does it sound like you're smiling, and you'd take great pleasure in stripping my clothes off?"

He clears his throat, and the bed moves again. "Because I'd have a good time looking at you."

This makes me smile. He's so damn cheeky, and smug. "I'll be out in a bit. Let me get ready."

"I'll wait. I'll call for Frank to bring my coffee in here. FRANK!" he yells loudly.

"Hey, give the guy a break. He doesn't need to be running after you all the time."

"Oh, look who's woken up with a backbone." He smugly glares at me.

Anger rises inside me. "You did not just say that." I sit up in bed.

Jude chuckles and crosses his left leg over his right one.

"Sounds like I did. FRANK!" he calls again.

"Jesus, you're a pain in the ass. Leave the poor guy alone. He does enough for you."

"Then get up."

"Ugh," I grumble as I swing my legs over the side of the bed. "Go away, leave me in peace."

He shakes his head. "I'll leave you alone when you get in the shower." He smells toward me. "Actually, when did you shower last?"

I smack him on the shoulder, and he moves his body with the shove. "Alright, alright. I get it. I have to get up. I'll do it, but I'm doing it under protest."

"Duly noted, and disregarded. Hurry up, because Frank will have breakfast ready soon."

Standing to my feet, I head into the walk-in, grab clothes, and head toward the bathroom. Jude's still in my bedroom, waiting for me. "Go away," I call as I close the bathroom door.

"I'll be here when you get out," he yells back.

Ass.

"Where are you taking me, Jude? Is it work-related?"

He slides into the back of the car on the seat beside me. "No, it's not. It's somewhere I think you need to go."

Ugh, great. He's taking me to a shrink. "I'm not losing my mind," I blurt.

He swings his head around to look at me. "I never said you were." Judging by his body language, and the humor in his eyes, he finds my statement amusing.

"Then where are we going?" The car leaves the grounds, and I look out the window at the woodlands framing the road. Jude's house is isolated, away from everything. I suppose it makes it more difficult for him to be found if he's living in the wilderness.

"You're not even listening." He touches my leg, making me

turn to peek at him over my shoulder. "What? You have that look on your face."

"What look?" I ask.

"The one that says you're thinking about something."

"Huh?" I shrug my shoulders. "I'm not as transparent as you think I am."

He coughs into his hand, which quickly becomes a laugh. "Yeah, let's go with that."

"You're amused now."

"Yep." He smiles again.

This has me staring at him. His calm face and relaxed shoulders makes him look so much younger and freer. "Why are you still in this line of work, Jude?" Suddenly his face changes. His jaw jerks tight, and he narrows his eyes. He takes in a deep breath, then he exhales it slowly.

"It's not something I want to talk about," he says after a long, silent moment.

"But, there's got to be a reason. I mean," I gesture around the beautiful, expensive car we're riding in, "clearly you have enough money. I'd go as far to say you probably don't need to work another day in your life."

"I don't," he answers candidly.

"So, why do it then? Why continue. It's obviously not about the money."

"I've told you before, it's about the power."

I shake my head and turn to look at the passing landscapes. "Let's go with that." I smile, because I've thrown his words back at him.

"You don't believe me?"

"Yeah, I do," my voice has a higher than usual pitch.

He grumbles and turns his body toward me. "It's the one thing I'm good at."

"You're good at illegal activities?"

"I'm good at hurting people, and I enjoy it. The rest is a

bonus." He doesn't bat an eyelid when he speaks. He's so matter-of-fact about it that it shocks me. "I have influence, and I'm known. The power is intoxicating."

"But you're not a good guy," I blurt out, not being able to stop myself.

"Have I done anything to you?" He lifts his hand to scrub over his chin. The act is innocent, but damn sexy.

"Well, let's see. You kidnapped me."

"Semantics." He waves the same hand dismissively.

"You held me against my will."

"In the past," he quips.

"And . . ."

"Really there's no 'and.' I may have technically kidnapped you, but I've always protected you and made sure you were looked after." I tilt my head down at him as if to say, 'What the hell are you talking about?' "Other than when Enzo got to you, but even then, I didn't stop looking for you."

"I don't know what I'm going to do, Jude."

"We're going to find who gave you your power."

"What happens once we find them? Once they take it out of me? What if they can't take it out of me? What if I can never get rid of it? Do you know how dangerous this is? If they can't take it out—whoever *they* are – then there's really no other choice than to destroy me."

"You're not going to die. I won't let it happen."

"Jude, let's be serious here for one minute." I hold up a finger to indicate one, then point it at him.

"I've never been anything but serious when it comes to you, Lexi."

More questions arise from his statement, but those questions can wait for another time. "Jude," I huff in annoyance.

"Lexi," he mimics me.

"I'm serious. What I have is untapped potential. I'm getting stronger every day, with every vision I have I'm able to control it more. I don't know how far this can go. What if I can have visions without even touching people? Do you even realize what this could mean? The possibilities . . . the power."

He reaches for my hand, but pulls back at the last moment and places it on my thigh, giving it a gentle squeeze. "Then we'll figure it out together. I promise you, Lexi, I won't let anyone get anywhere near you again." He pauses and smiles at me. "How do you feel about being microchipped? That way, I can keep an eye on you at all times and I'll know where you are."

The question is ludicrous, and his tone is even more ridiculous. "Should I wag my tail and let you scratch me behind the ear?"

He laughs but his face splits back into seriousness. "Is that a flat-out no? Or are you willing to negotiate?"

"Negotiate? As in you can microchip my ass but not my neck? Or would you prefer the microchip to be in my tooth? The answer is no to microchipping. I'm not going to stray," I add with an obvious eye roll.

"Got it, no microchipping. Then, my negotiation is a panic button and a body guard." Grinding my teeth together, I turn to avoid him. "Good, no resistance."

"You're misreading my silence for compliance."

"It's to keep you safe."

"And the bodyguard will have a gun, right?"

He laughs again. And him finding what I'm saying amusing is beginning to grate on my nerves. "All my men have guns, so the answer is yes."

"I'm struggling with everything going on. Can we drop this conversation?"

He squeezes my thigh again. "For now, yes we can."

Bringing my arm up to the rest, I lean my elbow on it and balance my chin on my closed fist. *For now,* what an ass. He's going to bring this up again, and I need to be prepared with an argument as to why I shouldn't have a panic button and a bodyguard.

But in reality, maybe I really should have them.

Ugh, I don't know.

What a mess.

Closing my eyes, I try and push myself out of the headspace I'm in. I wish I had someone I could talk to about all this stuff. How I feel about it all, how I hate having people in danger all the time because of me.

Jude's lifestyle is already a dangerous one, but how does he do what he does and still sleep at night? The thought of Dallas hurting again, makes my stomach churn with worry. Guilt is pulsing strongly as I try to come to terms with everything.

"We're here," Jude announces.

Looking out the window, we're in front of a vault in a cemetery. Realization rapidly dawns on me.

We're here to see my parents.

"Jude," I say as I turn to look at him, tears stinging my eyes, my body shaking. "You brought me to see my parents."

"I did." He leaves the car, and walks around to my side. As I pull the handle he opens the door from the other side.

Swinging my legs out, the jitters overtake me and make my hands tremble. "Do I look okay?" I ask as I try in vain to fix my hair.

"You look beautiful." He holds his hand out to me.

My throat constricts and I blink like crazy to keep the tears at bay. *I'm not going to cry. I'm not going to cry.*

"Lexi?" Jude urges me with his offered hand.

"Yeah," I mumble. I grab his hand, and notice there's no vision. He looks down to where our hands are joined, then to me. "No vision," I reaffirm his unasked question.

His brows knit together, the concern on his face obvious. His lips break the serious straight line, and turn upward into a small smile. Perhaps I've mistaken the expression on his face. Maybe, it's not concern, possibly it's something else. Something much less sinister.

The huge stone building blatantly stares at me. The door to the vault is open, with a caretaker standing to the side. The building is old, like hundreds of years old and the name 'Murphy' is carved into the stone above the door. "I never knew they had this," I say aloud but more for myself.

"Your parents had an airtight will. Your mother drew them up, and it was detailed in what they wanted to happen once they died."

I smile at what Jude says, because that sounds exactly like my mother. "It doesn't surprise me," I say, smiling though sad. "What does surprise me is how quickly their bodies were released. I thought, being an execution, the coroner would hold onto them and not let them go."

Jude kicks at a few small pebbles outside the vault. "I may have helped with that process being quicker than ordinary."

I turn to look at him, tilting my head slightly to avoid the sun, but to get a clearer look at the expression on his face. "Why would you do that?"

"Their death was deemed an execution, and I know you wouldn't want their funeral delayed. So, I paid a few people to hurry up and release the body. No sense in keeping them away from where they wanted to be laid to rest."

My heart skips a beat. It flutters its little wings like crazy, then settles down. "You did this for them?" I look to the vault door, then back to Jude.

He shakes his head, and offers me a genuinely warm smile. "I did it for you."

Damn.

Why does he have to be so normal . . . and nice?

"Thank you, it means everything to me for you to step in and help them." I look back to the vault door, and notice the incredibly bored caregiver. "I'm not sure I'm ready to go in there." I squeeze Jude's hand.

He steps in front of me, and places his hands on my shoulders. Slowly he runs his palms up and down my arms.

"I'm here for you, whatever you want to do."

Swallowing hard, I look up into his deep, dark eyes. They really are black, there's no color to them. "Your eyes are so dark," I utter to myself.

"They're black." He looks away, embarrassed, before blinking for a few seconds. When he turns his head to look at me, something new flashes in his eyes. It's an emotion I can't describe. Something so severe and powerful, my own body doesn't know how to react.

The blood running through my veins quickens, as does the breath desperate to escape. Parting my lips, a murmur whispers past them. *What's happening?*

"I . . . um . . ." Before I say, or do anything stupid, I compose myself and stand taller. "I want to go inside." But, *do I?*

"Do you want me to come in with you?"

My gaze travels over his shoulder where I stare at the vault, knowing my parents are in there. The reminder of how they died catapults me back into reality. "I think I can do it on my own," I say, trying to find the courage to believe my own words.

He steps away and tilts his chin down. A flash of hurt passes before he lifts his head and offers me a smile. "I'll be right here if you need me."

"Thank you," I say as I turn to look at the vault again. Taking a hesitant step forward, my heartbeat increases as my palms perspire. Wiping them down my jeans, I pause and try to compose myself before I go in.

My pulse is thundering so forcefully I can hear it echoing in my ears.

I take another step forward.

Fear quickly rises, as does sadness and hopelessness.

My feet move on their own, and I tremble with an uneasy, scared feeling bubbling away inside.

I shouldn't be frightened because this is the resting ground of my parents. But this turmoil of emotions is coming at me, thick and strong.

As my feet continue on their mission to enter the vault, guilt trumps every other emotion. Moving up the few steps, I enter the vault. Inside lie two coffins, next to each other, with a third place free. One coffin is smaller in size, and lighter in color, while the bigger one is richer in shade. My father is on my left, my mother on my right, and a place beside her is set with a plaque reading, *'Our little girl is lost, please find your way home soon.'*

Hurt rips me to shreds, and tears burn my eyes. I clasp at my chest, and struggle to hold my bleeding soul together.

Running my hand over Dad's coffin, the ache inside erupts free. Sobbing, I fall to my knees, completely ashamed. Consumed with remorse, I bring my hands up to hide my face and break down.

Absorbed by guilt, I chant to my parents, "I'm sorry. I did this to you. I'm so sorry." The torture inside tears its way through me. It slashes a huge hole where my heart once lay. It destroys me, completely, totally, *utterly.*

I lift my head to glance around in this vault. It's cold and heartless and nothing like my parents. My mother was tough and the disciplinarian, but she was always fair and loving. Dad, he was my rock. He was my strength when I needed him most, and he was my hero.

Slumping further to the ground, I cry even harder. I had only seventeen short years with my parents before they were ripped away from me in a callous and cold-hearted murder, ordered by a monster. I've now lost hope. Hope that one day my Dad would walk me down the aisle, or that my Mom would hold her first grandchild. Hope of having them in my life until they passed in their sleep holding hands. It's all been brutally torn away.

And all because of me.

I killed them.

I killed my parents.

"I'm so sorry," I whisper to them again, hoping they find it in their hearts to forgive me. "I'm so so sorry," I weep over and over again.

Collapsing completely to the floor, I lay my head on the cold concrete floor and cry. Overwhelming pain wraps around me. Nothing can mend my broken heart. Nothing can take the guilt and agony away.

Closing my eyes, I wish for death to take me. I deserve to die. I should be in a coffin instead of them. It's because of me, *me!*

I want Satan to open the floor and swallow me down. I hope he hears my prayers. To take me and bring them back. But I know they can never live again.

"I promise you my soul, please take me and bring them back," I try to make a deal, my life for theirs. "Please, use my soul, destroy it, ruin it, just take it."

They were massacred at too young an age.

Because of me.

"I'm sorry," I cry again, too ashamed to open my eyes and face the reminder of their merciless deaths.

My tears run dry, but the sadness runs deeper. It consumes me whole.

Two strong arms engulf my limp body and effortlessly lift me from the ground.

"Lock the door and leave me in here," I beg.

He says nothing. Instead, he carries me out to the car, where he slides me into the back, and rests my head on his lap. The motion of the car does nothing to calm me. Inside I'm hysterical, screaming how it's my fault how they died because of me.

On the outside, exhaustion has taken control of my body, and I'm lifeless.

Jude draws lazy circles on my back, while he talks to the driver and tells him to make the temperature inside the car warmer and turn on soothing music.

My heart is hurting. More, now I've seen what I've done to my parents.

"Jude," I say softly, hoping he heard me.

"Yeah, sweetheart," he responds in a gentle and caring voice.

"Kill me."

He sucks in a deep breath and I can feel his eyes boring into my head. "No fucking way," he replies.

Closing my eyes, I let more tears fall. "Please," I plead with him.

"No," he adamantly answers.

I gasp for breath. His hands are there to console me, but my heart is shattered to the point I don't think I can ever come back from this.

When we return home, Jude tries to carry me inside, but I shake my head.

With my head hanging low, I drag my feet into the house and toward my suite. I don't bother changing into anything, I simply collapse on the bed, hugging my pillow, and cry.

Jude takes my shoes off, and covers me with a thin blanket.

As I close my eyes and fall deeper into the pit of despair, I hear Jude talking low into his phone. Turning, I see him sitting in the chair he's dragged to be beside the bed. Drawing my brows together, my mind and body fills with questions, he holds a finger up to me.

When he finishes, he turns his phone off and sits back into the chair. "Why are you here?" I ask.

"Because you need me."

"I need you to kill me," I say with conviction.

"Don't ask me to do something I can't do."

"Then why are you here?"

"Because you need me," he replies again.

"Get out." I turn over, refusing to look at him. But I don't hear him moving. I count to ten in my head, then turn to see him still sitting in the chair. "Get out!" He shakes his head. "GET OUT!" I shout at him. He shakes his head again. Frustrated, angry, guilty, and hurting, I throw the blanket back and leap off the bed. "Get out!" I yell so hard my throat immediately hurts. He shakes his head. I grab the pillow off the bed, and throw it at him.

"Alexa, please . . ."

"Get out," I keep yelling even though my throat is protesting. I grab another pillow, launching it him. "Just get out!" He shakes his head.

I reach over and grab a book, heaving it with everything I have.

I'm angry at him for not killing me. I'm fuming at myself for causing so much hurt to my parents.

I'm livid that I never got to say goodbye. But most of all, I miss them so much it's unbearable.

My whole body hurts.

Jude leaps off the chair and embraces me. But I want to keep hitting him. He pins my arms by my body, and uses his body to shield me from myself. "It's okay," he says softly. "It's okay," he keeps repeating.

Eventually I collapse, not having the energy to fight him.

Or even to fight myself.

I'm not sure how it happens, but before I know it, the darkness inside my heart overtakes my body and shuts down every part of me.

CHAPTER 12

Thursday

IT'S BEEN TWO days since Jude took me to see my parents' grave. It feels like death's hand is closing in around my soul. The emptiness grows with every passing day. I can barely drag myself out of bed. I know I'm only barely functioning.

I'm a bad person. My parents died because of me.

I miss them so much.

Saturday

"MISS LEXI, MR. Jude is worried about you, and quite frankly, so am I. Come out to the kitchen to have something to eat."

"I'm not hungry," I murmur and pull the covers further over my head.

"Please, come have something," Frank pleads with me.

"Not hungry," I say in a smaller tone and curl into myself.

Tuesday

"GET UP. YOU stink and you need to eat," Jude commands.

"Go away."

"Get up." He rips the blankets off my body, and a horrid stench reaches my nose. I haven't showered since the day of the vault, but, I don't care. Nothing will mend the hurt in my heart.

"Go away," I say again, bringing my knees up to my chest to hug them.

"Get up," he says, angry now.

Turning my neck, I notice his stance. His feet are planted and he isn't going away in a hurry. "Fine. The quicker I do what you want, the quicker you'll leave me alone." He holds in a smirk. I crawl out of bed and stand. "Happy now?" I place a hand to my hip.

"Whoa," he dramatizes as he steps back and waves his hand in front of his nose. "You smell so much worse than I thought. Please, before my nostrils burn from the stench, go shower."

I poke my tongue out at him and roll my eyes.

Taking myself to the bathroom, I turn on the shower, strip and get in.

The warm water does feel great against my skin. The mist rising in the shower looks almost mystical and magical. As the water pounds on my back, I relax against the wall. Closing my eyes, I take several deep breaths. My head flops backward and the warm water falls over my head and face.

There's something healing and soothing about water. My heart picks up in pace, and suddenly, rejuvenation begins to sprout. Washing my hair, I let my mind go blank. For the first time in ages, I don't think of the hurt I've brought on my parents or even to Dallas.

When I finish washing myself, I step out, wrap my hair in a towel and get changed into something clean.

The stink that draped me is gone.

Walking out to the bedroom, Jude's sitting on the chair while Angus, the housekeeper, is changing the sheets on the bed. "You look like you have some color in your face," Jude says as he stands and makes his way over to me. "You look nearly normal."

While my soul is consumed with darkness, he manages to drag a smile from me. "Nearly?" I ask as I sit in the chair, flip my head over and towel dry my hair.

"Well, just calling it as I see it."

"Thank you," I sincerely reply. "I feel somewhat normal. Except for the whole . . . you know?" I flick my head back and eye Angus. Waiting for him to finish, he gathers the dirty sheets off the floor and leaves the room. "I feel kinda normal. I'd feel better if my parents were still alive, and if I hadn't gotten them killed." I let out a humorless chuckle. The ache inside still hurts, but at least it's not soul-consuming.

"You didn't kill them." Jude sits opposite me and links his fingers together. "Enzo did. And, *I* killed him."

"An eye for an eye?" I ask.

"Something like that. He was a cocky bastard who deserved what he got. If it wasn't me, then it would've been someone else."

I say something that surprises even myself, "I wish it was me who pulled the trigger."

Jude lets out a deep sigh and runs his hand through his hair. "Killing someone changes you, Lexi, and I never want you to change that way." I watch as his features darken. The interesting thing is how they tell a story.

One of sorrow and remorse that quickly changes to something more. Possibly triumph. Whatever it is, he's thinking about the first time he killed, and his reaction intrigues me. It shouldn't, but some masochistic part of me is strangely fascinated by it. I want to ask, but then I don't want to know.

Does this make me bloodthirsty?

Does it taint my values and change the type of person my

parents raised me to be?

Taking a few deep breaths, I choose to not ask any more questions. It's best I know nothing, because if I do, my opinion of Jude might change for the worse.

"Are you hungry?" he asks after a few moments of silently reminiscing about his past. Shrugging, I keep my eyes on him, and don't really answer. "I'm not a mind reader, Lexi, either you're hungry or you're not."

"What I am is hurting and lost." I use my arms to hold myself up on the chair while I cross my legs, then sit on them. "Do you think the pain will ever go away?"

"I think what we need to do is focus on what is, rather on what's gone."

I raise my shoulders and let out a low growl. "I can't get it out my head, Jude. Because of me they're dead. I can't stand living with that. I can't bring myself to breathe, knowing *I* killed them!" God, I rip my hands through my hair and feel like screaming at the top of my lungs.

"It wasn't you. You're a product of whatever happened to you when you got your appendix removed. You didn't give permission for them to put that in you. And I highly doubt your parents would've let it happen. So, none of this is on you, it's all on the people who did this to you."

"If only we knew who 'they' are." I exhale, hopelessly. "Not that it matters."

"Why doesn't it matter?" He sits forward, his body tense with concern.

"Because isn't it obvious? Whoever put this in me, clearly used me as a carrier, an experiment. They wanted me to have it, which means, I was chosen for a reason. They must've researched me, knew who I was, who my parents are . . ." I look down at the floor, saddened. "Were," I correct myself.

"Hmm," Jude grumbles. He's staring at me. I can tell he's seriously considering what I've said.

"If you think about it, it makes sense. They wouldn't want to give this," I tap my head, "to just anyone. They'd want to make sure they're giving it to someone who . . ." I stop talking and think about the severity of the situation. I look up at Jude and meet his worried eyes. "Do you think this has all been manipulated by them?"

He shakes his head. "I think at first it may have been, but when I took you, it changed everything."

I scoff at the word 'took.' "You mean when your men rammed into the car and kidnapped me?"

"Again, Lexi, semantics." He waves his hand frivolously at me.

I can't help but smile. He's really growing on me. I suppose that's a good thing, considering I have nowhere to go. Without realizing, I become quiet and retreat into myself. I can't help but think of Dallas and the danger that will always stalk her because of me. My heart was healing for a split second, but now it's back in little pieces. "I have to say goodbye to Dallas," I whisper quietly.

"What?" Jude's forehead wrinkles with doubt.

"I need to say goodbye to Dallas. It's not fair for me to put her in danger anymore. I need to find a way to tell her."

"Lexi, this isn't a good idea."

Tears prickle at my eyes, and my heart fills with sadness. "I didn't get a chance to tell my parents I love them. I don't want to miss the same opportunity with Dallas, because who knows what'll happen to me?"

"Nothing will happen to you," he says with confidence.

"Jude," I sigh, frustrated. "You can't be around me twenty-four-seven. And whoever got to me once, is probably working out a way to get to me again."

Jude's shoulders straighten, and his jaw jumps with tension. "No one is going to get to you. No one." Jude quickly becomes agitated as he stands to his feet to pace. "I need to make a phone call," he says, leaving me in my bedroom.

Watching him walk out of my room, I'm left even more

confused by his sudden exit. But then again, that's the way he is.

I finish drying my hair with the towel, then head into the bathroom to comb it and use the hairdryer. Once I'm finished, I take myself back into my bedroom. Jude's once again sitting in the chair, watching the door to the bedroom. His intense stare makes me jump back, momentarily frightened. "You scared me." I grasp my chest. "You look so serious."

"I'm thinking."

"About?"

He looks at me and sighs dismissively. "Nothing." His demeanor rapidly changes as he stands. "Frank's made pizza."

My stomach growls in response, and suddenly I'm starving. "Pizza," I say softly. "Yum." My stomach grumbles again, telling me to eat something.

"Come on." He walks over to me, and with his hand to my lower back he guides me toward the kitchen.

When we enter Frank's domain, he turns to see us, and a huge smile graces his aged, weathered face. "Miss Lexi, I'm so delighted to see you," he happily announces.

"I haven't been in a good headspace, Frank."

"You're here now, and that's all that matters." He whizzes around the kitchen, clanking pots and pans, making a coffee for Jude and pouring me a juice. "Sit, sit, sit." He points to the chair. "I've made pizzas!" he declares proudly.

"How many have you made?" I look over to the kitchen counter and see it perfectly clean.

"Three. I figured you'd be hungry."

"I doubt I can finish one piece, let alone all three."

"Hey, I'm hungry," Jude says as he slaps my leg. "You're not going to be a pig and not share, are you?" Frank chuckles and I smile at Jude's easy attitude.

"I'll share, if I have to." Silence falls in the kitchen, and this makes me revisit what I was thinking about before. "I need to say goodbye to Dallas."

Jude sighs and clenches his jaw together. "It's not a good idea. It's not safe."

"But you told me nothing is going to happen to me. I can't stay here forever. At some point I need to get out and start living. I can't be frightened by the 'what ifs.' I have to move forward with my life. I can't let the world decide my fate, I have to decide it for myself."

Jude grumbles lowly, and pulls at the shirt collar around his neck. "Until Ronan finds the people who did this to you, the safest thing for you to do is stay here."

A smile pulls at my lips and I shake my head in disbelief. "They got to me here before, they can get to me here again."

Jude obviously doesn't like to be reminded how I was taken from this very room. Clearly, he feels like he failed. "Just . . ." he starts but quickly stops. "I need to find these people first."

"Jude," I reach to grab for his hand, but pull back. "I need to say goodbye to Dallas."

"They may be watching her."

"And if they are, then your people can find out who they are with very little effort. Kinda kills two birds with one stone."

He crinkles his brows together and scoffs at me. "You sound so old when you say things like that."

"What can I say? My parents were a huge influence in my life." I shrug nonchalantly, but kick myself at the reminder of what I've done to them.

Frank brings three pizzas out and places them on the long wooden table. "I hope you're hungry," he says enthusiastically toward me. It's definitely not a question, more a statement.

My stomach growls again. "I think my stomach answered you."

"Eat, eat." Frank exits the kitchen, leaving Jude and myself on our own.

I inhale the first piece of pizza, and add a second to my plate. "This is good," I say as I shove more in my mouth. I notice Jude's not eating, instead he's watching me and smiling. "Not hungry?" I ask as I keep eating. When I demolish the second piece like it's nothing, I take a breath and look at Jude. "You made a big deal about how you're hungry, and now you're not eating, you're just staring at me. That's creepy, even for you."

He smiles, then turns his head muttering something ineligible to me. Then he adds, "I'm enjoying being here with you."

Flip. Oh crap! Jude's said something nice and it's making my heart flip. Why can't he be an asshole? Why does he have to be nice to me? It would make it a lot easier to not like him if he was consistently a bastard.

"Huh," I exhale.

"You being here, it calms me."

Flop. Stop it heart! "Huh," I mumble again.

"You make me not want to be such an asshole." *No! Be an asshole, then I'll hate you.* "And I like having you around."

"Okay," I manage to *not* say what I'm thinking. *Shove pizza in your mouth, Lexi, then you can't say anything.* I lean over and slide a third slice onto my plate. "I . . ." *shut up, girl.* I lift the pizza quickly, and bite off the biggest piece. As I chew, I internally scold myself. My *stupid* self. I shouldn't feel anything for him; he got me into this mess to start with. Who am I kidding? He's probably saved me from ending up in some facility where I'd be poked, prodded and tested, just another lab rat.

Jude's eyes are glued to me, and no wonder. I'm grunting my responses and have so much food in my mouth I must look like a squirrel with a year's supply of acorns stuffed in its mouth.

"For someone who's not afraid to say what she thinks, you're fairly quiet."

"Eating." I point to my mouth.

Jude nods his head, and reaches over to the pizza. "I'm glad you're eating."

He starts eating and suddenly the kitchen falls quiet. He's looking at his plate, and I'm trying my hardest not to look at him. When the lack of conversation finally plays havoc on my mind, I turn in Jude's direction. "Jude, we have to talk about this." I point to him, then me.

"What's there to talk about?" Ugh, typical male.

"Why are you so . . ." I look past his shoulder and try to find the right word for how I'm feeling. The struggle is real, because I don't want to say too much in case I'm reading the signs all wrong, but I can't let this go either. When I find the right words, I make eye contact with him, " . . . protective of me? Especially now when you say you won't use me."

"Whoa," he grumbles under his breath and sits back in his chair. Clearly, I've put him on the spot, and he has to find the words to tell me why he's the way he is toward me.

"I've seen what you're capable of, I *know* what you can do, but I don't know why you're the way you are with me."

It's Jude's turn to look past me and focus on a spot over my shoulder. His brows draw in and he bites on the inside of his cheek as he formulates his response. "You intrigue me," he finally says.

And of course, that's not what I was expecting to hear. I had no firm expectations, but come on . . . really? "I intrigue you?" I ask almost mockingly. "That's the best you can come up with?"

Jude stares at me. "You do intrigue me. You're sassy, you'll argue with me if you think I'm wrong . . ."

"When I *know* you're wrong," I correct him.

He clears his throat, and an amused smile lights up his face. "As I was saying, you'll argue with me if you think I'm wrong. You've been thrown into a world of chaos and you're choosing to adapt instead of laying down and letting it defeat you. And not to mention, your incredible strength."

"My strength?" I scoff at him. "I'm forever in tears because people around me keep getting hurt or killed, and I feel so bad for anyone who *will* be hurt or killed because of me. How can you say I'm strong?"

It's Jude's turn to mock at me. "Lexi, you once lived a life where you were ordinary."

"Thanks," I say and grit my teeth.

"Shut up and listen." He glowers at me warningly. "You used to be a girl who was like everyone else. You woke in the morning, probably texted or snapchatted, or whatever app you used with Dallas. You'd go through every day like the one before it."

Clamping my mouth shut, I opt not to tell him off for trivializing the way my life was.

"Then, suddenly, not through your choice, you've gone from an ordinary girl, to an extraordinary woman. You have something no one else on this planet has, and your power all lies with you. You've been thrust into a corrupt world, and you're learning how to live within it without compromising who you are, and without it consuming you. So, to answer you, yes you may cry, you may even crumble, but you'll never let it define the person you truly are."

Swallowing hard, I suddenly forget about *everything.*

Diverting my eyes so I'm not staring at this man whose ferociousness is bigger than life itself, I try and formulate some type of response to him. "I'm not the person you're describing, Jude. I'm *nothing* like her."

"You may not see it yet, but soon you will. And when you do, you won't be oblivious to your strength. You're a warrior, not the prey."

I shake my head, choosing not to believe a single word of what he's saying. It's simply not true. I lift a piece of pizza and take a bite. "Whatever," I respond.

"Yeah, whatever." But he doesn't sound convinced. He has so much confidence in me.

Pity, I don't.

CHAPTER 13

"MISS LEXI, MR. Jude needs you ready to go," Frank announces when he enters my room.

"Where am I going, and why couldn't he tell me himself?" Come to think of it, I haven't seen much of him since the pizzas two nights ago.

Frank smiles at me, his wrinkled face lighting up. "Oh no, ma'am, I can't say anything about anything."

I turn off the movie I'm watching and stand from the bed. "You can't say anything about anything?" Frank backs away from me, a huge smile on his face. "Frank?" I pester him while following him simultaneously. "Frank?" I say again, busting to know what he knows.

"I can't say nothing, Miss Lexi. Nothing." He smiles even wider.

"Tell me," I persist.

He holds both his hands up, shakes his head and backs away further. Now I feel like a crazy person as I chase after him, trying to get him to tell me. "I can't say anything, Miss Lexi. Please don't force me to tell you," he says seriously.

Damn him and the fact I like him. "Fine," I huff. "I hope it's a good surprise."

"You'll love it. Dress warm though, the weather's changing." He's right, the seasons are changing and I can feel the nights are getting cooler.

"Okay," I say, finally accepting Frank's silence about where I'm going. Heading back to my room, I pull a pair of jeans and a light sweater out of the immense closet and take myself to the bathroom for a quick shower.

When I get out, I fix my hair, dress and look at my reflection in the mirror. The jeans hang low on my hips, and I turn to get a better look at myself in the mirror. Groaning, I run my hand over my nearly concave stomach. "Ugh," I growl. "You look terrible, Lexi. You need to get more food into you," I say to myself. It's not like I don't like food, or I'm trying to lose weight, it's with all this crap going on, and Enzo nearly starving me, I seem to be dropping weight too easily.

Casting another look over myself, I straighten my shoulders and hold my head high.

"Lexi," I hear Jude's voice calling me from somewhere outside of my suite.

"Coming," I reply.

Slipping my feet into a pair of low boots, I head out to find Jude leaning against the wall near the front door looking down at his phone. Clearing my throat, I eagerly wait for him to drag his gaze away from the screen. He doesn't disappoint when he lifts his head to look at me. "Don't you look beautiful?" he asks as he pushes off the wall and makes his way over to me.

"Thank you." I brightly smile at him as I accept his words.

Standing in front of me, I can't help but appreciate his form snugly fitted inside his tailored suit. Whoa, a girl can look.

He leans down, and gently places a soft kiss to my forehead. Closing my eyes, I'm getting drawn into a vision, but I push back, not allowing it to take me to his immediate future. It tugs on me, wanting to immerse me in a world I just don't want to see right now.

Fighting it, I refuse the vision. Instead, I stand still and accept the soft, sweet kiss Jude is offering me. My hands snake up to hug him around the waist, while his hands caress the curve of my lower back.

He pulls away, and his darkened eyes keep me hostage, the blaze in them whispering softly to me. He takes a deep breath, narrows his eyes, and turns his head. "We need to go," he says in a low, strained voice.

I'm affecting him.

And I know he's affecting me.

There's a part of me that wants him to touch me, but there's another part, which says this entire scenario is wrong.

I'm just not sure which voice is louder.

"Okay." I pull my hands back, and tuck them into my jeans. Jude motions to grab my hand, but quickly retracts it when he sees me shove my hands in my pockets.

I'm screwed up enough with everything as it is, having feelings toward Jude isn't really an extra complication I can deal with.

Jude leads me out, where one of his cars is waiting for us. "Ronan," Jude says as he unbuttons his suit buttons and guides me to the back of the car.

"Jude," Ronan replies with a curt nod.

Wow, talkative.

I slide onto the bench seat with Jude next to me. Ronan shuts the door and walks around to the driver's side. "Is Ronan taking us?" I ask.

"Your powers of observation are exceptional," he teases me.

Rolling my eyes, I tilt my head and give him a 'shut up' look. He chuckles, which makes me shake my head. "Why's he coming?"

"Don't you like me, Alexa?" Ronan asks from the front.

"I don't know you. You might be an ass." I shrug my shoulders.

"You don't have to know me to know I *am* an ass." He laughs at himself, which makes a small smile creep up on my face too.

"Well, then you're no different than Jude."

"Oh man, no wonder you like her," Ronan says over his

shoulder to Jude.

Jude's features drop when he sees me smiling broadly, proud of myself at my clever remark. He shifts in his seat and turns his head to look out the window. "Just watch the road," he barks playfully toward Ronan. Ronan of course, chuckles even louder.

"So, are you going to tell me where we're going today? Actually, where were you yesterday? I know you don't go to 'normal-people' work, because let's face it, you're far from normal."

"Normal is in the head. My normal and your normal are on various points of the spectrum."

"Well, doing what you do isn't exactly a job most people aspire to."

"I do," Ronan calls from the front seat.

"Again, not normal." I make an obvious point of twirling my finger around near my head.

"Normal is subjective," Jude adds.

"No, it's not," I argue back.

"Really? And you're normal?"

I bite on the inside of my lip, chewing it for a few seconds before I answer. *Damn him.* "I used to be."

He shakes his head at me. "I'm sure you think you were, but I can guarantee you were so much more than normal, even before you got your powers."

I shiver when he says the word 'powers.' Jude catches the tremor and leans forward, removes his jacket and drapes it over me. "I'm not cold," I say as I take a deep breath. "It sounds so weird when you said my powers. Makes me think of Iron Man and Wonder Woman. They have powers, I have an ability."

"Even the word power isn't the right description for you. It's not . . ." He scrubs his hand over his chin, thinking. " . . . powerful enough to describe who you are and what you're capable of."

Sitting quietly, I don't respond. Instead I wait until the tension passes. "Where are we going?" I look out the window and try to gain a sense of direction.

"Somewhere," Jude replies.

"Will you tell me?"

"When we get there."

"So basically, me asking is futile?"

"Essentially, yes."

"Then I'll be quiet and wait to get where ever it is you and Ronan are taking me."

"Technically I'm taking you there, 'cause I'm driving, but Jude told me where to go. And I set it up."

Ugh, Ronan is as annoying as Jude. I look out the window, and watch as we pass through the countryside. We enter the area I used to live with my parents, and my heart picks up in speed, but quickly slows with the realization that my parents are no longer alive.

The scenery changes with every passing minute, and after what seems like forever, Ronan takes a turn onto an isolated road. The trees become denser as we exit suburbia and enter an expanse of greenery with cute little cottages.

Ronan travels for about ten minutes, before slowing and pulling into a long driveway that takes us to a beautiful, rustic home, with a wide timber-covered porch out the front, and a beautiful garden of luscious flowers. Lining the driveway up to the quaint house are rows of citrus trees with fruits hanging off them.

"Where are we?" I ask once Ronan's parked.

"Somewhere I know you'll enjoy."

Getting out of the car, I look around and take a deep breath in. "Can you smell that?" I ask as I immerse myself with the beauty around me. The aroma coming off the flowers, mixed with the zingy smell of the citrus trees, really makes the most captivating scent.

"LEXI!" I hear the familiar, but definitely missed voice of Dallas.

Swinging around, I see Dallas barreling toward me. She jumps off the porch and runs at me at full speed. Without thinking, she throws herself in my arms and immediately, I'm being dragged into a vision.

She's sitting on her bed, with her head down. Tears are falling from her eyes, and she's wiping them away. She leans over to grab a tissue, and I get a glimpse of how blotchy her face is.

There's a knock on the door, and I step back into the corner of the room.

"Come in," Dallas calls.

The door opens, and her mom pokes her head in obviously gauging what's happening in here. "Can I come in, Dallas?" her mom asks as she hesitates by the door.

"Yeah," she responds.

Her mom meekly enters, and goes over to the bed, where she sits beside Dallas. "I know it's hard," she says and embraces her daughter. Dallas cries into her mom's shoulder. "I'm sorry, sweetheart. I know how much you loved Alexa."

"Loved?" I whisper and step forward.

Dallas looks toward my direction, and tilts her head to the side. Her mom is still hugging her, but Dallas's eyes are searching forward. Dallas pulls away from her mom, but her eyes flick over to me. "I just need some time," she says offering her mom a kind smile.

"Okay." Her mom stands and walks toward the door. "But don't stay in here crying all night. I know you'll miss her, but I'm worried about you."

"Thanks, Mom." Her mom leaves and closes the door behind her. Dallas stands from her bed, "Lexi, are you here?" she asks looking in my direction.

"I'm here," I reply. And I'm ripped back into the now. "Damn it!" I shout.

"What's wrong?" Dallas asks.

I can't tell her how I think within the next few hours I'm going to die, that'll destroy Dallas, and saying goodbye will be hard enough as it is. But now I know this will be the last goodbye I'll ever say to her. "Nothing," I say with a huge lump in my throat.

"What did you see? Oh, my God, is something bad going to happen?"

Yes. "No." I smile. "Trust me, if it was bad I'd let you know." No, I wouldn't. "Anyway, what are you doing here?" I look at Dallas, and notice her cheeky smile. "Did you plan this? With him?" I turn and point to Jude who's looking all smug and cocky. *And cute.*

"Not exactly." Dallas drapes her arm over my shoulders and we start walking toward the little house.

"I don't get what's happening. And why aren't you at school?"

"Jude kidnapped me."

"What?" I turn to look at Jude, the fire inside me is seconds off erupting. "What the hell?" I yell as I storm toward him. "You kidnapped her? Jude, what are you thinking?" Someone chuckles from behind me, but it's not Ronan, it's Dallas. Turning to look at her, I swing around again to Jude and stare at him, then back to her. "What's going on? Why are you both laughing?"

"Because when I went to the bathroom this morning, Jude was in there waiting for me."

"Ewww," I respond. Turning, I look at Jude and screw my face at him. "I know you're a stalker, but waiting for her in the bathroom?"

"It was the only way I could get to her."

"Wait, why?" Oh man, my head is spinning.

"Because I had a plan." Jude steps forward, leans down and kisses my forehead. No damn vision this time. Ugh, am I defective?

"Will someone please tell me what's going on? I feel like I'm in an episode of American Horror Story."

Jude's hands rub gently up and down my covered arms. He leans down and whispers in my ear, "I wanted you to get your goodbye."

It dawns on me. It hits me right in the chest, a pain so deep it feels like a knife is striking over and over again. This is my goodbye to Dallas, because I can never see her again. It's just too dangerous for me to be in her life. "Oh."

"You have until two. Then we have to take her back, so no one suspects anything. She was supposed to be in school, but she's not."

"Her parents will find out," I say worried for Dallas.

"Trust me, Lexi, they'll never know."

"How?" I want to know the ins and outs, but I doubt Jude or even Dallas will tell me. "Just tell me no one is getting hurt."

Jude lets out a deep laugh, throwing his head back in a carefree manner. "No one is getting hurt. We had to do it this way, so Dallas wouldn't know. But she was on board from the moment I told her I was taking her to see you."

Even though I'm so happy I'm getting to see my best friend one last time, it still leaves a sinking feeling in the pit of my stomach. Because her mom said 'loved' instead of 'love.' Taking several deep breaths, I choose not to tell Jude what I know.

If keeping her safe means I need to die, then that's exactly what's going to happen.

If today will be the last day of my life, then I'm going to spend it with the best person in the world. *Dallas.*

"Okay," I say as I stare at the picturesque cottage in front of us. Walking over to Dallas, I snake my arm around her waist and lean in to kiss her cheek. The vision starts dragging me in, but I pull away before I can be forced to watch Dallas cry about how she 'loved' me. "What is this place?"

"This is for you and Dallas." Jude walks ahead of us, holds the front door open and waits for us to enter.

"This is the coolest place ever," Dallas happily announces.

We enter, and although Dallas has already seen inside, I haven't. The first thing I notice is the calming music playing in the background. I look around the pale-colored room and notice the four framed posters of a ying-yang, a heart, pastel flowers in a vase, and the last poster is of a large water-colored heart. "Are we in a day spa?" I ask looking around, trying to take in all the surroundings and textures.

"Welcome back, Mr. Caley," a woman dressed in a white flowy dress says to Jude.

"Is everything set?" he asks.

"As you instructed." She gives him a small nod, then a smile. "They're in good hands."

"I know," he adds.

"What's going on?" I ask.

"Mr. Caley has booked my spa for the day. The entire staff are here for you. We'll be starting off the day with a massage, then we'll be moving onto a pedicure, and manicure, followed by a mud bath, then ending it with another massage and a facial."

Shit. Panic rapidly spreads. People will be touching me, which means I'm going to get everyone's immediate future. I know Jude meant well, but I can't relax when I'm going to be getting dragged into all these peoples' visions. "Everything sounds fantastic," I breathe out. My eagerness isn't for all these treatments I can't have, but for the fact I'm spending the next four hours with Dallas.

"But?" the woman asks me picking up on my reservations.

"Other than the mud bath, I can't participate in anything else."

Jude touches my shoulder, and I turn to look at him. "They know not to touch you," he whispers.

"They know?" An alarm rings in my ears. If they know, then that means I'm susceptible to someone else taking me and using me. "Jude," I whipser in a warning tone.

"They've been told to use gloves." He lifts his eyebrows, looking between me and the lady who runs this place.

Suddenly, easiness washes over me. He's silently telling me, he hasn't said anything to them about my visions, just that they need to wear gloves.

Blowing out a sigh of relief, I smile and look at Jude. "Thank you," I say, deeply appreciative of his consideration for me.

"Well ladies, this is where I leave you. I'm sure Amy will look after you both." Jude turns to face the woman who'll be looking after us.

"Of course," she says with enthusiasm. "If you two would like to follow me."

Peering over my shoulder to Jude, he winks at me before giving me a sweet smile. "Ronan and I will be waiting outside."

"This way," Amy says and leads us down a long, well-lit corridor to a room on the left. The room is dimly lit, a striking contrast to what I've seen of the house so far. There's a subtle aroma of jasmine floating in the air, while soothing music plays in the background. "Mr. Caley was insistent I tend to you, Alexa, and this is Jacinta who'll be looking after you, Dallas." A young woman comes into the room, she's dressed identical to Amy. "He also told me of your skin condition, but don't worry, no need to be ashamed of it." My skin condition? What did he tell her? "I have special gloves made out of super soft bamboo."

"Okay," I respond.

"Bamboo doesn't sound super soft to me," Dallas pipes in.

"Trust me, they are. Now if you two would like to go into the bathroom, you can strip down to your panties, and slip on the robes we have hanging in there. Then come back out here and lay on the beds. Jacinta and I will step out and give you some privacy. We'll be back in a few moments." They both exit the room and I'm left looking at Dallas.

"Thank you," I say to her. "For being here. It means the world to me." *Because this is our last time together.*

She steps close to me, and pulls me in for a hug, being especially careful not to touch any part of my skin. "I love you, chicky. There's no way I'd miss out on it."

I pull out of the hug and head toward where Amy pointed, finding a small bathroom which'll be quite difficult for two people to use simultaneously. "Why did you trust Jude when he showed up to 'kidnap' you?" I air quote kidnap, and chuckle to myself.

"Because you trust him. You sent me to find him after . . ." She swallows hard and looks down at her feet. "After Enzo. You sent me to find him to help me, and he did. It's a no brainer, Lexi. He told me what he wanted to do, and I willingly went with him."

"You have a lot of faith in a man who could easily kill you."

Her lips turn up into a huge grin, the happiness traveling up to her eyes. "He likes you too much to kill me." Entering the bathroom, I close the door and strip down, then slide the robe over my shoulders. Leaving the bathroom, I find Dallas is already laying on her stomach on the bed, and the only thing covered is her butt. I can't resist myself, I walk over and smack it hard. Her butt jiggles, and she bursts into laughter. "Leave my ass alone, sister," she spits toward me, laughing.

Getting on the other bed, I sit on the edge. "What do you mean he likes me too much to kill you?"

"If he didn't have an interest in you, he wouldn't have come after you. When I got to that sunglass store you directed me to, the chick, whatever her name is, was hesitant to call Jude. But, I yelled so loudly she had to or I would've made a bigger scene. She called him, and handed me the phone, when I told him where I was, and who I was, he told me he was on the way to collect me."

"So?" I shrug my shoulders, what's this got to do with anything?

"He told me to wait inside the store, and not to go anywhere. He was in the store about ten minutes later." I shrug again. "He ushered me to the car, and started bombarding me with questions. Everything was about you, and who had you. He asked me if Enzo had hurt you, or . . ." she pauses for a second, " . . . raped you."

Swallowing all the saliva gathering in my mouth, I turn my

head to not look at Dallas. "What did you tell him?"

"I told him everything. Everything I knew, that is," she corrects herself quickly and softly. "I told him how Enzo kept you in the room, how the men would look at you, how they'd lick their lips when they'd see us, and how they made no secret of what they wanted to do."

"Are you two ready?" Amy calls as she enters.

"Yeah," I answer on behalf of both of us, but in my heart, I want to say no so Dallas and I can talk. This is the first, *and last,* time we'll talk since Jude rescued me.

Taking the robe off, I rest it over the end of the table, climb up and lay on my stomach. Letting my arms dangle over the edge of the bed, I close my eyes and wait. "I'm warming some lotion up between my hands before I apply it, okay?" Amy asks.

"Yeah," I answer. My mind is racing in every direction possible, because I want to know what Jude's reaction was when Dallas contacted him.

Amy applies her hands to my back, and she's not wearing gloves, because I'm drawn into a vision. I fight it, I don't want to be here, but the vision keeps dragging me into it. God, I don't want to be in here. Closing my eyes, I count slowly in my head, relaxing my shoulders and my body, controlling the depth and speed of my breaths.

As I pull myself out of the situation, I hear someone say, "Alexa Murphy . . ."

"What?" Opening my eyes, I look around the room I've been pulled into. Taking in my surroundings, I know exactly where I am.

A painting of pastel flowers in a vase.

Ying-yang.

Damn it, I'm here, in the front room.

"When did she leave?" I look at the man who's talking with Amy, and he has no face. His features are all blended into one another, there's nothing recognizable on him. I couldn't pick him out if I saw him again.

"She left about two, maybe three hours ago, and then someone came to get the friend."

"Her friend, who?" he asks as he types on his phone.

I tiptoe over to the faceless man and look on the screen of his phone, but just like his face, his screen is blank. What worries me is Amy isn't alarmed by the faceless man, which means he isn't faceless to her, only to me.

Which makes me believe he knows about me and what I can see and he's concealing who he is so I can't recognize him.

This changes everything . . . this has now become scary.

"Who are you?" I ask in a voice so small, I'm positive no one can hear it.

I look to Amy, she's made no movement to indicate she's heard me. But, the faceless guy, he steps back cautiously and makes no sudden movements, until he yells out the door, "She's here now."

My heart beat accelerates as I stand in the room looking around me. I have to get out. I need to get out of this vision, now.

Closing my eyes, I start to calm my thumping heart. "Get out," I say to myself.

"She's leaving, get in here now!" he yells again.

I'm back on the table, and I turn to look at Amy. Shocked, she steps backward. "You're shaking," she says.

Dallas lifts on one elbow, she draws in her brows before her eyes alternate between myself and Amy. "Give us a minute," she instructs them.

When the door closes, I reach out and grab a nearby folded towel, holding it to my body while I shift into an upright position.

Dallas does the same, and we sit on the beds facing one another. "They know," I say.

"Who knows what?" Dallas tone is filled with worry.

Jumping off the bed I start to pace inside the room. Something is wrong, very wrong. Throwing on the robe, I head out where

Amy and Jacinta are both waiting. "Is everything okay?" Amy asks, her eyes appear concerned.

I hold a finger up to her, and make my way outside. Ronan is leaning against the car looking down at his phone, and Jude's in the back with door open, on his laptop.

The moment they both see me, Ronan draws his gun, and Jude's out of the car, up on the porch beside me. "What's wrong?" he asks as he indicates for Ronan to go into the cottage and check things out.

"We have to go," I say with urgency.

"Why? What's happened?" He runs his hands down my arms and pulls me in toward his body. "You're trembling, Lexi. What did you see?"

I know what I have to do. I have to say goodbye to Dallas. I was hoping on these next few hours with her, so when I finally did say goodbye, she'd recall this day as one of the best in her life.

I hate for her to remember it like this.

"They're coming," I slowly say to Jude.

It takes him all of five seconds to know who I'm talking about. "How long?"

"A few hours." Tears pool in my eyes. This will be the last time I see Dallas.

Jude nods his head, then searches for Ronan. "Okay," he responds. His own stance changes, his shoulders dip and he puffs out a caught breath. "You have to say goodbye to her."

Nodding, a tear falls from my eyes. *I know*. He doesn't need to tell me what I have to do. It's the only thing I can do to keep her safe. "I know," I say, swallowing back the hurt desperately wanting to escape. My gaze drifts away from Jude's. I don't want him to see the ache inside me.

"I'll give you ten minutes, but then we have to leave."

Silently I head back inside. Dallas is standing in the cute, serene waiting area, her arms wrapped around her body. She's wearing one of the robes provided by the spa. "Are you okay?"

she asks as she approaches me.

My eyes meet Amy and Jacinta, who are both standing against the wall, their brows drawn in, watching us. I jerk my head to the side indicating the room we were in to get our massagers. I wait until Dallas is inside the room before I close the door, and flick the lock. "I have to go."

"What? What happened?" Dallas steps back until her body finds the wall. She slumps against it, worried.

"They've found me."

"Who's they?"

"I wish I knew. But they know who I am, and they're after me. And they're coming here."

Dallas stares at me, and I'm doing everything I can to hold in the tears. "Alexa," her soft voice twists the knife further into my heart. "What aren't you telling me?"

I have to say goodbye, or her life will forever be in danger. "I'll miss you," I say, as the tears prickling my eyes finally break free.

"What?" she questions, skeptically. "Jude's set this up, he can do it again."

A huge lump lodges in my throat as I hold back the sobs. I lift my chin, my eyes find hers. I search them, silently begging her to not realize there'll be no more. "Okay," I respond, but I sound unconvincing, even to me.

She stares at me, and a tear rolls down her cheek. "Alexa," she whispers. I try not to give anything away, but I'm struggling to hold the hurt in. "There's not going to be a chance to do this again, is there?"

I clasp my hands together trying to stop the shaking. The tremble moves through my body, quivering. She's realized this is it for us. Now I need to be brave enough to tell her the words. I shake my head, electing to take the cowards way out.

"Lexi," she pleadingly whispers. Her begging twists the knife already piercing my heart. But I have to do what's right for her. "Lexi," she says again.

I cast my eyes away from hers, focusing on one of the paintings. Breathing in a few times, I lift my eyes to meet hers. "I have to say goodbye," I finally admit. *The knife turns again*. My heart hurts.

"What do you mean?" Her tone is soft, *she knows*.

"I can't put you in danger anymore. It's not fair to you."

We hear someone clear their throat, and we both look to the door where Jude's unlocked it with a key and is patiently waiting. He gives me a curt nod, silently telling me we have to go. Dallas turns to me, her eyes brimming with more unshed tears. "Stay with me. My parents will let you move in."

God, I love her. "There are people who are on their way here, to get to me. And these people know what I can do." She crinkles her forehead, wordlessly asking who they are and how they know. "My life has now changed, Dallas. It'll forever be . . . different."

"We can figure out how to get this out of you. Maybe the people who are coming will help you . . ."

She sounds so hopeful, but deep down inside, I know she's not naïve enough to believe that. "I need to find out who they are on my terms, under my circumstances, not theirs."

"We can go to the police."

"Did you go to the police when you got back after Enzo kidnapped you?" Her eyes drop to the floor. "And why didn't you?"

She swallows and lets a tear drop before quickly wiping it away. "Because you told me not to. I don't know who to trust anymore. I told my parents I ran away and was living on the streets, they were just thankful they had me back, I never told anyone."

"I have to do this, I have to walk away. It's going to be one of the hardest things in my life, but I have to—in order to keep you safe."

"Move in with me," she says again. This time with more fever. "We'll figure it out."

"Alexa," Jude calls from the door. We both look over to him, and I give him a small nod.

"Until I figure out what this is," I tap my temple, then add, "he's the only one who can protect me. He's the only one who has the means, and the nerve to pull the trigger in order to protect me."

Dallas cries, because we both know, as good as her intentions are, she could never kill anyone. And neither of us is innocent enough to think Jude wouldn't. "Please, stay with me."

"I can't," I whisper.

I take a step away from her toward the door where Jude's waiting, but this isn't the way we should end our friendship. She's been my best friend, and to walk away like this is truly going to break my heart.

Turning, I head back to her and throw my arms around her. The instant I do, I'm locked into a vision where she and her parents are watching TV. The news flashes up, and there's a picture of me. The caption below it reads, *'Kidnap victim found dead.'*

My heart leaps into my throat, and I clasp my hand over my mouth. Dallas cries into her mom's shoulder while her mom embraces her and kisses her forehead.

I don't need to see any more. I can't bear the thought of hurting Dallas. Dragging myself out of the vision, I hold onto my best friend.

"Alexa," Jude encourages once more. "We have to go."

Pulling away, I wipe at the tears running down Dallas's face. The vision tries to pull me in, but I fight it, *and I win.* "I love you," I whisper. I don't tell her how my life will end soon, I refuse to tell her about my future. "Promise me something."

"What is it?" she says between sobs.

"Forget me."

She howls even more, and I can't help but let the sadness bleed from my soul. Dallas is the best girlfriend a person could ever have, but now the time has come to leave her.

"I can't," she cries. "Please, reconsider." She steps forward, and I step back.

The quicker I say goodbye, the better for her. "I love you," I say as I lay a kiss on her cheek.

Wrapping my arms around my body I head out to where Jude's waiting for me. "Are you okay?" he asks as he places his jacket over my shoulders. I shiver in response, wipe at the sensitive skin beneath my eyes and shake my head. "Here." He holds the back door open for me, and when I get in, he leans down and smiles. "I'll be back in a minute." Closing the door, I watch as he speaks to Ronan, Ronan nods and then rounds the car to get into the drivers' seat.

Jude heads to Dallas, whose flushed cheeks are tear-streaked. My core twists with anguish, but it's better this way. Jude talks to her, she nods her head in response. He steps away from her, but she lurches forward, grabbing his upper arm. He turns to look at her, and now it's her turn to tell him something.

Jude hangs his head while he listens to whatever she's saying, and then he nods. His lips turn up into a smile, before he looks at her and says one more thing. I want to know what they're saying to each other. I want to be there, to hear their words.

I try and focus in on his mouth, to try to read his lips. The only thing I think he says is, 'I promise, I will.' He promises he will, what?

He leaves her and heads down to the car Ronan has idling. I look past Jude's shoulders and notice how Dallas is hugging herself, but she doesn't look as broken as I expected. Don't get me wrong, the tears are flowing down her cheeks, but she looks as if she's accepted me leaving.

"What did she say?" I ask as we head down the driveway. As the car gets further away, I watch Dallas getting smaller by the second. I don't turn forward until I can no longer see her standing in the doorway.

"She told me to make sure I look after you."

The swelling in my throat increases, and the stabbing pain in my chest becomes more hurtful.

"I'm going to miss her so much."

Jude places his hand on my thigh and squeezes. "There's something Ronan and I have been considering."

The tears finally stop, and I take several deep breaths to compose myself. "What have you been thinking?"

"Ronan and I have been planning your death."

I don't even react, I saw it in the vision. "I don't think she heard you," Ronan says from the front of the car.

"I heard," I breathe. "But I also knew it was coming."

"How?" Jude asks. I turn and tilt my head at him.

"Really?" I question. "Really?" I say again.

"So, it was successful then?" Jude asks.

"The vision I saw was a news report that my body had been found. Whatever you have planned, makes the news."

"Excellent," Ronan proudly announces.

"Does anyone want to fill me in on your plan for killing me? Or are you just going to pull over and shoot me?" I ask, deflated by everything.

The car fills with stoic silence. They're both not telling me something. "Boss," Ronan says. "She thinks we're actually going to kill her."

"We're going to stage your death, not actually kill you," Jude clarifies. "We need to make sure anyone you were connected with can no longer be a target."

"You'd do that for me?" I ask. He diverts his eyes, darting them away from me. For a big, strong man, he's suddenly become quite reserved. "How?"

"We've lined up somebody who's going to help us out."

"Absolutely not!" I shriek. "You're not going to kill an innocent girl for me. No way!"

Jude now relaxes back and shakes his head. "We're not going to kill anyone, but someone owes me a favor. He's got a dead body, and he's agreed to help."

Confused, I screw my nose and silently question him. What is he talking about? "Huh?" I query.

"All you have to know is this girl is already dead."

"Did she die because of me?" A sick feeling churns in my stomach.

"No, she died of an overdose."

"Ewww," I grumble. "Wait . . . she didn't die of an overdose someone gave her to kill her for this reason, did she?"

"Stop panicking, Lexi. No, she wasn't given a bad hit, she was a junkie."

"How are you going to make her look like me? DNA? Fingerprints? All of those things won't be me."

Jude chuckles, and so does Ronan. "We have favors owed to us," Ronan says from the front.

"Do I want to know?" I ask.

"Probably a good idea if you don't," Jude answers. At which, Ronan lets out a huge laugh.

"Then I don't want to know." Jude squeezes my thigh once more.

Jude and Ronan speak to each other, and I choose to zone out and not listen. Even though they're talking, I'm surrounded with cold silence. An ache inside me is trying to burst through, a pain so sharp and deep, I don't think time will help with healing.

My life has been so drastically altered. It's been thrown into a continuous spin, and all I can do is hang on and pray that one day, some kind of normality will return.

But I've lost everything important to me in less than six months. My parents have been killed, and now I've had to say goodbye to my best friend so I can ensure she stays safe. I don't want her to suffer the same fate as my parents because of me.

I simply couldn't live with myself if I was the cause of her death too.

Exhaustion finally creeps up on my body. My eyes begin to

tire, as my eye lids grow heavier and heavier. I know we're not far from Jude's house, but I can't seem to keep them open.

Why does the car always make me tired? Is it the motion? The warmth?

My head flops back, and my entire form heaves a sigh of relief. Closing my eyes, I sleep, dreaming of the life I once had that no longer exists.

CHAPTER 14

"HI, FRANK," I say as I enter the kitchen. My nose is assaulted with delicious aromas, and I can't wait to see what Frank's creating.

"Good evening, Miss Lexi." He prepares dinner while I make my way over to him.

He's stirring something in a saucepan, and I peer over his shoulder. "What are you making?"

"The meatloaf is in the oven and the mac and cheese is nearly finished."

"How about I finish dinner and you sit?"

He shakes his head while smiling. "Oh no, Miss Lexi, it's my job to look after you, not the other way around. And besides, it makes me happy to know you're being looked after."

Frank is a genuinely beautiful man. With every passing day, I discover something new about him. He loves cooking; that's a given. But he also loves playing chess. I look over to the long table and see the chess board set up and ready to go. "I have a feeling I'm going to kick your ass, Frank," I say as I sit on the opposite side, tapping my fingers on the counter.

Frank looks up from the stove and raises his brows at me. "Are you challenging me?"

"Not at all, I'm just saying, I'm going to kick your butt," I cheekily reply.

"Oh no, not gonna happen on my watch." He tries to come across as arrogant, but Frank is the sweetest old man I've ever met. "Just you wait 'til you've eaten, then I'm taking you down," he adds.

"Do you know if Jude's joining us tonight?" It's been days since I've seen Jude. He disappeared the morning after we returned from the failed attempt at the day spa, and I've only seen him in passing.

"He hasn't given me instructions to cook for him," Frank replies in a small voice.

"Okay." I breathe out, quite disappointed how Jude's vanished and hasn't even told me where he was going or when he'll return. A twinge of hurt grasps my heart, I had hoped I meant more to him. "How long before dinner?" I ask, distracted by my bruised ego. Jude isn't even bothering to talk to me.

"Not too long."

I stand from the table, and start making my way out of the kitchen. "I'm going for a walk."

"Dinner will be ready in half an hour," Frank calls as I leave the kitchen.

When I get out to the foyer, I look around and try to figure out where I should go. I've been living here for a while now, and I've yet to discover the entire house. But I don't feel like staying in, so I make my way through the large sunken lounge room, out the back door, past the huge pool, and toward the meticulous, green gardens. It's late and the sun is sitting on the horizon, nearly gone for the day.

Down at the back of the property, I sit on the grass and let my hand run over the pristine sprigs. Lying down, I gaze at the sky, and watch as a few stars try to sparkle through the darkening sky.

"Do you think we'll ever find an answer?" I ask the sky. "Do you think it could ever be taken out of me?"

Linking my fingers together, I place them beneath my head and watch as the sky darkens. The moon is huge, and bright, and surprisingly close.

"What happens if they can't?" But then, an intriguing thought comes to mind. "What if I don't want them to remove it?" God, what am I saying? If I don't have them—whoever 'they' are—remove it, it means I'll have this thing for the rest of my life.

But, what if, since I have this thing, I use it to benefit people? Ugh, how frustrating. Because I know I'll always be used, or people will try to take me so they can use this gift I was given for their own advantage. I don't want to be a pawn in someone else's deadly games. What if I can hone into this, really master it, and use it to help?

"Ugh," I grumble to myself, even more discouraged then I was when I first arrived out here. "What do I do?" I ask myself.

"What do you do about what?" I tilt my head up, looking at Jude upside down. He approaches me, and sits on the grass next to me. I follow him with my eyes as he plonks down in his expensive suit with his ultra-trendy, expensive shoes. "What do you do about what?" he asks again.

I turn over, leaning on my left arm, and balancing my head on my fist. "I'm just thinking out loud."

"About what? Maybe I can help you decide."

"Well, no you can't. But, I'm thinking about what to do."

Jude rakes his hand through his hair. "About?" he asks persistently.

"About this ability I have." He chuckles. "What's that supposed to mean?" I sit up and cross my legs. But my adrenalin is pumping and I'm ready for an argument with him.

"You're not going to do anything about it."

"Wait up, what do you mean?"

"It's something most people would kill to get their hands on, and you have it. You have the golden egg, Lexi, you aren't giving it away."

"Hold up, Jude, you're not telling me what to do here."

"Looks like I am," he says in a cavalier manner.

No way. He is *not* going to tell me what I should or shouldn't do. "Jude, you do realize, this is my body, my life, and I'm going to make decisions for myself."

"Don't be stupid, Alexa."

What the hell? "Did you just call me stupid?"

"Chill, will you?"

"What?" My blood hammers furiously through my veins. "Jude, this has nothing to do with you."

"It has everything to do with me." He laughs condescendingly. He damn well laughs at me!

"How does it involve you?" I stand to my feet, and place my hands to my hips. Holding my head high and puffing out my chest, giving a more dominant, feisty vibe. Jude also jumps to his feet and moves in front of me. "Intimidation doesn't work on me."

"God knows I've tried." He screws his face up trying to lighten the situation. But this isn't going to go away. I want to know what makes him think he has any choice in what I do.

"This doesn't involve you."

"Of course it does."

"No, Jude. It doesn't. This is all happening to *me*. I'm the one who was given this, not you. I'm the one whose world has fallen apart, not you. I'm the one who's had her parents killed because some asshole wanted to teach me a lesson, not you. I'm the one they're after, not you." Annoyed and upset, I poke my finger into Jude's chest with every point I'm making.

"It's got everything to do with me."

"Ugh," I grunt loudly as I turn to walk back toward the house.

"Don't walk away when we're having an argument."

"This isn't an argument. It's you being a stubborn ass."

"You're still walking away." He catches up to me easily, and walks beside me.

"Go away. I'm so damned angry right now."

"I'm not going anywhere, I live here."

We get to the house, and I slam the door after I enter, leaving Jude outside. I head to my bedroom, but I know he's following because of his heavy footsteps behind me. "Go away," I say as I enter my suite and try to slam the door in his face.

"No. You're being ridiculous."

"Why, because I want to live a normal life? What's ridiculous about wanting to wake up and be able to go out without having to look over my shoulder for the rest of my life?"

"Yes, that's exactly right. You're being stupid and ridiculous."

"Seriously." I storm away from him. "Just get out," I yell, pointing my finger toward the door.

"No," he roars as he approaches me.

"At this moment in time, I'm furious, and I can't talk to you when all I hear is bullshit coming out of your mouth. Maybe later, when I calm down, we'll be able to have a conversation, but I fail to see how the hell this involves you. This is my decision, and my decision alone."

He takes another step closer to me, and I plant my feet firmly to the floor. I refuse to move, and I absolutely refuse to let him bully me. "This is about me too, Lexi."

"No!" I yell at him, wiggling my finger in his face. "No, this has nothing to do with you. It's all about me. Not you. You're not the one who's being affected by this."

"Like hell I'm not. You're my responsibility. You're living with me." He takes another step closer to me.

Did he just say that out loud? "I'm not your responsibility."

"You think you can survive out there on your own? You think me being here isn't stopping every person with ulterior motives from taking you? It's because of me you're safe, it's because of me you have somewhere to live."

"I can handle myself!" I shout.

"You think you can, but you can't. You're naïve if you think you could."

"Naïve? Are you kidding me, Jude? I survived Enzo. *I*

survived him."

"And I came in and saved the day."

The anger inside me is bubbling so hard it's on the verge of spilling over. "No, you came in and got me out of there, but *I* saved myself."

He steps closer to me, he's so close, I can almost feel his breath on me. "I saved you," he says, cockily.

Bam, and just with his ego, and his stupid admission of being my savior, my anger breaks the surface. I slap his face, hard. His head swings to the side, but he straightens and glares at me. A red hand print is rising on his cheek. "Oh, my God," I whisper, completely stunned at myself for hitting him.

"Without me, you'd still be at Enzo's."

Why is he continuing to taunt me? I smack him again. "I'm not even sorry," I say, standing taller.

"You belong here."

Just shut up! Why is he still talking? And why is my body reacting the way it is? My heated blood boils, while my heart leaps to the back of my throat. Why am I feeling all these crazy emotions? In a split second, I lift my hand to hit him again, but he grabs onto my wrist, tugs me so forecefully I smash into his body, and crashes his lips to mine.

I'm being dragged into a vision, but I'm enjoying—no, I'm hating—no wait, I'm enjoying—*ugh.*

"Stop it." I pull away and step back from Jude. "What the hell did you just do?"

"I kissed you," he suavely adds.

"Why?"

"Because you needed to be kissed."

I step backward, he steps forward. I step back again, he steps closer. "Stop coming closer."

"But I want to kiss you again."

I comb my fingers through my hair, tugging on the ends. "I don't care what you want." I liked him kissing me. No, wait!

What am I thinking? No, I didn't.

Yes, you did.

He steps closer, I step back, my back finds the wall and I'm cornered, having nowhere to go. "Don't," I whisper looking him straight in the eyes.

He rests his hand on the wall beside my head, he leans in and softly smells my hair. "Are you sure you don't want me to kiss you again?"

Oh, my God, what the hell is happening to me? No . . . I mean yes, I mean . . . *damn it* I don't know what I mean. My chest feels like it's heaving, as my breath rapidly escapes past my lips.

His scent is right here, invading me. His body is hard, leaning into me. Everything about him is drawing me into his dangerous web. My mind screams at me to run, but my heart already knows what it wants. I've been entangled in his life since the moment I saw him.

Slowly I lift my hand and grasp his tie. Without breaking eye contact, I pull him into me. His mouth hovers over mine, our eyes are glued to each other. He looks between both of mine, the hunger in his own growing with every passing second.

"Are you sure?" he asks, a mere hairs breadth away from me.

"No," I whisper. "I'm not anywhere near sure."

He leans in further. His taut chest pressing into my breasts. Our exposed skin isn't touching, *but I want it to.* "Then I won't kiss you." He lowers his nose to skim my jaw then down the column of my neck. He's touching me, and I'm desperately fighting the vision that's trying to pull me in.

Instead, I focus on the now, and how my heart is frantically leaping. How my palms are sweaty and all I'm yearning for is his mouth on mine. "Don't kiss me," I say, absolutely lapping up the attention he's giving me.

"I won't." I feel his smirk against my skin. It feels to me like he's familiarizing himself with me. He's taking his time, smelling my neck, licking my hyper-sensitive skin. Finally, after what seems like hours he pulls away, leaning his forehead on mine. "I want to kiss you," he whispers before kissing my nose.

Yes! "No," I whisper. Stupid body, why does it have to react this way? Why does it have to want him?

"Not until you tell me you want it too."

"A mobster with morals." The moment the words are out, I instantly regret them. He's always kept that side of him away from me . . . except the time with the driver. . . . and what I see in the visions.

"While I'm here, I'm just Jude," he says not at all fazed by what I said. But I know I shouldn't have said it.

"I'm sorry," I whisper my apology. "I shouldn't have said that about you."

He pulls away completely, and goes to sit on one of the seats. "You're simply stating a fact."

Leaning against the wall, I push off and hesitantly make my way over to sit beside Jude. "You know . . ." I breathe in, my cheeks suddenly flushing at the memory of him kissing me, and me wanting to keep kissing him. "I was getting pulled into a vision, but I was enjoying . . ." I clear my throat and redden even more. " . . . it so much I stopped the vision so I could keep . . ." Fidgeting I look away from him. " . . . kissing you."

Why does my face feel like it's on fire? Oh yeah, probably because it is.

Jude chuckles loudly. "Was that uncomfortable for you?'

You have no idea, buddy. "What? No, why?" *Hell yes!*

"Your entire face is crimson. Candy apple red."

"Oh shit," I mumble and cover my face with my hands. "No," I finally say after a moment of having my head down. But, I can still feel the fire burning.

"Then you do want to kiss me again?"

Yes! "What?" He chuckles at me. "No, I don't," I say as my head nods 'yes.' Jude laughs again at me. "I'm hungry, dinner should be ready now." Standing to my feet, I leave him in my suite and head out to the kitchen. I have to get out of here.

I find the kitchen empty, two plates covered with silver domes placed on the long kitchen table. Crap, Frank's already served everything, cleaned up, and left the kitchen. I feel so bad for letting him down. Even the chess set is packed up. Disappointment runs through me. I've let Frank down, and that in itself upsets me.

Walking over to the table, I sit and lift the silver dome. Beneath is dinner, meatloaf with mac and cheese and greens. I sigh as I stare at the plate of love in front of me. He made this for me, and I can't even play a game of chess with him or say thank you.

"What's wrong? Don't you want it? Throw it out and I'll take you to dinner," Jude says as he sits in his seat and dismissively pushes his plate aside.

"Don't do that. Frank works really hard for you, he tries to make sure we're fed properly. Don't push it away like it means nothing."

"It's just food. Frank doesn't care if I eat here or out."

"Listen to yourself. Of course, he'd care. He wouldn't want to waste his time making us something to eat if all we're going to do is push it aside. So, no, I don't want to go out to some super expensive restaurant when we have perfectly good food here." I bring the plate closer to me and pick at my food. Truth be told, I'm not hungry now because I know I've let Frank down. I've treated him like just a member of the staff, and he's so much more than that to me.

"If it means so much to you, I'll eat Frank's dinner." He picks his fork up, and begins eating, quickly shoveling it into his mouth.

My eyes are glued to Jude. He's eating super fast, and he has cheese sauce on the corner of his mouth. In a cliché moment, I lean over and wipe it off. Ugh, I feel like I'm in one of those romance movies where their eyes meet, the music becomes lush and soft, and he leans into her and kisses her. I burst into laughter at the ridiculousness of it all. "What?" he asks through a mouthful of food.

I laugh some more and the romantic movie has now become a Mr. Bean moment. Nothing romantic or tender about this at all. "Nothing," I laugh again while still picking at my food.

Once dinner is finished, I stand and take my plate over to the sink. Rinsing it off, I stack it in the dishwasher. Jude leaves his on the table. "What?" he asks when I shoot him a look of disbelief.

"Seriously?" I ask, my eyes traveling between him and his plate. He shrugs indifferently and steps away from the table. I stop him before he leaves the kitchen by standing in front of him and placing my palm to his chest. The vibration of his heart beneath his shirt throbs strongly against my hand. This excites me, and makes me want to keep my hands on him. "Come on." Titling my head to the side, I pleadingly gaze into his eyes.

"Oh, for fuck's sake," he mumbles under his breath as he turns and grabs his plate. "This is what I pay Frank for." He takes his plate over to the sink and half drops it, causing a loud clanging sound. "Don't think I'm washing it up," he sternly says to me.

"Hey." I hold my hands up yielding his macho stupidity.

"Wanna watch a movie?" he asks. "I haven't shown you the cinema room."

"You have a cinema room?" Why doesn't this surprise me?

"I have a lot of things here." He smiles broadly at me.

"Anything illegal I shouldn't know about or any part I shouldn't go to?" My heart pounds angrily. *Please say no.*

"This is my home, Alexa, not my place of business. I don't keep anything illegal here."

Phew. I exhale a sigh of relief. "Well, that's good."

"And especially not now that I have a permanent house guest, one I know is incredibly curious and would go on a mission to find anything illegal."

"I don't know what you're talking about." I look away before he figures out that's *exactly* what I'd do.

"So, how about a movie?"

I've had way too much excitement tonight. Even though a part of me wants to be near Jude, another part of me is saying to take things slow and not rush into anything. "I'm going to go to bed." I step away from him, and before I know it, he's grabbed onto my upper arm and has me colliding into his chest.

His lips are on mine and my mind is spinning. A whirlpool of emotions is being evoked. And a vision is desperately trying to make a connection with me, but I keep pushing it back, not wanting to see anything.

Fever quickly rises between us. My heart beats strong as his mouth commands mine. He's soft and gentle, though demanding and knowledgeable. I'm loving every moment of this kiss. I never want it to end.

His hand snakes down to my lower back. He lifts my t-shirt, possessively splaying his hands on the small of my back. He pulls me in closer. My body is reacting to him, in a way that is starting to worry me.

Pulling out of this scorching hot kiss, I lean my forehead on his chin. Closing my eyes, I bring myself back to the now, missing the intense and heated kiss immediately. His fingers are still caressing the skin of my lower back. *I like it.* The vision is still there, trying to grab me and drag me under. I concentrate hard on not allowing it to take me. I don't want to leave this moment.

I feel safe.

"I need to go for a shower," I whisper, but hope he doesn't let me go.

"Okay." He kisses my forehead, his lips staying connected to my skin for long minutes.

He doesn't want to let me go; his hesitation is obvious. I don't want him to release me either, but I'm nowhere near ready for this thing between us to progress. So much has happened to me, I need time to get my head on straight before I take this further with Jude.

"Okay," I respond.

"Okay," he says again, and this makes me smile.

Pulling away from him, I don't say anything. I turn and walk to my suite.

Once I'm showered and changed into my pajamas, I slide into bed and turn a movie on. My eyes instantly drift closed, and the sound of the movie immediately becomes white noise.

A persistent cough wakes me from the deep sleep I was in. Opening my eyes, they burn with pain. My coughing increases as I try and adjust my eyes to the darkness of my room. The television is off, the room is shrouded in heavy blankness.

But a scent catches in my nose, and I sniff at the tell-tale sign of something burning. It's a cross between electric and wooden. Slipping out of bed, I head out of the room and into the suite.

I reach for the handle, and open the door to the suite. A thick cloud of smoke sits high near the ceiling. The thick, gray fog is growing quickly. "Shit!" I yell as I fall to the floor and crawl my way over to Jude's room. We have a fire in the house. "Jude!" I yell as I bash on his door. I hear nothing. "Jude!" I beat on the door again, trying the handle only to find it's locked.

I get nothing.

"Alexa," both Frank and Ronan yell at me as they approach.

"Jude, his door is locked and he's not answering," I cry, frightened at what's going on in his room. "What's happening?"

"Get back." Ronan moves me, steps back and lays a boot into Jude's door. "Frank, get her out." Frank tries to make me leave, but I shake my head all while Ronan kicks the door again, this time flinging it open.

He runs in, and I follow straight behind him. "Miss, Alexa," Frank says.

"Go, I'll be there in a moment," I say to him. His face is stubborn, he's not leaving me again. "Go!" But he doesn't. He stays with me, ready to pounce and pull me out of this.

The crackling of the fire in Jude's room licks the walls. Thick orange and red flames engulf part of his space, and I look around to see where it's coming from. It takes me all of a second to see the car hanging out of the wall. It looks like a ram raid. Someone's managed to drive their car into the house. "What the . . . ?" Frank murmurs as we both stare at the car.

There's a man in the driver's seat, slumped unmoving over the steering wheel. "What's happening?" Looking around, I try and make sense of the scene. All I can see is fire, and the car and no Jude. "Help Ronan find Jude," I yell to Frank.

He looks just as lost as I am. He heads toward Ronan, and I'm left near the car. There's a small fire coming from the engine, and I know it's only a matter of time before it explodes. I need to see what's happening. I go to the driver's side. The window is shattered. I touch an exposed part of the driver's body that isn't covered in blood. I notice his chest heaving rapidly.

I get nothing.

Now's not the time for my ability to leave me. I take my hand off him, and then lay it on him again. Closing my eyes, I get dragged under. I'm in his vision. I'm in blackness, complete and utter darkness.

I pull out of the vision and look around me, trying to figure out why I'm getting nothing.

It's then I see it, sticking out from beneath his shirt – a wire. A red and blue entwined wire.

I move him, so I can see better, but I have a sick feeling in my stomach I already know what the wires mean. Strapped to his chest is a homemade device.

A bomb.

Turning, I run into Jude's room. He's lifeless on the bed. Ronan is trying to lift him, Frank's helping too.

"Get out now!" I yell. Running toward Jude, I have no time to notice his unconscious state. "The driver, he's a suicide bomber," I scream at Ronan and Frank.

Both look at me quizzically for only a split second. Ronan

kneels onto the bed, grabs Jude, and slings him over his shoulder. "Go, we're right behind you," he yells.

Frank and I crouch down and try to get out of the house which is filling with smoke at an alarmingly fast rate.

I try to look behind me, but the thickness of the smoke is preventing me from seeing anything. "Go, go, go!" I hear Frank's voice.

I make my way to the door, and out into the yard. The crackling of the fire behind me is becoming louder and louder. I try to turn to see where Ronan is, where Frank is, *where Jude is.*

The boom happens before I have a chance to see anything. It's so loud, and so forceful it propels me forward. A sharp pain bites my shoulder, and something scrapes at my cheek, leaving an intense sting behind.

The explosion was so powerful it threw me to the ground.

Turning, I search for Frank, Ronan, and Jude.

I see nothing but thick clouds of smoke bellowing from the house. The red flames are now caressing the exterior walls.

They're nowhere to be seen.

CHAPTER 15

MY HEAD IS pounding as I try and stand. There's another, smaller explosion, this one makes me squat down and protect my head, in case something comes flying over. It's instinct, to avoid any debris that could potentially hit me.

I stand again and look around. There's so much mess, so much devastation. It feels like I'm sitting in a cinema and watching an action movie.

Blanketed by blackness of the sky, the only illumination is the scorching fire encompassing the house. I see some of Jude's men laying lifeless on the ground.

Panic quickly closes in around me. My lungs burn as anxiety overtakes me.

"Jude!" I yell as I stumble around and try to find my coordination. My ears are ringing, making it difficult to hear if anyone is calling for me. "Frank!" I shout louder. Still, I'm getting nothing. "Ronan." *Ringing.* "Jude!"

"Alexa," I hear someone calling me. But I can't work out who the someone is. "Alexa."

Turning in the direction of the voice, I see Ronan staggering toward me. "Where's Jude?" I ask as I look around.

"Are you okay?" he asks, not answering my question. He grabs hold of my upper arms and squeezes. The long-sleeved shirt I'm wearing prevents me from getting a vision. Thank God, because I doubt I'd be able to handle seeing something right now.

"I'm fine. Where's Jude?"

"Are you okay?" he asks again with complete disregard of my question. I don't think he can hear me.

"I'm fine. Where the hell is Jude?" I peer past him, trying to locate Jude. My heart beats like crazy as I try to see him. But he's nowhere to be seen. Shit, is he dead? "Where's Jude!" I yell, but I don't wait for a response. I take off to the other side of the house, trying to see through the smoke filling the air.

"He'll be okay," Ronan replies.

I make it around the side and see Jude lying on the ground.

My heart stops.

He doesn't look okay.

The blood in my veins chills, as ice shoots through me.

"Oh, my God, he's dead," I whisper as tears prickle my eyes. Everything freezes; time stands still. My pulse is rapidly beating in my ears and my breath is coming thick and fast.

Walking over to him, I kneel beside his body. It takes me a few seconds to notice his erratic breathing, and a few more for it to comprehend.

He's not dead.

"Alexa, I told Ronan to get you out of here," his voice is rough and he looks like shit. Even his clothing is wrong. He always dresses sharply with a tailored suit, or at the very least tailored pants and a dress shirt. But now he's covered in black ash, and his sweatpants and t-shirt are filthy.

"You look like crap," I blurt.

He manages to smile between coughs. "Are you hurt?" he asks me as he lifts his hand and runs it down my cheek. Closing my eyes, I lean into his hand, thankful for him being alive.

And I'm drawn into a vision. We're in a sterile white room, he's lying in bed and Ronan is sitting on a chair in a corner of the room.

This concerns me. Why is he here? I step further into the room and look around. The door opens and a male doctor comes in. "Mr. Caley," he announces while looking down at some paperwork in his hand.

"Yeah," Jude replies.

"All your tests seem okay. We just want to keep you here overnight to assess you for any complications."

Jude rolls his eyes and sits up in bed. "This is bullshit; I'm fine. Get me out of here."

"I can't do that, I need to make sure you don't have any further complications."

Jude swings his legs around and places his feet on the ground. "Nah, not happening, doc. Sign the papers, I have somewhere to be."

"No," the doctor asserts himself. "I'm not giving you the okay to leave until tomorrow." He's one stubborn doctor. But then again, Jude can hold his own.

"Listen here, doc . . ."

The door opens and I come in with Frank. The doctor turns to look at me and Frank, then swings around, smiling, at Jude. "I'll see you in the morning, Mr. Caley. Rest up for now." He leaves and Jude mumbles angrily under his breath.

"This is bullshit," Jude says louder.

Knowing Jude's okay, I force myself out of the vision. "You're a pain in the butt," I say to Jude, opening my eyes.

"What did I do? Or . . . should I say, what will I do?"

"You're staying in the hospital tonight, Jude. Don't argue with the doctor."

"What doctor?" He looks at me confused, but within a few seconds realization dawns on him. "I won't," he replies while lying back on the lawn, still coughing.

I look around, let out a deep breath and shake my head. "What's going on?" I turn to face Ronan before my eyes settle on Jude.

"It happened so fast." Ronan's running his hand through his

hair while he shifts from foot to foot. Judging by his reaction, I believe him when he says it happened fast. "We were ambushed."

"What happened? Why the fuck is my house on fire, Ronan?" Jude asks him.

"I'm not entirely sure yet, but I think it's because . . ." he pauses and looks over to me.

"Because of me?" My hand goes to my chest and instantly I feel guilty. I want to ask why, but I have a feeling I'm about to hear the answer.

"We must've been getting close," Ronan replies to my unasked question.

I squint and look away. "That doesn't make sense. Why would they send a suicide bomber in to kill us? If they gave me this, then that means they gave me this for a reason. Why would they kill me?"

"They're not interested in killing *you,* Alexa," Jude says.

"Wait . . . you mean they were trying to kill you? But, why?"

"Because I stand in the way of them getting to you."

Oh shit. They're trying to eliminate him to get to me. This means, Jude's in danger. I turn and look at Ronan, my head is spinning with everything. "You're all in danger, because of me. *Again.*"

Jude grabs onto my thigh and squeezes it. Before he speaks, Ronan jumps in to say, "The car's here. We're taking you to the hospital, Jude."

"I'll be fine." He coughs heavily, the smoke still in his lungs.

"Please," I beg him. "Just go to the hospital."

Jude looks at me, and the stress stretched across my face must be enough. "Okay. But you're not leaving my side."

If it means getting him the proper treatment, then I'm fine with his ridiculous demand. "Deal." I try and offer him a smile.

I get out of Ronan's way as he and Frank help Jude up. Jude's heavy coughing worries me. Smoke inhalation can be dangerous. Turning, I look at the house. Part of the frame is burning bright, the walls crumbling beneath the burn. We're damn lucky we got out.

I have so many questions, but I doubt I'll be getting any answers until we find whoever did this.

The car pulls out of the driveway, and I see the watch tower. The two men who were on duty tonight have bullet holes in their heads. This was orchestrated carefully, though I can't help but wonder why they didn't just swoop in and take me. Why crash a car into the house with a suicide bomber inside?

It was obviously their intention, but they didn't succeed. They can't have put all this thought into getting me, just to leave me here. They would've had a contingency plan, so why didn't they take me? What stopped them? Who stopped them? What is going on?

The ride to the hospital has me assessing and questioning everything. Jude's coughing is making me angrier and angrier. Not at Jude. He's just a casualty in this hot mess. But at the fact that with each passing day, I'm no closer to finding these people.

We get to the hospital, and Ronan goes ahead. He does whatever he does, and before I know it, Jude's being shown to a private room. *Money talks.*

Jude continues coughing, and I sit on the chair in the corner and let the anger inside me bubble away. Frank enters the room and looks toward me, then Jude. Standing to my feet, I head over to Frank, throw my arms around him and hug him. "You okay, Miss Lexi?" he asks.

I do everything to hold onto my anger. But somehow it bursts through in the form of tears. "I need something to eat," I say.

"Lexi?" Jude questions. His distressed voice sends me over the edge.

I don't let go of Frank. Frank is like a father figure to me. He'll never replace my dad, but at the same time, I trust him like I trusted my father. "How about I take Miss Lexi to get something to eat?" Frank suggests to Jude.

Turning, I look to Jude and see the worry carved into his face.

His shoulders are stiff and high, and his eyes beckon for me not to go. I stare at him and wait for his answer, silently begging him to let me go.

Jude's understandingly concerned. "Only to the cafeteria, nowhere else. Don't take her out of the hospital. I'm holding you responsible if anything happens." Jude points to Frank.

"Nothing will happen on my watch," Frank responds with confidence.

"Don't leave Frank's side." I nod my head in agreement. He huffs and he looks as if he wants to say something else, but he doesn't.

"We'll be back soon, Mr. Jude."

Frank and I head toward the door, and Jude adds, "Take care of her."

We leave the hospital room, and Frank turns to his left, leading me down the hall. We get to the elevator and I press the down button for the floor where the cafeteria is located. When we get in, we're isolated. All I want to do is curl up into a ball and forget my life.

But if I forget my life, then I'm forgetting the bad *and* the good. I'm not ready to let go of the good yet, I'm not sure I ever will be ready.

Silently we arrive to the floor, and we head toward the cafeteria. I find the most secluded spot, which isn't hard considering the early hour, and sit in the corner. Frank orders something, then comes back with a sandwich for me, a hot chocolate, and a bottle of water for himself.

"What's going on in that pretty head of yours?" he asks, pushing the sandwich toward me.

Picking it up, I break off a small corner of the bread and nibble on it. "How much about me do you know?" He's in the thick of it, he may as well know everything.

"I know Mr. Jude is very fond of you."

I sigh and look away. "That's not what I mean, Frank."

I catch his gaze, and this time it's his turn to avert his eyes away from mine. "I know you're a very special young lady."

Swallowing hard, I nod my head. "How special?"

"You can do things others can't."

I nod my head again. "I *can* do things no one else can."

"You're different, but in a way people can't see." Spot on, my friend. *Spot on.*

"I have the ability to see a person's immediate future with a simple touch."

"Oh," he grumbles and his brows raise.

My heart races as I wait for more of a reaction from him. He chews on the inside of his cheek and stares down at his water. "Is 'oh' the only thing you can say?" Holding my breath, I wait for his response.

"You said immediate future?" I nod. "How immediate?"

"I haven't figured out the time constraints, but I always see the person in the same clothes they're wearing. I figure, it has to be only a few hours ahead." I think back to when Jude killed Enzo, and realize the vision I saw was only moments ahead. I crinkle my brows and slump my shoulders, staring at the hot chocolate.

"How did you get it?" Frank's question makes me push my thoughts to the back of my mind, and return my focus to him.

"I don't know. But, recently I had appendicitis and when I woke, I was able to see a person's future. Scared me to death, because when it first happened, I had no idea what was going on."

"Did you die while they were operating?"

"They said I had complications. I never asked. I think I didn't want to know."

Frank rubs his chin and furrows his brows together. "Tell me more about it. This is interesting. How do you see the future?"

"I really don't know how to explain it, but it's like I'm being dragged into a tunnel, where on the other end, there's a movie playing and I'm behind the camera recording it."

"What can you do while you're in these . . . apparitions?"

"At first, I couldn't do much, but I'm getting stronger with each passing day."

"How so?" He leans into the table, careful to look around to make sure no one is within listening distance.

"Now I can move around easily in the vision. I can talk and people can hear me. I'm getting better at resisting going into a vision . . ." I shrug and say, "I'm learning to control it instead of letting it control me."

"Ah," Frank says as if an epiphany hits him. Moments pass as he focuses on his water. "What you're saying is you're lethal?"

What? Lethal? "I'm not lethal." I nearly want to laugh at his silly comment. But I think about it. The more I discover, the more dangerous I become.

"Miss Lexi, you're potentially an incredible dangerous person. You just told me you're learning to control this power you have. If you can harness it, learn it, understand it, then you'll be one of the most dangerous people in the world. Can you imagine what someone would do in order to get to you so they can use you?"

"I never saw myself as dangerous. Instead, I thought this was a hindrance, something that killed my parents and got my best friend kidnapped. I thought what I had was a gift, then a curse . . ." I break off my sentence, caught in the middle of the hell playing in my mind. "I thought Jude could protect me. Maybe that's my naivety coming out." Exhaling deeply, I grasp the truth. He can't protect me.

No one can.

Ideally, he'd be able to keep me safe. He was the one who saved me from Enzo. But this, this now is much bigger than either of us.

"Miss Lexi, whoever knows about this will move mountains to be able to use it. I suggest you don't go telling too many people."

"Ordinarily I'd agree with you, but I believe this was given to me while I was knocked out to have my surgery. So, it wouldn't matter who I told or didn't, whoever gave it to me, already knows about me." Frank's forehead wrinkles in concentration. "The house being bombed . . . most likely happened because of me. What I can't work out is, they're obviously organized, they knew what was going to happen, so why didn't they take me and leave all of you behind? It doesn't make sense. Maybe I'm missing something."

"Maybe the house being bombed wasn't about you. Maybe it's about Mr. Jude."

I shake my head in frustration. "It still doesn't make sense. Why go to that extreme to kill Jude?"

"Hmmm." He twists the lid to his water bottle, takes a swig then places it on the table. He's thinking, and so am I, but nothing is making sense.

"It could've been for Mr. Jude because the car was in his room."

"But that could be to kill him and take me."

"Or they have no idea about your *talent,* and the intention was just to kill him."

"Talent?" I roll my eyes. "Let's go with that then." I offer Frank a weak smile, but the turmoil in my head doesn't allow me to muster energy for anything else. "I'm scared, Frank."

"It's no wonder. I'm scared too, and I'm a grown man."

"What do I do?" I plead with him to give me some direction.

"Miss Lexi, I hate to say this, but I have no idea. For now, stay close to Mr. Jude, Ronan, and me, and take each day as it comes."

I breathe out several times in frustration. The thing I hate most about this situation, is the uncertainty. Someone else is holding all the cards and we have to wait until they're ready to show them before we can make our move.

"We need to get back to the room," Frank says reaching out to touch my hand, but he stops himself and looks into my eyes.

"It's okay, I understand." I pull my hand back.

Standing, we head back to Jude's room. When we open the door, Ronan's sitting on the chair in the corner. The doctor's in here with them and I'm in the vision I had. The doctor looks at me, then back to Jude, a sly smile lifts his features. "I'll see you in the morning, Mr. Caley. Rest up for now."

He leaves and Jude mumbles angrily under his breath, "This is bullshit." The door closes behind the doctor who really isn't interested in Jude's response. "We're not staying here." Jude stands, and instantly relapses into a coughing fit.

"You have to stay here for observation, doctor's orders," I steely instruct him.

"What? How do you . . ." He looks over to Ronan and shakes his head. "Of course, you'd know."

"Lie down and stop being a pain in everyone's butt. He told you to stay here, so you're staying here. Get over it," I snap, exasperated with everything.

Ronan looks up from his phone, and Frank backs away before quickly adding, "I'll be waiting outside, Mr. Jude." He exits, closing the door behind him, leaving Jude staring at me.

"Before you say anything, I'm tired, I'm frustrated and I'm angry. So, can you do me a favor and just stay here for tonight instead of marching out to set heads rolling when you've got smoke inhalation."

"Alexa."

I hold my hand up to halt whatever he wants to say. "Please . . . for me?" I drop my voice and let my chin fall to my chest. "Just for tonight." If something happened to him because he left the hospital against the doctors' orders, it would be the end of the slim sliver of sanity I'm desperately trying to hold onto. "Please," I beg again.

The room is filled with silence. Everyone in here is quiet. I've pleaded and begged, and now we're waiting for Jude's decision. "Alexa." Sighing, I cover my face with my hands. I'm not crying, but I want to. This is all too much for me to handle. "Get out," I hear him instruct Ronan.

"Got work to do." Ronan walks out, leaving just Jude and me in the room.

"What's wrong?" he asks and steps closer to me.

"Someone tried killing you, or me, or both of us. And it's . . ." Closing my eyes, I take several deep breaths to calm my thoughts. " . . . it's too much for me to handle. Everyone around me is suffering because of . . ."

"Don't say it's because of you."

Opening my eyes, I notice how Jude's stepped closer to me. "But, it *is* because of me."

He wraps his arms around me, and pulls me in for a hug. "It might feel like that, but it's because of what was done to you. A huge difference, and definitely not the same thing."

"Jude." I breathe out as I step closer into his body. A vision is nipping at me, wanting to take me under, but I'm refusing to allow it. "Please stay here tonight. Tomorrow you can leave. Besides, it's late or early, whichever way you look at it." With my head on his chest, I can hear his heart's steady beat.

"I'll stay, but on the condition you stay with me."

I simply nod my head against his chest.

CHAPTER 16

"GET ME A coffee," I hear Jude grumble.

Stretching, I open my eyes and see Ronan standing opposite Jude. "I'll get Frank to get it," he replies.

"Morning," I say as I stand and stretch again. Sleeping in a chair is extremely uncomfortable. Jude tried to give me the bed, but I refused it.

Jude smiles at me, and Ronan nods his head sharply. "Ronan's going to get me a coffee. The coffee from the cafeteria is shit, I want a proper coffee."

Ronan rolls his eyes. Evidently, he thinks it's a task that's beneath him. "I'll come with you, I'm kind of hungry."

"For fuck's sake," Ronan mumbles. "I'm not babysitting her." He points toward me.

Whoa, what's happened for him to become so passive-aggressive toward me. "Hey, I'll stay here," I reply as I hold my hands up, complying with his tantrum.

He groans in frustration. "It's been a hard night, Alexa." I guess this is his way of apologizing.

"It's cool." I stretch again and look at Jude. "How's the coughing?"

"Alright." He shrugs one shoulder and heads in the direction of the bathroom. "I'm going for a shower, get Frank to get me a real coffee considering you won't do it."

"Oh, I'll go with Frank then," I announce, jumping to my feet in a sprightly way.

"Wait up." Jude stops walking and turns to face Ronan and me. "You're staying here," he orders.

Here we go again. "No, I'm hungry, so I'll go with Frank to get you a coffee, and I'll get something for Frank and me to eat."

Jude flicks Ronan a look. Ronan sighs and grumbles beneath his breath. "I'll go with them."

Jude nods triumphantly and I feel like a school kid who's in trouble and needs her big brother everywhere she goes. *Whatever,* I'm hungry.

"Let's go," Ronan says as he holds the door open for me.

"Sorry you have to babysit me." We head out of the room, and find Frank slumped in a chair, sleeping.

"Wake up, Frank." Ronan nudges him.

Frank's up on his feet in seconds and falls in beside me. "Mr. Jude okay?" he asks in a sleepy voice.

"Typical pain in the ass. So, yes, he is," he answers to Frank. "And, don't you be sorry," he says, looking over his shoulder toward me. Ronan is walking so fast, I nearly have to jog to keep up with him. When we get in the elevator, he pulls his phone out and searches for something. Man, he's obviously in a shit mood. "There's a Starbucks nearby. We'll go there and get everyone what they want."

When we get down to the entrance, the driver who bought us to the hospital is waiting for us. "The car's this way," he says pointing out the front of the hospital.

We all get into the car, Ronan in the front passenger seat, Frank and I in the back. Frank taps my leg and makes a gesture as if to say, 'why's Ronan being an ass?' I shrug my shoulders and turn to look out the window.

We get to the coffee shop, and the driver parks a few spots away. Ronan, Frank, and I all get out. My stomach rumbles loudly. "Sorry," I mumble when Ronan glares over at me. "I'm hungry." Ronan's coming across as really pissed off. And I have no idea why. Screw this shit. I'm not going to take his crap. "Hey." I grab onto his arm, stopping him from walking into Starbucks. "Why are you being such an ass today? Has something happened?"

He runs his tongue over his teeth while screwing up his mouth. "There's a lot of shit going on."

"I know that, I even know most of it has something to do with me."

"Jude's on the verge of losing the . . ." he stops talking and looks around, making sure only I can hear him. "Jude's on the verge of losing everything he's worked for."

"How?"

"Because shit's happening."

"Like what?" I push.

"Shit you don't have access to."

"Seriously? Shit I don't have access to? You are aware that I can find out anything I want at any given moment in time." I place my hand on my hip and stand my ground.

Ronan steps back, and smirks at me. "I see it," he says with his eyes wandering over my body.

"What?" Man, this guy is making me so mad.

"I see why he likes you. I get it. You don't back down. You're strong, for a chick."

"For a chick?" My temper flares. What is it with Ronan today? I was liking him, but now he's turning into an ass. "For a chick?" I say again. I straighten my back, clench my jaw and step forward. Ronan regards me with humor, which makes me even angrier. "I'm not strong, Ronan, but I'm damn powerful." The hair on my arms stands to attention. "Probably the most powerful person you'll ever meet. I'm the queen, the king, the rook, and the bishop all rolled into one. No one stands a chance against me."

Holy shit.

Did I just admit my own worth to myself?

Ronan blinks at me, his body stiffening. A smirk stretches his features. "Yes, you are. About time you realize it, too." He walks away from me into Starbucks.

Slowly, I make my way in, where Frank's already in line. The line isn't too long, only eight people ahead of us. "You okay, Miss Lexi?" he asks and looks over to Ronan who's dragged out a chair and is sitting in it.

"I called myself more powerful than a queen, a king, a rook and a bishop." I take out my hair tie, run my fingers through my hair and tie it up again. "What was I thinking?" I mumble to myself.

"You were thinking exactly what I think of you. You're a force to be reckoned with." He chuckles, and we shuffle forward as the next person gets served.

Frank is talking to me, but I'm not listening. Instead I'm zoning out to him, and thinking about me. Maybe I *am* lethal. Maybe I'm exactly what I said I was. I'm a queen—she has the ultimate power of being able to steal whoever she wants. I'm a king—I need to be protected and guarded. I'm a rook—fast and strong and considered a major player. And I'm a bishop—moving around to protect the power within the game.

"Do you know what you want, Miss Lexi?" Frank taps me on the shoulder, to ask.

My veins fill with shards of ice cold. The hair on the back of my neck stands while a wave of realization washes over me. I am powerful. I. Am. Powerful.

"Miss Lexi?"

"Um . . ." Looking up to the board, out of the corner of my eye, I notice Ronan moving toward me.

"Get Jude a coffee, and I'll get one too." Ronan looks up at the menu board. "And a breakfast sandwich."

"Which one?" Frank asks.

"Whatever." Ronan takes a roll of cash out of his pocket, and gives me three twenty-dollar bills.

There are a few people working behind the counter, and when it's our turn we get called by a young guy. "How can I help you?" he asks.

He's young, maybe my age or a year or so older. He's got short blond hair, fair skin, and black eyes. I thought Jude's eyes were dark, but this guy has the darkest eyes I've ever seen.

"Can I help you?" he asks again.

Frank gives him his order, and nudges me to tell the barista what I want. "Miss Lexi."

I stare at the guy, something about him is familiar, but not. "Pumpkin bread and hot chocolate."

He enters my order, all the time glancing at me. I want to know who he is and why I'm drawn toward him, like a moth to a beam of light.

"Miss," he says as his eyes find mine.

"I'm Alexa," I say as I hold my hand out to him.

He lifts a brow and stares at my offered hand. "Nick." Hesitantly he extends his hand to me.

Our skin touches, and I get . . . nothing. Not a goddamn thing. Focusing on this moment, I'm still standing in Starbucks without going in a vision. Nick looks at me. There's a twinge below his right eye.

He pulls his hand back, and looks down at the point of sale screen. "Is that all for today?" He turns around and starts preparing the coffees. His head is down, as he works to get our order ready.

There's something about him. I don't know what it is, but something is happening here.

Frank's talking to me, but my eyes are glued to Nick. The inside of the store quietens; the voices of the patrons fade into nothing.

Turning to look around, I notice Ronan's sitting at a table, still on the phone. There are now only a few people milling around in here.

Something's wrong.

I look to Ronan and he catches my stare.

My stomach knots. My arms form goosebumps.

A black car slowly drives by. A man with dark glasses looks into the store.

I look back to Ronan. He hangs up and stands. He can see how uneasy I am.

Turning, I look to Frank, then Nick. He's still making our coffees, when I notice his entire back shudder. He drops what he's holding, and he turns to face me. "You brought them here."

"What?"

"Get down!" he yells at the top of his voice.

Everyone freezes. A frantic fear rises rapidly as the air erupts with a crackling intensity.

Ronan throws himself at me, and Frank falls next to me.

At first it sounds like a car is back firing, but I quickly realize the sound isn't a car backfiring.

Gun shots.

Ronan is nearly suffocating me as he shifts his weight to cover more of my body. It's all over in a few seconds, but it feels like hours. There's someone screaming, and Frank asking me if I'm okay. Ronan lifts off my body, grabs my arms and yanks me up in a single movement.

"What happened?" he asks me.

Swinging around to look for Nick, my eyes dart everywhere.

He's no longer behind the counter.

He's gone.

Seconds before the gun fire started, he said to me, *'You brought them here.'* How does he know about me? But most importantly, who is Nick?

CHAPTER 17

"WE'VE GOT TO get out of here before the police arrive." Ronan ushers me out through the front doors toward our waiting car.

"Wait," I try to protest, looking over my shoulder in case I catch sight of Nick.

"No time to wait. Get in the car." He pushes me in, Frank follows and Ronan jumps in the front. The car is in motion before Ronan's even shut the door. He pulls out his phone, and dials someone's number. "Have you got the tracker on us?" He waits, and I keep looking around us. "Hack into the store and delete all footage."

How deep do Jude's pockets go? Who is Ronan talking to?

"Get me a suite at the Ritz Carlton," he stops talking, looks over his shoulder to me, then adds, "actually, get me two suites."

"Wait!" I yell as the driver zooms down the road.

"What is it?" Ronan asks.

"The guy from Starbucks. I just saw him running, he's heading down there." I point out the window, and toward a narrow lane way we passed.

"Who cares about him?" Ronan states. "We have to get you somewhere safe."

"Ronan, please. He knows about me. He had a vision, he saw

them coming before they got there. He knows something."

"I don't care."

"Ronan!" I yell. "Then let me out. I'll find him and try to figure out what's going on."

Ronan looks at me and his jaw tenses as he lets out a deep breath. "Turn the car around, let's find this kid."

The driver spins the car, and I hold onto the handle above the door while the force of the car spinning around nearly throws me across the car. *Thank God for seat belts.*

I keep my eyes open as we near the alley where I saw him. As the driver turns in, I can't see Nick anywhere.

Suddenly, I see someone running in my peripheral vision. That someone is Nick.

I jump out of the car, and head toward him. "Nick," I shout.

"Alexa, get back in the car," Ronan barks from behind me.

No way, I need to find Nick, figure out what he knows, and who he is. "Nick!" I yell again. He looks over his shoulder at me, then speeds up. Damn him and his fast running. But he's no match for Ronan, who passes me, catches Nick, and tackles him to the ground.

"Where are you going, punk?" Ronan has him down, with a knee in his back.

"Ronan!" I yell once I catch up to them.

"What?" He looks up at me, and shrugs. "You wanted him, I've got him for you."

"Just, get him up." I step back, and Ronan lifts Nick by the back of his t-shirt. He looks at me angrily.

"Do you know what you've done?" he spits toward me with fury.

"I don't have any idea what's going on. The only thing I do know is you're like me."

He chuckles at me, and tries to get loose of Ronan's restraint. "You're nothing like me." He smirks arrogantly.

"You can see the future. But, I noticed you don't need to

touch. I need you to tell me what you know and how you do it."

"I'm not telling you shit. You brought them to me, which means now I need to run again.

Stunned, I stand and stare at him. "We can protect you," I blurt.

"What?" Ronan says.

"What?" Nick says at the same time. Both stare at me in disbelief.

"Come with us, we can help you," I offer again.

Nick looks over his shoulder to Ronan, then back to me. He tries to loosen the hold Ronan has on him, but he realizes it's a fruitless attempt because Ronan is one strong guy. He pushes Nick toward the car, which has backed up. The passenger door's still open. Frank's sitting in the back while the driver keeps an eye on our surroundings.

"Do I have a choice?" Nick asks as Ronan pushes his head down and into the car.

"Nope," he answers sarcastically. "Get in, and if he looks like he's going to try to get out, I *will* shoot him." He looks me straight in the eye, and I know by his tone and his look, he's deadly serious.

"Try not to, I think he's useful," I whisper just before sliding in beside Nick.

Ronan and the driver both get in, and we head down the alley, like we haven't just snatched a guy off the street.

When we get to the hotel, Ronan opens the glove department, takes out a set of cuffs and gives them to Nick. "I have two words for you. Bullet. Brain. You try to run, and I'll kill you. Put them on." He pointedly looks down at the handcuffs.

My stomach churns with anxiety as I watch Nick shake while he secures the cuffs. Man, Ronan is terrifying. I never realized *how* menacing, until this moment. I feel like I should apologize to Nick, but then I'd be undermining Ronan. And if I'm being honest, I need answers. And I think Nick can help me understand what's been happening to me.

"Park the car below. I'll go and check us in, then I'll come down. Shoot him if he moves," Ronan instructs the driver. The moment he's out of the car, we take the driveway down to an underground parking area.

Ronan's threat to kill Nick makes me believe he's deadly serious.

We wait in the garage in complete silence. Nick is searching around him, looking at the lock on the car door and trying to map out his escape route. "He'll kill you," I say, desperately trying to hold him here.

He searches my eyes, then slowly closes his own. I watch as his body shudders, exactly like it did back in Starbucks.

He's in a vision.

Watching intently, I lean into him, wanting to touch him to see what he can see. But, I have to hold back, because I can see the future a few hours ahead.

Except for that one time with Enzo. Maybe I can focus and go into his vision. Taking deep breaths, I too close my eyes and focus on my heart rate. I feel it increase, then it slows. My breath comes out softly, and I lift my hand to touch his.

The moment I make skin on skin contact, I'm being tumbled into a tunnel. A passageway of darkness. There's a vision at the end of the long path. It's bright and I can see it, I just need to get there.

With pure determination, I head toward the vision.

I'm thrown into the garage where we're waiting. Nick is standing outside the car, watching. The moment I land beside him, he turns to look at me. "How did you do that?" he asks. He steps back and looks around the isolated garage.

"I have to see what you can see," I answer, trying to step closer to him.

"How did you follow me in here?" he nearly shouts at me.

"Don't run, Nick. I need answers, and you can help me."

He looks around again, and we both see Ronan walking toward us. "If I run, will he kill me?"

I don't know. Probably. "Yes." I need him to stay.

He looks me up and down and clenches his jaw tightly together. "I'll stay."

And just like that, he vanishes. I pull myself out of the vision, and bring myself back to the now. "Thank you," I say to him.

"I'm not doing this for you, I'm doing this because I don't want the gorilla to kill me." He pointedly looks toward Ronan, who's walking toward us.

Good enough reason for me. "Thank you, again," I say, trying to impress upon him how important this is to me.

He flicks his eyes away and grumbles.

"Are you going to give me any problems? I've killed younger for less," Ronan says to Nick.

"Nah," he disdainfully scoffs.

"Good." Ronan steps back as I exit the car. He then grabs Nick's shirt and drags him out. Frank follows quietly, not saying anything but watching what's happening. "Behind him," Ronan says to the driver who obediently stands behind Nick. "Frank, to the side."

"Yes, Sir, Mr. Ronan." Frank isn't a body guard, well I don't think he is. But, he still does what Ronan tells him.

"Lexi, you go ahead, we're on the entire twentieth floor. We'll take the rooms at the end of the hall, twenty-fifteen, and twenty-sixteen. Here." He hands me the key to one. "You're in fifteen. Where do you want him?" He pulls on Nick, making him stumble.

Pleadingly, I stare at Ronan. "In my room."

We get in the elevator, and Ronan reiterates to Nick, "Make one false move, and your brains will be all over this elevator." Man, Ronan means business. The tone, his harshness, the fact he's manhandling Nick, I know he'd kill him.

We exit on our floor, and thankfully no one is in the corridors. We get to my room. I open the door and Ronan roughly pulls Nick in. "Can you take the cuffs off him?" I ask.

"No, he'll try to escape."

He won't. For some reason, I trust him, and I don't think he'll try to run. "If he does, then shoot him in the thigh." I feel sick giving those instructions.

Ronan smirks at me. "I'll shoot alright. Here, across the hall," he says to Frank and the driver, whose name I still don't know, handing them a card key. Both leave, closing the door behind them. "Turn around," Ronan instructs Nick. He takes the cuffs off him, and goes to stand by the front door.

"Can I get something to drink?" Nick asks, too petrified to move toward the small bar-fridge.

Heading to the bar-fridge, I open it, grab a bottle of water, and throw it to Nick. At the same time, Ronan's phone rings.

"Yeah," he answers. He listens for a few seconds then says, "We've picked up a stray, I'll send Frank and Mike to get you." Oh, Mike must be the drivers' name. "Yeah, you'll see when you get here." I look to Ronan and draw my brows in together. "She's fine. She was the one who insisted we pick up the stray." He must be talking to Jude. "I'll send them now."

He hangs up, and looks down to his phone. Then he looks up at both of us. Walking over to the sofa, I sit and wait for Nick. His shoulders are up high, and his spine is rigid, probably with fear. "Sit," I offer toward one of the arm chairs in the small sitting area.

He looks to Ronan, then me. Slowly, he makes his way over to an available armchair and sinks down into it. "What do you want to know?" Taking the lid off the bottle, he has a quick drink then sets the bottle on the table beside him.

"I have a million questions, but I have no idea where to start. Can you wait until Jude arrives?"

"Do I have a choice?" he snidely asks.

"Well . . ." I shrug. "No, you don't."

Ronan keeps an eye on Nick, who keeps looking around the room, trying to plan his escape. But every time his eyes find Ronan, who's glaring at him, I can see he changes his mind.

"How long have you lived here?" I finally ask after the silence becomes unbearable to me.

"For a while," he replies.

"Do you move around a lot?"

He chuckles and nods. "You will too."

"How long do you stay in one spot?"

He huffs an angry sigh. "Until I know they've found me."

I'm itching to know who 'they' are, and how they find him. I'm desperately wanting to know everything. How he got his ability, how he stays ahead of them, how he lives . . . this is driving me crazy.

Standing, I begin to pace the length of the sitting room. So many crazy thoughts are going through my mind, I need to know everything.

As I pace, Ronan stands solidly by the front door, keeping his eyes on Nick. I can't help but let all these emotions bounce through me. But, I keep it together, instead I let my nervous energy escape by pacing.

There's a knock on the door, Ronan doesn't turn to answer it, instead, he makes a phone call. "Yeah," he says into the phone. He hangs up and opens the door.

Jude waltzes in, his eyes landing on me first, before taking in Nick. "Are you the stray we've picked up?" he asks Nick.

"Jude, please," I beg.

He looks over to me and sighs. "Keep an eye on him," he says to Ronan while pointing toward Nick. "Alexa, come with me."

We leave the room and head across the hall to the other room. Frank and Mike are both lounging in arm chairs when we enter. The moment they see Jude and me, they jump to their feet. "Mr. Jude?" Frank asks. "Is everything okay?"

"Go to the other room," he tells them. Both leave, and Jude turns to me. "What's going on with the kid?"

"He's like me, Jude. He can see the future, but differently. He said I led 'them' to him. He said . . ." I become overwhelmed as I'm talking. Excitedly, I bounce up and down, and all I want to do is get back to the room so we can figure out what's happening.

"Okay, okay. Calm down a moment, and stand still. You're giving me a headache from watching you bounce."

Shaking my hands out, and rolling my neck, I take several deep breaths so I can calm my frantic heart down. "He's like me, Jude. Do you know what this means? He may have answers."

"And he may not. Don't get ahead of yourself."

"But . . . but . . . what if he does? What if he knows who's behind this? What if he knows if it can be reversed?" Shit, now that the answer is so close to me, I'm really not sure I want it to be reversed.

Crap, crap, *crap.*

"He may have answers, or he may not. You have to be prepared for disappointment."

"He said I led them to him. He has to know who 'them' is. He just has to." I sound like an obsessed teenager. I suppose, I am.

"Okay, this is what we're going to do. We're going to go in there and we're going to question him. We'll see what he knows, then we'll go from there."

"Jude, don't kill him."

He smirks and looks away. "I won't." Yeah, right.

"And by don't kill him, I mean don't order anyone to kill him either."

The other side of his mouth lifts with sarcastic laughter. He runs his hand to the back of his neck as he stares at me. "Alright," he agrees. "But, I can't guarantee I won't hurt him," he quickly adds.

"Jude," I beg of him. "Please, this is important to me. If he doesn't want to cooperate then we're in no worse place than we were before him."

"You drive a hard bargain, Miss Murphy, but as you wish. No hurting, and definitely no killing."

"Okay," I respond suddenly wary of how quickly Jude

accepted what I've requested from him.

"Come on." He jerks his head to the side toward the door, and waits until I've reached it before he opens the door, steps through, looks around then gives me the okay. We enter the suite, and Ronan gives Jude a small head nod, before he looks at me and winks. "Problems?"

Ronan shakes his head. "Nothing. The kid hasn't even moved."

Jude walks over to Nick, who's looking between us. "Jude." He holds his hand out to shake Nick's.

"Nick." They shake hands and I move to stand beside Jude.

"So," I start, eager to know everything about Nick and his power. "I have no idea where to start. Um . . ." I look to Jude.

"How long have you had your ability?" Jude asks.

Nick looks uncomfortable and uneasy. "Just over a year."

"Do you know how you got it?" I move to sit in the arm chair beside him so I can listen intently.

"I had an operation." He rubs his throat. "Had my tonsils removed. Very routine, apparently."

"I had an operation too." I quickly recall the first time I awoke after my operation. "What happened?"

"When I woke, everything was different. I was seeing things happening before they actually happened. It was like I had precognition of things."

At the exact same time, we say the identical thing, "Déjà vu."

"Exactly. I thought I was losing my mind. I had no idea what was happening around me. I'd see someone do the same thing twice."

"Who . . . how . . . what . . ." I have so many questions.

"Some guy and his assistant came in to see me, and they were asking me questions."

"Did he have a beard? Was he wearing a suit?"

"Yeah, kinda older?" Nick asks. I confirm with a head nod. "There was something off about his assistant too."

"I know this is weird, but was she wearing heels?"

"That's exactly what I noticed. She had on these incredibly high heels," Nick responds.

I look to Jude, as excitement begins to bubble. It sounds like they're the same people who came to see me. "He said his name was Doctor Smith."

"He told me his name was Doctor Patterson, but when my doctor came into the room, and I asked about Doctor Patterson, he said there wasn't anyone there by that name."

Sitting back in the chair, my mind is moving at a hundred miles an hour. It's so fast I can barely think straight. "That's kind of what happened with me." I look over to Nick, who seems to want to ask me questions too. "Do you think there's more of us out there?"

Nick shrugs. "I've never met anyone else, until you." He leans forward and stares at me. "The first thing I noticed about you were your eyes. They're incredible." Jude mumbles irately from where he's standing. "What I didn't notice was that eye . . ." He points to my right. " . . . is nearly entirely blue, but has the smallest sliver of green. It almost looks like a colored contact, with a fragment that isn't colored."

"I did have green eyes. Now, I have a green eye and a blue eye." I point to the respective colors.

"Freaky, but super cool." He smiles at me. "When did your eye turn blue?"

"It started off with a small amount of blue, but the stronger my visions got, and the more I can do with them, the blue seems to take over."

"What exactly can you do?" he asks me, interested.

"At first I wasn't able to do much, but once I really accepted it, I've been doing a lot. I'm getting better at it, I'm able to pull out of a vision, or I can make myself go into one. I can move around, talk and be heard."

"What do you mean by you can talk and be heard?"

"Exactly that. I can go into a vision, and I can talk to whoever is there and tell them things. They don't hear it immediately, they hear it later, in the near future."

Nick shakes his head. His mouth is screwed up in confusion, and he's blinking at me, puzzled by what I'm saying. "How do your visions work? Aren't they like mine?"

"I see the future by a few hours, I haven't worked out the exact time limits yet. But I do know I'm starting to control myself so I can see anything in the future."

"So, like tomorrow?"

"No, what I mean is I've been able to see from a few minutes to a few hours. It's always been hours, but lately, I can concentrate and see minutes."

"Wouldn't that mean, if you keep practicing, you might be able to see days or even weeks ahead?"

I shrug, not really knowing what I'm capable of for sure. "I don't know," I add.

"How long have you been like this?"

"A few months, not long."

He narrows his brows at me. "And you can do all of what you've said?" I nod my head. "You have untapped potential." I shrug again as if to say, 's'pose so.'

"Have you met anyone else like us, Nick?"

"No. You're not even like me, you're so much more. You're like a two-point-o version of me. An upgrade."

"If you and I exist, then there have to be more of us."

"Why would there be when you have unlimited power?" Chills run over my body. I don't like the way he said that. It freaks me out, makes me feel like I'm more of a target, like my life is never going to be my own.

"I need to clear my head," I abruptly say as I head into the adjoining room. I notice there's a sliding door to a balcony, so I go out there, needing a few minutes to myself. My heart is racing crazily, and I'm nervous as hell. Nick has frightened me; he's confirmed what I was most anxious about.

"Hey, are you okay?" Jude asks as he joins me out on the balcony, sliding the door shut behind him.

"Uh, let me think on that one," I sarcastically retort. "He's said what I've been thinking, and that scares the shit out of me."

"We'll face it together. I won't let you get hurt."

I chuckle at Jude. "It's not about me getting hurt."

"Then what?"

"Jude . . ." I cross my arms in front of my chest, and straighten my back as I stare into his darkened, worried eyes. "Whoever gave this to me will kill you to get to me. I have no doubt at all in my mind, you'll be dead soon, and they'll take me."

"You underestimate me and what I'm capable of."

Offering him a weak smile, I huff in frustration. "This actually isn't even about you. It's about me, and the promise of my ability. It's what I can do with it. They're not even interested in you, Jude. If you hold no value to them, they *will* kill you. Because whoever did this, has more power, more authority, and more skill then you do. They'll get to me, and they'll kill you in order *to* get to me."

"I can handle myself," he cockily replies.

"There's a fine line between confidence, and arrogance. And right now, you're being arrogant and not listening. Look how everything has turned out so far. If you think you can take care of yourself, then you're a fool who's going to end up dead."

His face drops as do his shoulders. "I can handle myself," he declares again.

He's trying to be protective, and I get it. He wants to show me he can protect himself and me. But the reality of the situation is, he can't.

These people, whoever they are, are more powerful, have deeper pockets and can get to anyone. "I think the only way for us to move forward, is to figure out how we find them." I'm careful to insinuate 'us,' because I want Jude to think he's moving forward with me.

But tonight, when he's asleep, I'll be leaving him so I can go in search of the people involved.

Jude seems to accept what I've said. "Okay." He nods his head. "Then let's get back in there and find out what we can." He gestures to the sliding glass doors, and waits until I'm inside before grabbing me by my upper arm. "Promise me you're not going to become a lone ranger and try to find these people without me."

Damn it, I thought I was hiding my intention behind my words. I muster every ounce of acting ability I have before I open my mouth to say, "I promise." God, I hate lying, but if it means I can get to them before they get to me, then I'm going to do whatever I can to make sure no one else is going to get hurt because of me.

CHAPTER 18

NICK, FRANK, RONAN, and Mike are all in the other room. Jude decided he was going to sleep in here with me. He's in the shower, and I'm perched in the recliner in the sitting area, trying to decide how I'm going to get out of here without arousing Jude's suspicions.

Leaning over, I open the small fridge, grab a bottle of water and a candy bar. I place them beside the fridge, so I can take them with me when I leave. But I know this isn't going to be enough for me to last a few days out on the streets until I find these people.

Regretting my next actions, I try to reason with myself that it's not stealing. I head into the bedroom, where Jude's wallet, phone and watch are on the bedside table. "Sorry, Jude," I whisper.

Opening his wallet, I see he has a wad of cash in there. Easily a thousand dollars, maybe even more. A sickening twist churns my stomach. I hate stealing, even as much as I hate lying.

"You're doing this to save them," I say in a low voice to myself. "To save him," I correct myself.

Damn it. Why do I have to care about Jude? Why does he have to mean so much to me?

Stop it.

I shouldn't go, I should stay here and find them with Jude.

If you stay, he'll die.

Looking at the money, my mind argues with itself. Part of me wants to take it and run, and another part of me is screaming to stay and let Jude be involved in finding them. But I know what they're capable of, that means they'll stop at nothing to get me.

I have to run and hope Jude won't follow.

Pushing my feelings of guilt to the side, I shove most of the cash in my pocket. "Sorry," I say allowing that last twinge of guilt to course through me.

There's no other way.

The water turns off, and I quickly put his wallet back as I found it. I hate myself for doing this, but this is the only way I can move forward and maybe, lead a normal life.

But my stomach and heart are both telling me, *normal* isn't in my future.

Sitting up on the bed, I cross my ankles and attempt to look relaxed, though inside, my body is playing havoc. My damn heart races, while the blood pumps so furiously around my body I swear I can hear it echoing in my ears.

"You having a shower?" Jude asks when he emerges from the bathroom with a towel wrapped low around his hips.

Whoa. I'm taken aback by the sight of him fresh from the shower. I glance at the water dripping off the ends of his hair, and I gulp. He looks good. *Real good.*

Swallowing back the sudden desire constricting my breathing, I look away and shift on the bed. *Stop it, Lexi!* "Yeah, when I'm ready." *After I finishing perving on you.*

He crosses between the bed and the TV, and I catch a glimpse . . . okay an ogle, of how far down the towel is. And when he turns, I *may* be eyeballing the defined planes of his back muscles.

Crap, am I salivating?

Bringing my hand up, I run it over my neck, while my eyes are vigilantly watching how fluidly his body moves. The muscles in his back slightly contract and bulge when he runs his hand through his wet hair. Enthralled by his body, I feel myself leaning forward toward him.

Jude turns and catches my riveting gaze stuck on him. "Oh, so you're enjoying the view?" he cheekily asks.

"Hell, yeah. Wait, what?" My face burns with embarrassment. Burying my face into my palms, I try to hide the awkwardness charging through me.

Jude laughs, which makes me want to peek through my fingers to look at him. But, I know my face is bright red, giving away my humiliation. "I like that you looked."

Oh God. *Please don't respond, Lexi.* "I liked what I saw." Shut up, woman. *Shut the hell up!* I hear him clear his throat, and I decide to not be ashamed. So, I lift my head and stare at him. Big mistake, huge. Because my eyes are drawn to his obvious arousal toward me. "Shit," I mumble and look away. Sliding off the bed, I head out to the sitting room. "I'm going to order room service, I'll order something for you too."

I don't hear his response, but I swear I can hear him laughing as I close the door.

"What were you thinking?" I scold myself. Slapping my forehead, I take a moment to gather my wits. Finally, I'm calm enough to feel the redness in my face die down.

Picking up the menu, I can't really concentrate on it while I still see images of Jude with a towel slung low on his hips. The first thing my eyes see, is what I'm going to order.

Burgers. Yep, they'll do. Picking up the phone, I dial room service and give our order. Once I hang up, I contemplate going back into the bedroom, but I know if I do, I'll want to touch Jude, and I'm in no way ready for a relationship with him. I have too many other things I need to focus on, like finding the people who've given me this ability.

"How do I find you?" I ask aloud, but to myself. If I were them, obviously, I'd be tracking me. But, with Jude in the way, then it's quite possible they've lost the track. I sit on one of the chairs, tapping my finger on the table. Looking out to the peaceful, sleepy city below, my brain races as I think of a possible way to get them to come to me, instead of me trying to find them.

If they were searching for me, then maybe I can go somewhere they may be watching. But, where would they think I'd show up at? Maybe, my parent's crypt? Or home? Or maybe even back to Dallas's?

Dallas seems to be the most logical choice.

Yeah, I have to get to Dallas's place. How am I going to get there though? And what am I going to do once I'm there? I'll get a cab from the hotel, and when I get there, I'll wait. I won't knock on the door, because I don't want to involve her or her family any more. I'm purely going to use them as my gateway to hell. I have a feeling I'm about to enter those gates, and I probably won't leave alive.

With my newfound determination, I head into the bedroom, where Jude's relaxing on the bed in a t-shirt and boxer briefs. "Where did you get clothes?" I ask looking down at the same clothes I've been wearing.

"You don't listen. Frank went and bought us clothes, and I told you he had. But you were too enthralled with what Nick was saying." Do I detect a hint of jealousy in his voice?

I think back to this afternoon, and of course, he's right. "Oh yeah," I say as I play a little movie in my head of when he told me.

He points toward the bathroom. "The bags are in there."

"Thank you. I've ordered dinner, burgers. They should be here soon." I step closer to the bathroom. "I'll go have a shower."

"Okay."

Closing the door, I rustle through the bags and find a pair of jeans, a long sleeve t-shirt, socks, undies and even a light jacket. Taking the cash out of my pocket, I slide it into the back pocket of my new jeans, making sure the bills aren't visible.

Standing beneath the stream of water, a million thoughts jumble around. When they come to me, what will they do? Who are these people? Why did they do it to begin with? What are their intentions? What will they do with me once they have me? There's no one coherent plan, only thoughts about going to them, meaning I'm about to step into the lion's den. I hope the lion doesn't bite . . . at least, not right away.

Once I've come to terms with the situation I'm about to step into, I'm ready to face whatever the consequences are going to be. Moving out of the shower, I dry myself and get changed into the clean clothes Frank purchased for me.

The moment I open the bathroom door, a beautiful aroma gently wafts past me. My stomach grumbles in response to the delicious smell coming from the front of the suite.

When I enter, Jude's watching TV with our dinner sitting on the small round table. "You could've eaten," I say as I take my seat at the table.

Jude turns the TV off, then heads over toward the table. "I wanted to wait for you," he replies.

"It looks great, doesn't it?" I pick my burger up and sink my teeth into it. Jude nods, but something's off about his behavior. He's unusually quiet. He picks at his fries and stares down at the burger. "You okay?"

"I'm worried about Nick."

"Why?"

"I've been thinking about everything, and I have this feeling he's not being entirely truthful about a few things."

"Like what?"

"I have no idea. He's just . . . off. Either he's hiding something, or he's lying about something."

"How do you know?"

"Being in my business, you learn to read people. The more I think about him, the more I think he's putting on a façade."

"When I touched him earlier, I didn't see anything like that."

Jude sits back in his chair and rubs his chin. "Maybe he's as good at the vision thing as you are; or maybe he's better at it than you. Or, he's maybe learned how to show people what they want to see."

"Jude, I think you're reading into this much more than necessary. *He* ran from us. *He* tried to get away from us."

"Maybe because he wanted you to chase after him." He shrugs.

"That's ridiculous. Who'd get themselves caught on purpose?" *Ugh, me.*

"I'm just saying, I don't trust him."

"You don't have to. We heard what he had to say, and I suppose tomorrow we can ask more questions." Although, by tomorrow I hope to make contact with *them.*

Jude scoffs and raises his brows at me. "Yeah."

Hmmm, why is it I get a feeling Jude means more than what he's telling me? Leaning over, I touch his hand and force myself into his vision.

I'm in this room, and Jude's pacing. Ronan's in here with him while Jude's angrily trampling the length of the room. He's dressed in what he's wearing now, and the curtains are still opened revealing the darkness of the night. There's no hint of the sun rising, which means it's still late at night. "I knew she was going to do this," Jude spits toward Ronan.

"Is that why you . . ."

"Don't say a word. She could be watching us right now."

Ronan cautiously glances around the room. *What have those two done?* Ronan steps forward and places his hand on Jude's shoulder. "We'll find her," he says in a softer tone, which is so contradictory to the man he is.

Jude's phone rings, and he holds up a finger to Ronan. He swipes his finger across the screen and answers the call with a short, curt, "Yeah."

I step closer to try and see the name on the screen, but with the phone to his ear, I have to wait for him to pull it away.

Suddenly, I'm back in the room, with Jude staring at me. "Did you see what you wanted?" he asks mockingly. He knows I touched him to see his future, the unfortunate part is, he knows me so well so he's able to prepare himself.

"Not exactly what I wanted to see, but it'll do."

Jude picks his burger up and takes a massive bite. When he's chewed, he stares at me. Apparently he wants to ask me something. "Are you going to tell me why you wanted to see my future?"

Crap, I wasn't expecting a question so forward. But then again, this *is* Jude. Quickly, Nick pops into my thoughts. "I was afraid you were going to kill Nick."

Jude huffs and shakes his head. Damn him. He knows I'm lying. "Are you really going to stick to that?"

"It's the truth. I wanted to make sure you're not going to kill him because you think he's suspicious. And, I'm worried for him. I would hate for someone else to die because of me. And he seems like a good guy," I say.

Jude lets out a forceful gush of air. His gaze rolls over me, and I feel myself about to break down and tell him the truth about everything. I'm literally on the verge of opening my mouth when Jude's lips twist. "Do you know how I know when someone's lying?"

Oh crap. "No," I meekly reply. "How?"

"The person talks way too much. Giving me more information than I asked for."

"I wasn't babbling." I snap toward him defensively. Shit, if I didn't give it away in my answer, my reaction just did.

Jude finishes his dinner and stands. "I'll take the sofa, you can have the bed."

Double crap. That means he's sleeping out here, and I have to get past him in order to leave via the door. "Considering it's because of me you've lost your home, it's only fair I sleep on the sofa, and you take the bed."

He shakes his head at me. "No, I insist. I'll sleep here and you take the bed."

If I argue with him, then I'll prove him right in whatever suspicions he has. "Okay. But I think I'll watch TV first."

Hopefully he'll fall asleep, and I can sneak out.

"Great, I'll join you."

Take a damn hint! *Go away.* "Okay." I stand and make my way over to the sofa, where I slump down. Jude flicks through the channels before landing on a movie. I'm not paying attention to it. Instead, in my head I'm going over my escape route. There's a staircase at the end of the hall, near the elevators. I'll take the stairs down a few floors, then I'll take the elevator the rest of the way. Knowing Jude, he'll be able to get his people to hack into the security system of the hotel and track where I'm going. Damn it, that means I've got to leave through the kitchen. A back exit.

It's the only way I'll be able to get a head start before Jude and Ronan come after me. Possibly I'll get to *them,* and that way, I'll be able to keep Jude safe.

The moments drag on quietly, and every time I look at the clock on the wall, it appears the hands are moving backward. Sheesh, hurry up and fall asleep, Jude. My own eyes get heavier and heavier, but I'm on a mission, I need to get out of here.

The longer I stay, the harder it'll be for me to leave. And, the more of a chance *they'll* kill everyone to get to me.

Every time my eyes close, I wake myself up and discreetly glimpse over to Jude. The tension in the room is an obvious sign that he's watching me watching him. He's making sure I don't run, I'm making certain he's asleep when I *do* run.

My window of opportunity is closing, I'm getting edgy knowing I need to get out of here.

Jude stands, and heads into the other room. "Tired? Going to bed?" I try and make my voice sound disinterested.

"Going to the bathroom."

Yes! This is it, my opening. Maybe it'll be the only break I'll get, so I'm going to go the moment I know he's in the bathroom.

I listen closely to Jude's footsteps, and when I hear the door to the bathroom close, I jump up and silently make my way to the other room. Looking around to make sure he's actually in the bathroom, I make a run for it. I get to the door leading out to the hallway.

Opening it slowly, I look down both ways. No one is here. Closing the door as quietly as I can, I run.

I run so hard I nearly fall over my own feet. I get to the stairwell, push on the heavy door and bolt down the stairs. Thankfully going down steps is much easier on the thighs then going up. I keep running, until I see a huge 'sixteen' painted on the wall near the door for the floor.

For some reason, I run past it. Huffing, and nearly out of breath, I make it down to the twelfth floor, push through the door and look around. No one is in the hallway, which means I can run as fast as possible to the elevators. When I get there, I call it, and wait until it comes up from the ground floor.

Getting in, I put my head down and don't look at anything around me. Elevators have cameras. At some point, Jude will look for me in here. The elevator pings when it gets to the ground floor. Stepping out, I glance around. The guy at reception is looking at his phone, he only looks up when the doors close and make the pinging sound again.

I see signs for the restaurant, so I head that way in hope of finding an exit door. There are a few staff in here, who look like they're cleaning. "Excuse me," I say to a woman with a chef's hat.

She's an older person, maybe in her thirties, with dark circles beneath her eyes. She looks like she hasn't slept in a month. "Are you okay, sweetie?" she asks while looking behind me.

"Is there a back exit?"

Her forehead crinkles, and I can tell she's concerned I'm here this late at night alone. "Are you running from someone?"

Shit. Touching her hand, I launch into a vision. The chef is in a room, it looks like a family room. She's walking the length of it with a tiny baby in her arms. The baby is coughing and crying. "Shhh, Ava, it's okay." She feels her forehead and painfully groans. The baby keeps crying, and the chef stops walking.

"She only got like this in the last hour," a man says from behind the chef. He looks so stressed himself, his appearance is disheveled, his eyes are darkened from lack of sleep and stubble pokes out from his chin.

"Why didn't you take her to the hospital?" she asks.

"I gave her some baby aspirin. I was waiting for them to work."

I let go of the chef's hand, and I'm instantly transported back to now. "Can I please go out through the kitchen exit?"

"Are you in trouble?" she asks. "If you're in trouble, I can call hotel security, they'll help you."

"Please, don't. Trust me, I'm not in that kind of trouble. I just need to leave."

She looks me over, her eyes going to every inch of exposed skin. Finally satisfied that I'm not running from trouble, she ushers me out toward the back. "This way." When the door opens, I look down the dark alleyway. "Go left, then right. That'll take you out to the main street."

"Thank you," I say. "By the way, in a couple of hours Ava is going to get really sick. Take her to the hospital right away."

I leave her standing in the doorway, with wide eyes and a gaping mouth.

When I get out to the main road, I run in the opposite direction of the hotel. Getting around the corner, I see a row of cabs. Letting out a sigh of relief, I go to the first one, open the back door and slide in.

I sink down as far as I can, only being able to look through the glass.

"You okay?" the guy asks as he turns in his seat to look at me. "I don't want no trouble."

I take out the wad of cash, and thrust fifty dollars at him. "I need a ride."

He takes the fifty, and turns to face forward. "Where to?" he asks as he starts the cab and takes off down the street.

I turn to make sure Jude's not chasing after the cab. In a way

I'm relieved he's not, but I'm kinda upset he hasn't realized I'm gone.

Or maybe he has, and he's relieved I'm no longer a thorn in his side.

"You wanted this," I say to myself.

The cab driver looks at me through the mirror. "You didn't say where to?"

Disappointed, I give him Dallas's address. With my head leaning back against the headrest, my eyes start to water. Hurt fills my heart, but deep down I know this is the right thing to do. I shouldn't be selfish and hope he'd notice I'd snuck out. That's the whole point of sneaking out. For him not to know I'm gone. This is to protect him.

The comforting feeling of knowing he's safe now doesn't translate well to my heart. A knife twists in it, and the wound it was already sporting grows deeper.

It hurts like hell.

When we near Dallas's house, I stop feeling sorry for myself and push through the pain to try to see the positive in the situation. No one else will ever be put in a position of fear on my account again.

"Can you go around the corner and stop please?" I ask the driver. He nods his head, and slows, finally coming to a stop about a block away and around the corner. The fifty I gave him was more than enough, and he hands me the change. "Keep it."

He salutes me, and when I get out he leaves quickly.

I have no idea what to do. I'm hoping someone's watching Dallas's house, because if they aren't then I'm not sure how I'm going to find these people. The taillights of the cab disappear, and I'm left isolated. Standing in the dark night, I look up the street, then down. If they're here watching Dallas's house, I have to make my presence apparent.

I stroll past her house, get to the end of the block, then turn and walk past it again. "Come on," I say as I look around for any type of movement.

Nothing.

I walk past her house again, and I hear a dog barking from down the road. My heart beats quickly at the possibility of it being *them.* Standing in the middle of the sidewalk, I look toward where I hear a dog barking, but can't see anything. The dog stops barking, and I lose hope of it being them. The dog was just barking to hear itself.

"Come on," I whisper.

Turning, I'm face to face with a masked figure.

My heart jumps with fright.

My skin is instantly covered in a fine layer of goosebumps.

Adrenaline pumps through my body.

"We've been looking for you," says a deep, throaty voice.

Before I have a chance to respond, something sharp is stuck into my neck. Within seconds my eyes become droopy, and I pass out.

This isn't the way it was supposed to happen.

CHAPTER 19

BLINKING, I LOOK around me. My head is spinning, and my stomach is churning. Bile rises to the back of my throat, and I swallow the sensation of wanting to throw up.

My hair is falling over my face, and when I try to lift my hand to sweep my hair away, I find it weighted and restrained.

Groggily, I try to focus on the room I'm in. It's white and sterile, with no windows.

It's impossible to be centered when the room is spinning and you feel like you're going to throw up. "Hello," I call as I blink as many times as I can in an attempt to focus.

"Don't move around too much. The drug we gave you takes time to wear off," comes a robotic male voice over a speaker.

"Where are you?" I ask, still seeing everything through hazy vision.

"We can see you, Alexa. You're in no danger."

What an odd thing to say. They can see me and I'm in no danger. Why are they saying I'm not in danger, because they've got me restrained?

My eyes are slowly beginning to focus, and I notice I'm not in my clothes. I'm in loose, white pants, and a white t-shirt. It feels all very . . . experimental. But, I suppose that's exactly what I am. An experiment.

"I came to you. So why am I restrained?"

"For your own protection."

I let out a humorless chuckle. "I haven't hurt myself since you gave me this future-seeing thing. Why would I hurt myself now?"

For my protection . . . *my ass.*

They've got me restrained because they don't want me losing control and hurting them. I rattle the cuffs against my hands, and find they're incredibly secure. "Alexa, please don't. We don't want to sedate you again."

Rolling my eyes, I stop trying to break free. "Then take these cuffs off. *I* came to *you,* remember?"

"Until we establish you're not a threat, I'm sorry; we can't."

"Can't or won't? Two very different things. If I came to find you, then by process of elimination you have to agree I'm not a threat."

"We've been discussing this. Why did you attempt to find us?"

"Attempt? I did find you. If I didn't go to Dallas's house, you would've had no idea where I was."

I keep blinking, and finally my vision is clearing.

"We knew where you were."

This guy is pissing me off. His condescending tone is irking on the side of irritating. "Is that right? That's why *I* came to you?"

"We were assembling a crew. The only obstacle was the fact Mr. Caley had hired out the entire twentieth floor of the Ritz Carlton. But, rest assured, Alexa, we were only a step behind when you decided to run."

My stomach twists with anxiety as my blood cools to ice. My hands shake and heart hammers. Shit. *Jude.*

My first reaction is to worry for Jude. I got out of there so no harm would come to him, and now, it seems that it doesn't matter if I stayed or left, he was only ever an obstacle.

Panic bubbles away, while the chaotic thoughts in my head

struggle to form a sane plan. I need to pull myself together, not let my heart get in the way. I'm here for a reason. I have to push my emotions to the side and focus.

I stare down at the floor, and take several deep breaths. *Get yourself together, Alexa.*

"I want you to remove the cuffs."

"We can't until we establish your stability."

"What you've done to me has caused so much hurt. I don't want it to create even more. I have no reason to cause you any problems." *Please, believe me.*

"We'll ask you a few questions, and we'll go from there."

The only thing I can do is answer their questions. I really have no choice in the matter. "What do you want to know?"

"Your ability hasn't been tracked the way we were hoping. We'd like to test it, and see exactly what you can do."

Crinkling my brows, I look around the room and finally notice the discreet cameras positioned strategically. Eight that I can see, but there are probably more. "No need to test me, I can tell you what I can do. But, I'd like to ask some questions of my own." There's silence, negative confirmation that they're willing to answer anything. I count seventy breaths before I say, "Hello, is anyone there?"

"We're still here, Alexa. Your request has been denied. Now, to start, how far in advance can you see?"

"What? My request has been denied? Are you kidding me? You've got me shackled like a damned animal, and you're refusing to answer any of my questions? Guess what, you can go fuck yourself if you think I'm going to answer any of yours." They have to be joking. I'm so damned angry at them, and at myself. How stupid of me to think I'd get answers.

Squaring my shoulders, I decide if they're not answering any of my questions, then I'm going to refuse to answer any of theirs.

"Alexa, it's in your best interest if you . . ."

"If my hands weren't cuffed together, you'd be able to see what I'm doing now. Which, incidentally, in case one of your cameras is missing it, I'm flipping you off. Meaning, go screw yourself."

"Alexa," the voice warns over the speaker. I pretend to yawn and look around the room completely disinterested. "How far in advance can you see?" he asks again with a slight bite of urgency.

"I'm really tired now. I think I'll go to sleep," I reply. Closing my eyes, I try to get into a comfortable position, which is impossible, secured to a chair.

"Alexa, how far in advance can you see?" Nope, buddy. Not gonna get an answer from me. "Alexa, how far in advance can you see?" he asks again, his tone turning clipped and frustrated.

A woman comes over the speaker. "Alexa Murphy, you've been asked a question."

I stare at one of the cameras, cocking an eyebrow and smirking.

"Stop acting like a brat," the woman says.

"Then you shouldn't have given this ability to a teenager," I snap. Still smiling, and damn well pleased with myself, I sit against the chair and pretend to yawn again. I'm not answering their questions until they answer some of mine.

"Alexa!" the woman yells.

Pretending to startle, I open my eyes and smile. "Yes."

"Answer the question."

"When you answer mine."

"We'll be forced to sedate you and judge you as hostile."

Here we go again. "And then you won't have the answers you want."

They want stubborn, then I'm going to give them stubborn. They can threaten me as much as they want, but what I've worked out is that they obviously need me. If they didn't, they would already have killed me. I'm way too valuable to them without even knowing what I'm capable of. Once they find out what I can do, then I'll become a priceless asset.

No one says anything for a long time. They don't respond, and I don't feel any urgency to talk to them either. Both sides are quiet. At some point, someone will break. I'm hoping it's not me, because if I break now, they'll forever have control over me. And I refuse to allow them to manipulate me any more than they already have.

A low, dull ache develops in my shoulders from the way my arms are pulled behind me. Instead of telling them, so they can use that as leverage over me, I say nothing. With my shoulders hurting more and more with each passing minute, my brain yells at me to give them what they want.

But the pain is also a reminder of why I'm here to begin with. Because of them, I've been kidnapped, lost my parents, and my best friend was nearly killed. Stubbornness sets in, and suddenly I see past the hurt in my shoulders. Determined, I'm focusing on the suffering they've caused.

I stay like this for such a long time. My body is aching, my shoulders spasm, and my bladder decides now is a good time to pee.

There's no denying the deafening, intense silence in the room. But I refuse to let them get inside my head. I absolutely will *not* allow them to win this battle.

Time keeps ticking, and my body is protesting loudly. Every part of me hurts. My spine is tender and I can't shift my weight to get comfortable. My butt cheeks feel like I'm sitting on a cushion of pins, while my calves are cramping from not moving. Not to mention my bladder is now about to erupt. Inside my head I chant, *don't pee yourself, don't pee yourself.*

"Alexa," the man's voice says. In response to him calling my name, I look at one of the cameras. I don't say anything. "Are you ready to talk now? You're looking uncomfortable."

Screw them!

Grinding my teeth together, I feel a snarl about to rip through me. *Don't pee yourself.*

"Are you ready to talk?" he asks again.

Don't pee yourself.

"I'm ready to answer one question."

"How far in advance can you see?"

"I'll answer your question, if you let me go to the bathroom." *Please, don't pee yourself.*

"We'll let you go to the bathroom once you've answered our question."

There's no way they'll hold up their end of the bargain. Although I'll be completely humiliated, these stupid white pants will be stained yellow, and the smell will be sickening, I'm completely prepared to pee myself because I can't let them get the upper hand over me. "No." I take a deep breath and press on. "I'll answer the question once you let me go to the bathroom."

I move my thighs together, holding the pee in. If I don't get an answer in the next few seconds, I'm afraid of what'll happen.

Suddenly, the door opens, and a masked person enters. I notice their entire body is covered in clothing, so I have no opportunity to touch them. "Get up," says a male voice.

"Good one, Einstein. I'm cuffed," I sarcastically retort. *Idiot.* "Apparently, you don't have to be smart to work here."

He walks around behind me, takes the cuffs off, then grabs me by the shoulder of the t-shirt, yanking me up to my feet. "Go." He pushes on my back toward the door.

"Yeah, yeah," I snap toward him. "Are you all gutless wimps, or is there a reason you refuse to show your faces? Maybe you're butt ugly? Or maybe you have a cold sore festering that's so huge it's taken up half your face?"

He chuckles, but quickly clears his throat. "Go straight down the corridor."

The corridor is white, sterile and lifeless.

"Or maybe you're not hideously disgusting to look at, and you're a well-known celebrity. Oh, are you Tom Cruise? I love Tom Cruise. If you're him, can I have your autograph?" I turn to look at the masked man, and place my hands together like I'm praying to him. "Or, maybe you're Leonardo DiCaprio. Prrrr," I purr toward him.

"Turn left at the end."

"Okay, so you're not Tom, or Leonardo. Hmmm, are you a singer? Maybe you're Harry Styles, but you don't have a sexy English accent, so that eliminates Harry. Oh! I know who you are, you're John Legend. Man, can you sing."

"Bathroom is on the right."

I see the sign for the ladies, and I push the door entering the small bathroom with three stalls. Hurriedly, I go into the first cubicle and move to shut the door. The masked man pushes it open and stands right in front of me. "Do you mind?" I shriek. "You can wait over there, I'm not going anywhere."

"Sorry, instructions are I have to wait with you."

"Like hell you are. Get out." I push on his chest, but it's like he's made of solid stone, he doesn't budge. "Get out!" I yell louder.

"I'm trained to handle these situations."

"You're not watching me get naked from the waist down. I can't see your eyes, you might be a sick perve who gets off on watching girls pee." He plants his feet, pulls his shoulders back, and crosses his arms in front of his chest. "It's humiliating enough having you in here, can you at least give me some dignity and turn around?"

He lets out a strangled breath, but turns. "There."

Pulling my pants down, I sit on the toilet and of course, performance anxiety sets in. "You can't be serious?" I mumble to myself.

"Everything okay there?"

He looks over his shoulder and I pull my shirt down so he can't see anything. "Hey, eyes to the front." He quickly turns back. "Your presence is preventing me from peeing. And this is a huge problem when your bladder is about to explode."

"Hurry up."

"I can't hurry up. Not with you standing there, watching over me."

"Try anything and I *will* kill you." He steps forward and allows me to close the door. As soon as I lock it and sit back down, my pee is no longer being held hostage by my body. Instantly, I relax and finally pee.

Once I'm out, I wash my hands and wait for the masked heavy to give me instructions. He opens the door quietly and waits for me to exit. Looking down the first hallway, I notice a door at the end. My eyes search it so I can store it for future reference. "Where does that lead?' I ask, knowing I'm not going to get a straight answer.

"You can try and run, but all the doors require fingerprint recognition." He may not have given me an exact answer, but he has told me it'll be extremely hard to get out of here.

Heading back to the room in which I was being held, I walk around the expanse for a few seconds. He points to the chair and I roll my eyes. "Is restraining me necessary? It's not like anyone's in here with me." He points again. "Fine," I say as I stretch my back and take my seat. He cuffs my hands in front of me and leaves the room.

A minute or two pass before the woman comes over the loud speaker. "How far into the future can you see?"

I agreed to give them an answer for letting me pee. "I'm not entirely sure of the exact time. Maybe five or six hours."

"What are you capable of in the visions?"

I shake my head at the camera. "Sorry, I said one question for allowing me to pee. You want me to answer another question, you need to answer one of mine."

"This isn't how we work, Alexa," the woman responds.

"Then this is going to get nowhere for either of us." I shrug my shoulders. "Unless, of course, you answer one of my questions."

The silence fills the room once more. But this time, I'm not so worried about it, because I've been to the bathroom. I know they want information from me, so hopefully they'll talk. I could potentially be sitting here for hours, waiting this out. But if I give in, they'll always be able to do what they want without me knowing anything about them.

"What's your question?"

Crap, I wasn't expecting that. Not so soon. I have so many questions, I have no idea where to start. "How many of us are there?"

"About forty."

"Holy shit," I say sinking down further into the seat. At least forty of us walking around with this ability. "Are they all my age?"

"How exactly do you see the future?"

Damn it, I set the terms. If they answer a question, I'll answer one back. "I want the restraints to come off, and I want a face to face. I'm not talking like this any more."

It's the only way I'm going to get an opportunity to touch someone and try to get honest answers.

"Alexa."

"No! This isn't working for either of us. Take it or leave it. These are my new terms. I'll answer your questions, but I'll do it face to face with no restraints." Nervously, I wait for their reply. My stomach twists as I wait.

It's a long time before I hear the creak of the door. It opens, and I nearly fall off my chair.

My eyes must be deceiving me, while my mind struggles to form any type of comprehensive thought.

My heart pounds furiously as I watch the man walk in, drag out the chair opposite to me, and sit. My mouth dries and I'm completely speechless. How . . . what . . . huh?

CHAPTER 20

"ALEXA." HE CURTLY nods his head, his mouth turning up into a smirk.

"How . . . ?" I'm still unable to form a sentence. How on earth did he . . . I mean, what . . . ?

"You weren't expecting me?" A mocking sneer dances over his face. He knows damned well I had no idea he was involved.

"I . . . um." Shaking my head, I try to grasp what's happening. "Why?" The expression in his eyes says all I need to know. "Oh," I breathe out with understanding. "Money."

He nods his head, crosses his arms in front of his chest and raises his brows in confirmation. "That's exactly right."

"Does Jude know, Ronan?"

"He figured it out, but he's of no concern of mine any longer."

Fear takes hold as a sudden feeling of impending doom washes over me. "Where's Jude?" I ask, frightened to hear the answer.

"I shot him." His face is cold, and stoic. It's as if he never cared.

I lunge forward over the table, and grab onto his hands. I need to see for myself.

I'm dragged into a vision of Ronan's future, but I don't want to see the future. I need to see the past. It's something I've never done before, but if I'm capable of going into the future, I should be capable of rewinding it to see the past.

I just need to concentrate.

Ronan's in an office, sitting down and talking with someone. Instantly, I recognize the voice of the woman who's been talking to me over the speaker. She's also the same woman who came to see me in the hospital with the high heels.

But, for now, I need to get to Jude.

Closing my eyes, I focus on Ronan. It's as if I'm watching him in rewind. My mind is straining as I concentrate on rewinding time.

But, I can't make it work. I can't rewind the vision to see the past. I can only see what's happening in the future.

"Is he dead?" the woman asks Ronan.

"He's shot," he confirms while inspecting his nails. *Cocky asshole.*

She smiles at him, then looks down at paperwork on the desk. "You've done a good job. We're all satisfied with your work." Ronan clears his throat and crosses one leg over the other. "Is there a problem?" she asks.

"Payment. I was told I'd be receiving it when I brought the girl in to you."

"I'm waiting for confirmation of the job."

"I shot him, Nick saw it with his own eyes."

"Nicholas hasn't checked in yet. When he confirms the hit, I'll authorize your payment." Nick is involved too? Oh my God, I never stood a chance.

Bastard. He's supposed to be Jude's head of security. He sold him out for money. My anger froths inside of me as I watch the smug look emanating from Ronan. I want to punch that stupid, pompous sneer off his face.

"Then I'll wait." Ronan squares his shoulders and sinks back further into the office chair.

She looks up from her paperwork, and gives him a curt nod. "As you wish." She leaves his staring gaze, and continues with her work. A quick moment passes when she stops working, and glances up at him. "I have another job for you if you're interested. This kid is of no use to us. Her ability is minimal, and not what we need."

I step forward and look at the papers on her desk. I may not be able to go back in time to save Jude, but I can sure as hell look at what she has to save the next person.

"What's it pay?"

"The same."

"How old's the girl?" He juts his chin forward indicating the job.

"Thirteen. She hasn't made an impact on anyone yet. Her parents will miss her, but they'll learn to adapt."

Holy shit, how can this woman be so heartless? My own soul tears in two, and I'm praying Ronan doesn't take the job. How could he betray Jude? How could he kill a child?

"No fucking way, this one is thirteen. She's the youngest one. You're delusional if you think I'll take the same as the others."

The others? My heart splits with what I'm hearing. How many has he killed?

"It's what we pay the other slayers."

"The others who attempted to get to Alexa, but couldn't?" he snaps at her.

"That's only because she had Jude, and you. And now, you're on our team."

I want to pick up the pen she's been using and drive it through her eye. She's talking about taking a life, and has no remorse at all.

"I'm on the team of whoever pays the most, lady. But killing kids, that's not exactly high on my agenda. How many are there and how many do you want to get rid of?"

"This experiment has been going on for fourteen months. There are dozens out there, most of which we have eyes on. Some though, are useless to us and not what the organization needs."

The door opens, and the doctor who saw me at the hospital waltzes in. "Catherine, what's happening?" he asks.

My heart falls to the pit of my stomach. In this room is everyone I despise.

"I was offering Ronan a job. I'm impressed with what he's done for us. The other experiments, he brought us the girl, and he killed Jude."

My body collapses silently to the floor. He *killed* Jude! A million emotions overtake me. But the one hurting the most is sorrow. He's dead, because of me. *Again.* Everyone dies because of me.

"I've been monitoring the girl. Are you sure she can do what you say she can?" he asks Ronan.

"She's amazing. She gets stronger with each passing day, she's able to move around in her visions and communicate. But, I think the most impressive ability is the fact she's learning how to take herself out of visions and put herself into them. If she doesn't want to go into it, she somehow fights it."

"She can be selective?" the man asks, intrigued.

Stop giving them all my information! I want to yell at Ronan, but I also need to find out as much as I can, because when I escape from here, I'm going to take all of these assholes down. Every one of them will be made to pay for the hurt they're causing.

Ronan nods his head, impressed with the information he knows and is sharing with them. "She's powerful," Ronan adds.

"More than she knows, my friend." The fake doctor takes a piece of paper off the desk and reads over it. "We're not keeping her?" he asks Catherine.

"Her ability is weak at best. We don't need her."

"But she's young, she may show potential."

Catherine laughs, then adds, "We can't keep them all. We only want the ones who are capable. Only they can carry our mission forward."

"What mission?" Ronan asks. *Yes, what damn mission?* "Nick

told me it's for security."

Catherine and the fake doctor look at each other. A knowing gaze passes between them, neither say anything. "It is for security. Kind of," the fake doctor responds.

"The man who founded this project is brilliant," Catherine adds with admiration. I look between the fake doctor and Catherine, and I'm convinced she's the one in charge. When I met them at the hospital, I thought he was the boss. Now, I'm sure it's her. "He was developing a drug to suppress the memories of trauma patients."

"Why?" Ronan asks. "Why would someone who suffered a trauma want to suppress their memory?"

"Because some people can move forward, and others can't. The ones who can't often turn to drugs, crime, or even self-harm."

Ronan looks to the fake doctor, who's nodding his head, then back to Catherine. "That's a long way away from what you have here. I mean, there's a girl in there . . ." He points out the door, and I assume he's referring to me. " . . . who's able to see the future. How does someone go from what you've described, to her?"

"He created a drug, highly experimental. It couldn't pass the FDA testing, though."

"He worked tirelessly to improve it, and get it into the hands of the FDA. The lab rats were dying quickly; the drug was killing them," fake doctor says.

"He still had backers who believed in it, though. They sent in a brilliant young chemist who was a huge risk taker. He and the founder refined the drug, testing it first on animals, then they found humans to test it on."

They found humans? Who would agree to testing something not FDA approved?

"How did they find the humans?" Ronan asks the question I'm burning to know.

"Homeless, runaways." Catherine shrugs her shoulders

callously.

"And I thought I was a monster." Ronan chuckles, and shakes his head. "So how did it go from there to here?" He gestures with is hands.

"A lot of errors, and then a lot of successes. He found a strain of the drug to work on thirty-five percent of the recipients. However, since then there have been a few teething problems."

"What's happened to the other sixty-five percent?" Ronan asks.

"Most die. Some have lost their minds," she answers blankly.

Slumping against the wall, a tear falls down my cheek. I'm a damn experiment.

"You're quite open and honest with me. I find this surprising."

She looks at Ronan, her own evil smirk drawing up the corners of her lips. "You're good at what you do . . . but you're not irreplaceable."

"I might take this information you've given me, and go straight to the police," he cockily replies.

"I doubt your sister, Stephanie and her two sons, Jamison and Isaac, would like you to open your mouth. Especially considering Isaac would have no one to look after him. You wouldn't want him to be left to the system, would you? Down syndrome children don't thrive in the system," Catherine counters with her own threat.

Oh. My. Lord. Ronan has a sister who has kids. How did I not know this?

Ronan's face morphs in shock. He blinks several times before he shifts uncomfortably in his seat. My heart beats hard for Ronan, but I have to remind myself that he killed Jude and helped get me here, for money.

Suddenly, a deafening warning sounds.

"What's happening?" Ronan asks as he leaps to his feet.

Catherine's on hers in a matter of seconds too. Both her and the fake doctor move to the door, opening it to look out.

I run to the desk, and read over as many names as I can. Memorizing them to the best of my ability. There are pictures and statistics. I try to move the papers so I can see more, but my hand is translucent and glides through the paper.

"Damn it!" I yell.

Ronan turns to look toward where I'm standing.

And, I'm out of the vision. Ronan's managed to throw me off him, I find myself on my butt in the chair. "I can't believe you killed him," I spit toward Ronan.

"Nothing personal, Alexa. Actually, I like you." He stands and runs his palms down his trousers. "It's just business."

"I hate you! I hope you rot in hell," I scream at Ronan as he leaves the room.

Tears fall as I slump against the chair.

Jude's dead because Ronan sold him out.

"Alexa, tell us about your ability."

I lift my shackled hands and wipe the tears away. I ran from Jude to save him, and he died just the same. Tilting my head down, I silently cry for everything I've bought on everyone I loved. Innocent lives have been taken, because of me.

"Alexa," Catherine says again. "We have more questions."

I raise my head to look at one of the cameras. I lift my hands again, but instead of wiping at my tears, I flip the voyeurs the bird. "You can suck on this." Lowering my head again, my heart hurts with all the pain I've caused.

"Alexa!" Catherine harshly shouts through the speaker.

I refuse to talk. I'll be useless to them, they'll have no choice but to kill me. I won't do anything they want.

Lifting my head, I arch a brow and stare straight at the camera. "I have nothing more to say."

Cold runs through my veins. My heart is finally calm enough to know the implications of my words.

I've sealed my fate.

CHAPTER 21

I'M READY.

Ready to die. Ready to meet my parents.

I've been left in this interrogation room for a long time. I have no clock to tell me the time, but by my estimate, I'd say at least six hours have passed.

I've been given no food, no water, and no further access to the bathroom.

The cuffs are still around my wrists. They're uncomfortable, and the steel pinches my skin when I move. But I'm ready to die.

My entire body is protesting in pain. My feet have had pins and needles several times, and my spine is a constant, straining agony.

Although my body is tormented by pain, my mind is clear.

I will not help these people.

I won't be a part of whatever they're doing.

Staring blankly ahead, I blink as I wait for my executioners to show. They have to be in their conference room, or office, trying to find a way around me, to make me useful to them.

In the vision, the fake doctor said I'm more powerful than I know. That means if I won't cooperate, they'll have to kill me so I can't bring this organization to its knees. They can't just let me go.

I'm fated. I've made peace with it.

The door opens, and Ronan enters the room again. "Get up," he orders. I ignore him. I flick my gaze to him, then go back to staring at the wall.

I'm giving him a huge, fuck you, without saying the words.

"Get up!" He steps closer.

My gaze goes to his shoes, then back to the spot.

"I said get up!" He steps even closer, leans down and shouts in my face. With my game face on, I stare ahead.

Suddenly, Ronan grabs my t-shirt around the neck, and hauls me off the chair. "Should've listened, Alexa. This would've gone better for you." With a quick flick of his wrist, he snaps me to the side, slamming me into the edge of the table; pain shoots from my hip.

But, I remain quiet, refusing to show weakness.

If he's the one they've sent to kill me, I won't give him the satisfaction of seeing me hurt or cry.

Grabbing me by the shirt again, he drags me out of the room, roughly tugging me along the corridor. I hear a rip, and know he's torn the shirt. Looking down, I see skin exposed, and the top of my bra poking through the shredded clothing.

But with my hands still cuffed together, and my feet slipping as I attempt to find traction, Ronan is throwing me around like a rag doll.

"Should've just got up, Alexa," he angrily huffs as he manhandles me.

The pain is now searing in my hip, and I'm doing everything I can to hold in the tears. I hate him. I despise him with every drop of blood in my body.

We arrive to another room, where there's a toilet and a mattress on the floor. There's nothing else, not even a tap to wash my hands. He haphazardly throws me in there, making me slide along the floor until my back hits the wall. He then comes in, leans down and takes off my cuffs.

Shaking his head at me, I can see by the anger in his eyes, I'm about to cop a beating. Angrily, he lifts his hand and brings it down with so much force, it feels like my cheek splits. He lifts his hand again, this time backhanding me on the other side. His knuckles are huge, causing a sharp, burning sting across my other cheek.

Standing, he spits on the ground, looks me over and leaves the room. "Should've fucking listened," he says while closing, and locking the door behind him.

When I know he's gone, I stand to my feet and try to relax my body. My adrenalin is still pumping away furiously, and it takes me several minutes to finally calm down. Rolling my shoulders, I attempt to release the tension from my body.

Sitting still in the interrogation room for so long has wreaked havoc with my body. My muscles cramp, and I walk around attempting to loosen them. I also try to find where the cameras are in here. I half chuckle to myself, because they're easy to spot. There are undoubtedly a dozen in here, watching my every move. The room is sterile and white, and doesn't have a window, which will make attempting to tell time impossible.

"Ugh," I huff out a deep breath. "You may as well send Ronan back in here to end me."

"That's not necessary," Catherine says over a concealed speaker.

Suddenly, exhaustion hits me hard. I head over to the mattress, and lay down on it. I form a make-shift pillow by tucking my hands beneath my head. I have no more energy to fight these assholes today. I've been awake for what feels like three days straight, and in this time, I've been tricked, I've found out a man I trusted is not trustworthy, and my original kidnapper, the man who was becoming more than just my savior, is now dead.

Closing my eyes, I find myself too drained to think of anything. These people have emotionally, and physically depleted all my energy. They've burnt me out. I can't run anymore, I can't even try to get away from them.

They've ruined me.

They've broken me.

I give up.

The shrieking sound of an alarm startles me from my restless sleep.

"What's going on?" I ask the stark, white room. A shiver runs over my body as I try to blink the sleep from my eyes. The wailing sound of the alarm echoes deep inside my head. The sound is so shrill, it vibrates in my skull. I place my hands over my ears, hoping it'll drown out the sound.

It does, but only marginally.

"Hello?" I call out. Of course, I get no answer. "Wait," I say to myself, remembering back to the alarm being sounded when I was in the vision with Ronan.

The sound is still loud, but at least it's somewhat bearable. It's not ripping through my head like a large screw being shoved in my ear any longer.

Eventually the sound stops, and the door opens.

I hastily get to the other side of the room, trying to make myself one with the wall. Stupid, because there's no running from death.

A man stands at the door, his hands up in front of him as if he's showing me he's not a threat. "Miss Murphy?" he asks and takes another step forward.

"Yeah," I hesitantly reply, still having no idea who he is.

Behind him, I catch a glimpse of two women, who are like bodyguards to the man in the room with me.

What's happening? Who are these people? I search his clothes for any tell-tail sign of who he is. A logo, or a word . . . anything. He's dressed in jeans and a t-shirt, and has nothing on him to identify who he is or where he belongs. His gentleness tells me he's not like everyone else I've encountered here. I haven't been roughly shoved, or beaten, or even thrust into a car. I truly have no idea what is happening.

"My name's Emmett Baxter and I work at the FBI." He looks like an 'Emmett.' He's tall, with really broad shoulders, but a kind face. "Can I come in?" he asks as he softly steps toward me.

"What's . . . ?" I glance around his wide shoulders to the two women outside the door.

"It's a long story, and you're caught in the middle of it, but you're safe now."

It's almost like a weight has been lifted from me, instantly making my body relax. I let out a sigh of relief, and suddenly everything hits me at once.

I burst into tears and collapse to the floor.

Emmett rushes over to me, but I shake my head at him. "Please, don't touch me," I whisper. I'm not strong enough to keep from entering into a vision. And I have to try and hold on to the hope that this is real. I have to pray this isn't an illusion, or some kind of sick, twisted conspiracy to get me to talk, or worse still, to kidnap me . . . *again.*

"Alexa, the wound on your cheek needs to be seen by a doctor."

I reach up and touch where Ronan hit me, it only hurts when I brush it. "I'm okay," I say shaking my head. Emmett sits beside me on the floor. I look up at him, tears stinging my eyes. "Are you real?" I ask, not believing that something good is finally going to happen.

He draws his lips up in a sympathetic smile. "I am," he announces.

"Can I leave this place?"

He nods his head. "But we need to talk to you; there's a lot we need to discuss."

"Like filling me in on what's happening?" He chuckles, stands, takes a set of gloves out of his pocket and slides them on. He offers me his hand to help me up. I stare at his hand, dumbfounded. "You know?"

"We know."

What? How? *What?*

Taking his hand, he pulls me up to stand. I still have no understanding on what's happening. "We're going to transport you to our field office, where we can talk about everything."

Nodding my head, I walk out of the room and immediately notice the number of people and the commotion happening around me.

Catherine is being led away in handcuffs, and so is the fake doctor. Ronan is being lead out behind them.

I run toward Ronan, stopping when I reach him. The man leading him out tries to block me from him, but Emmett tells him to step aside. Ronan stares at me, as cocky as ever.

"You're going to hell for what you did to Jude," I spit toward him.

Ronan's smug look doesn't falter. Out of the corner of my eye, I see Catherine turn back to watch our exchange. He looks at her, then back to me. "Then I'll see him there."

The asshole. The damn bastard. I lose my shit at him, and slap him across the face. My hand stings from the force of the slap, and Ronan stares blankly at me. Redness immediately blooms on his cheek. Where did that come from?

"Take him," Emmett instructs the officer leading Ronan out.

I watch his retreating back, and wish I had it in me to hurt Ronan more than just a slap on the face.

Officers walk past me, their blue jackets with giant letters spelling 'FBI' stenciled on the back telling me, this *is* real. This isn't a sick joke, or another game. Some are carrying boxes out, and some have cameras and are taking photos.

Emmett stands beside me, watching me watching everyone else. "Take me away from here, and tell me what's happening."

"There's a lot to tell. Come this way." The two women who were at the door lead the way down a maze of corridors. We get to an elevator, where the doors are ajar. A man, also in an FBI jacket, is waiting by the elevator. The moment he sees us coming toward him, he steps into the elevator and stands to the back.

"Who are all these people?"

Emmett looks down to my ripped t-shirt, and turns to the guy in the elevator. "Give her your jacket."

"Yes, Sir." The guy quickly shrugs out of it, and places it softly around my shoulders.

"These people all work for me," Emmett answers.

"Are you their boss?" The elevator door pings shut and one of the women presses the button for the basement.

"My official title is Assistant Director."

"That's pretty high up, Emmett. I don't get why they'd send you, and not a special agent."

"You know your rankings."

I give him a look as if to say, 'are you serious?' "My mother was a judge, and a damn good one at that. My father was her bailiff."

"Then you'd know how sensitive this is. All these people have been selected because of the delicate nature of the case."

The doors finally ping open, and I'm met with one person I never thought I'd see again.

Frank's by the door, his arms wide open for me. "Frank," I cry, as I leap into them and hug him as hard as I can.

"It's okay," he whispers, kissing my hair.

"What are you doing here? What's going on?" I ask him, begging for answers.

"Not my story to tell, Miss Lexi, but trust me, when you find out, everything will come together."

"This way," Emmett states and points to an awaiting car.

Emmett opens the back door, and Frank lets go of me. "Trust me, you're safe."

I lean down to slide in, and I nearly fall out of the car.

What the . . . ?

CHAPTER 22

"GET IN THE car, Lexi," he says as he waits for me to slide in.

My brain isn't talking to my body though. I'm dumbfounded. How is he here? "I don't understand . . . you're dead." Somehow my heart kick-starts and I numbly fall into the seat.

Jude moves his head impassively. "There's a lot we need to talk about."

The door slams shut, making me jump at the sudden noise. I tear my eyes away from Jude to flash a peek at what's unfolding around me. But I can't seem to make sense of it all.

Jude's not dead.

Frank is in the front.

Emmett is driving.

And I'm dazed by the fact Jude is in the same car as the assistant director of the FBI and neither have their guns drawn. I quickly look to Jude, my eyes dragging down to his wrists, but find they're free and don't have hand cuffs on.

The spit gathering in my mouth is hard to swallow. I don't understand. "What . . ." I lose my words for a second as I try to make my head comprehend the madness surrounding me. "I'm really struggling with this." I point to him and Emmett.

Jude's eyes narrow in on me, looking directly at the cut on my face. "Who did this?" he asks as he gently grips my chin and moves my head to the side so he can get a better look.

"Ronan," I whisper. "He betrayed you . . . and me." My stomach churns with distress. I hate having to tell him, but he needs to know the type of man Ronan is.

Jude's lips quickly pull up into a smirk, then immediately the smile disappears. He nods, while staring at my face. His thumb tenderly skims over my cheek before he drops his hand. "No vision?" he asks.

Shaking my head, I look down to where my hands are knotted together. "I chose not to." Swallowing hard, I gaze up into his intense black eyes. His brows are drawn low, and there are dark circles lining the bottom of his eyes. "You look tired," I say.

He chuckles at me. "You have no idea."

He slides his hand down to rest on my thigh before slowly linking our fingers together. My body warms and all feels okay again. Jude's not dead, and this makes my heart smile.

"We'll be there soon," Emmett says into his phone.

With Emmett's words, I'm hauled back into reality. Turning, I view our environment. "Where are we going?" I ask. Looking behind the car, there are no less than three black vans following us. Panic takes over as my mind clouds with the thought of someone else after me. My hands shake and a cold sweat rips through me. *Not again.* "Emmett?" My voice comes out shaky.

"What is it, Alexa?" he asks looking at me in the rear-view mirror.

Jude turns to see what I'm long at and squeezes my hand. "It's okay, they're with us," he comforts me.

I let out a huge sigh; my heart finally calming. "Are you okay?" Emmett asks.

"I don't know, this is all too much." Tears brim as I try to hold in the frustration of the unknown. *Tell me now what's happening.* Lowering my head, I rub my free hand over my forehead, trying to release the tension without shedding any tears. I've cried way too much, I need to find another way to deal with all this chaos.

A better way.

"We're nearly there," Emmett announces.

"Anyone want to fill me in where 'there' is?" I snap too forcefully. "I'm over all these secrets."

"We've set up a field office close to the Facility. You're safe here, Alexa."

I don't know if I should be happy, or even more frustrated because I've yet to get any answers.

We arrive at a structure that could easily be mistaken for an office building. There's nothing extraordinary about it. It blends into all the other buildings around it. It's late in the day, the sun has started to set, and the chill in the air tells me it's going to be a cool evening.

We enter the building and Emmett guides us over to the elevators, where the FBI agent who gave me his jacket has already gone ahead of us and called the elevator.

The quiet is deafening to me, I need someone to tell me what's happening, but I have a feeling they're waiting to hit me with a sucker-punch. My mind is traveling at high speed. I want to know *now* what's going on. "Is anyone going to talk?" I finally ask, breaking the harsh silence.

"We will, as soon as we get a doctor to look at your eye, and you have something to eat and drink," Emmett replies.

Anger vibrates through me. I can feel the speed of my heartbeat picking up. "No," I say as I let go of Jude's hand and cross my arms in front of my chest.

The elevator dings open, and Emmett steps through, waiting for me. I follow, only because I refuse to ride the elevator on my own. I need answers, and I need them now.

"No what?" Emmett asks.

"No, I'm not going to see a doctor and I'm not going to eat and drink. I'm not going to have a shower, or get changed, or what other bullshit excuse you make up so you don't have to tell me. I'm sick and tired of being played from one side or another. You're going to tell me what's happening, and you're going to tell me *now*."

Both Jude and Frank raise their brows in surprise at me. Jude proudly sticks his chest out, and Frank gives me a small nod. "Welcome back, Miss Lexi," Frank declares with a smirk.

Emmett looks among the three of us. He too gives me a curt nod, steps aside and sweeps his hand toward the back of the open office space to a corridor. "Then let's get this started. Down there is my office."

My anger recedes, and it's then I notice the number of people milling around or hunched over their computers. In the center of the room are cardboard boxes stacked high atop each other.

Some of the people have stopped what they're doing, and are staring at me. Their eyes are glued to me as if I'm some kind of criminal.

Am I?

"Here, take a seat." Emmett indicates to one of the chairs in his office. Looking around, I notice the view of the opposite building behind his desk. His desk is filled with stacks of paperwork, messy and unorganized. Jude sits beside me, and Frank stands behind us.

"Okay, I want to know what's been happening," I say turning to face Jude first, then to Emmett who's now sitting behind his desk.

"Jude and Ronan came to us a short time ago."

Sharply I turn my head to look at Jude. "Why?" This had to be some heavy shit if Jude couldn't handle it on his own.

"Because you're important to me. And I was dealing with something which I had limited information on. I didn't know how far these people would go, how deep their pockets were, or how well-connected they were."

"But, you're Jude Caley. You're notorious. How could you need help?"

"I am," he announces proudly. "But, I'm also a businessman and I have to take advantage of an opportunity when it presents itself."

Suddenly, I feel sick. "Was I an opportunity?"

"No, but we had to think quickly on how to get you out, and how we could help ourselves while we were at it."

"We?" I question.

"Yes, we. As in Ronan and myself."

"Ronan?" I ask in anger. "Ronan did this to me, Jude." I point to my face. "And this." I stand and open the FBI jacket and show him the ripped t-shirt. "He also agreed to kill more people like me," I nearly shout at him.

"Yes, I know," Jude replies calmly. "Because that's what we planned he was going to do."

I flop back in my chair, mentally exhausted. "What? You told him to hit me?"

"I told him to make it look realistic. I told him now he had their trust, to keep it."

Blinking like crazy, I stare at Jude. I'm not entirely sure if my mind can comprehend what he's saying. A word tries to escape my mouth, but it sounds more like a grunt.

"If I may?" Emmett interjects.

"It's best if I tell her." Jude holds his hand up to Emmett, who gives him a nod and sits back in his chair.

"Before the house was bombed, Ronan was researching the hospital where you were admitted into for your appendectomy. He found that in the last twelve months a lot of teenagers, mostly females, had routine operations and then disappeared."

Tilting my head to the side, the word 'disappeared' has thrown me a curveball. "What do you mean by 'disappeared'?"

"The 'Facility' as they like to be called, were injecting teenagers with their product."

"Why teenagers?" I ask looking between Emmett and Jude. "And why females?"

"Because females are easier to integrate into society then males." I screw my nose at Jude's response, but I'm eager to learn more. "The ones who responded strongly to the drug would be snatched, and told if they work for the Facility, their families would be safe, if not, the Facility would kill their parents."

"Huh," I grumble. "Sounds like someone else I know." I pointedly look at Jude. Frank chuckles from behind me.

Jude shifts awkwardly in his seat. "The thing with them is, they killed the kids' parents anyway."

"But that still doesn't explain why they chose teenagers."

"They have fewer ties to society. They chose ones who weren't working, who hadn't really started their lives. They also chose ones who were healthy, other than the small procedure, injected them and watched as their abilities developed," Jude says.

"So, how did you find this out? Does this mean the hospital was involved?"

"Ronan. He started on their trail, and he kept at it until he found out what he could. He didn't know much about the Facility, and couldn't find out a lot about them because their tracks ended shortly after he found out about the teenagers they were targeting. As far as the hospital, Emmett said they're denying all knowledge."

I turn to Emmett, shocked and confused. "How do you come into it?" I point to Emmett.

"Jude came to us with an offer."

"What offer?" I shriek as I turn back to Jude. "What did you have to give up?"

"I'll get to that. But you need to know everything else before I tell you what's been sacrificed."

"Okay," I whisper. Knotting my hands together, I'm suddenly nervous about the outcome.

"We had no choice but to get Ronan to infiltrate them. He went after one of the teenagers, he . . ." Jude says.

My heart leaps into my throat. "He didn't kill them, did he?" I cup my hands over my mouth.

"No, but we made it look like he did," Emmett steps in.

"Wait . . . you're involved in this by now?" I ask Emmett.

Emmett nods. "This is where we came into it. Jude approached us, and told us about the Facility. They were already on our radar because they'd been rejected by the FDA and investors hadn't stopped funneling money to them. They went deep underground though, and we couldn't get to them. We went after Jude on a separate incident, and he countered with information about the Facility and made us an offer."

My head's spinning. "So, you went after Jude, but Ronan had already infiltrated the Facility. And in order for him not to be indicted, he gave them up?" I look between the two.

"I gave up something else, too."

"What?" I ask.

Jude struggles to tell me, he's quiet and choosing his words carefully. "A big supplier."

"A supplier? What kind of supplier?" I ask.

"One who is at the top of the food chain in human trafficking."

"Wait . . . you don't deal in human trafficking, not after what your father went through." I look to Emmett, hoping I haven't given away too much of Jude's story.

"No, but he's also a different kind of supplier. One who was annoying me." He smiles.

"Oh," I say as realization takes over. "Someone I know?"

"I think you asked him if he had shares in Viagra."

I'm quickly taken back to Enzo's party and the filthy, disgusting men in the house. "And the rest of the party-goers?" I know I'm getting side tracked, but I may as well know everything.

Jude sideways glances at Emmett. "We'll discuss them later," he says. Jude doesn't want to incriminate himself any more than he already is.

"Back to the Facility," I quickly prompt.

"Marcus," Emmett says. I look to him, puzzled, and

remember the bodyguard my parents hired for me. "The threat on your parents was all instigated by them, because they knew your mom would hire a bodyguard for you. They sent in Marcus to keep an eye on you, to see how you were developing."

"And Laura?" I ask about the female bodyguard.

"She wasn't part of it. Marcus, on the other hand, was reporting to them."

"The day you . . ." I look to Jude and carefully construct my words. " . . . smashed into the car, Laura was with me, not Marcus."

"He was on another assignment. He was taking care of someone who wasn't as receptive to the drugs as you've been," Emmett says.

I sigh because I know exactly what he means. "It was by pure luck that was the day I chose to . . . smash into your car," Jude says, being careful not to say 'kidnapped.' We're way past that now.

"And that meant, they lost track of me, and had no idea where I was." Slowly, it's all piecing together. "But, the bombing . . ."

"Wasn't them, it was . . ." He looks over to Emmett again, "someone else who was after me, not you."

"Did the Facility know who Ronan was?" I need to know everything.

"Ronan made himself known, told them he was my head of security, and accepted an offer to work with them, taking out the less powerful recipients. If they weren't showing potential, he was eliminating them."

"But he wasn't really, was he?" This time I ask Emmett.

"No, we've set up a safe house for them."

"But he said he shot you." I turn back to Jude.

"He did. It was all part of it. Just before we got to Nick, he had made contact with them, telling them about you. Ronan caught on to it, and was a step ahead. Ronan told me Nick was working for them, a spotter for the people who'd escaped from their sights."

"You knew all along?" I ask. Jude nods his head. "You knew I was going to try and find them?"

"I was hoping you wouldn't, but when I discovered all my cash gone, I knew then you were going to bolt."

My stomach twists with regret. "I'm sorry I stole from you. I didn't know how long I was going to be out on the streets."

"I would've done the same thing," Jude replies.

"What happened next?"

"With Ronan now firmly involved with them, he was leaking information to us. Getting us pictures, the layout, codes, everything we needed to take them down," Emmett says.

"You worked together?" I scrunch my nose. "The law and the criminal." Frank chuckles from behind me, and even to my ears, the statement is ridiculous.

"Sometimes we need to sacrifice the small things for the bigger picture," Emmett says.

"How many people were killed because of them?" I ask.

"The numbers are high, and climbing."

Catherine told me there were about forty people. Was that number watered down? Suddenly, I feel sick. Vomit rises to the back of my throat. Knowing people were dying because the Facility wanted to use us to make money, makes me sick. "We were nothing but vessels for them. They were modifying us to become cash cows for them." I sigh and look down. "Makes sense they'd choose younger people to go after. We're easier to manipulate into what they wanted, and I suspect we'd be easier to threaten so they'd get what they want."

"Unfortunately, you've described them perfectly, Alexa," Emmett says, confirming everything.

"What happens to Ronan?" I ask. "I saw him being taken away in handcuffs, by your people." I point to Emmett.

"He's an informant for the FBI, *for me.* It was part of the negotiations. He'll be released soon."

"And me? What happens to me?" I ask. "Where do I go?"

"There'll be an investigation, and I can guarantee you'll be part of that investigation."

I sigh again. Great, I'm going to be poked and prodded. This has always been one of my biggest fears. I'll never live in peace, I'll never have a normal life. "Everyone will know what I can do, I'll be a circus side-show attraction. Everyone will want a piece of me, wanting to know what I can do, and what I can see." Emmett nods his head. "And the others who are like me? What will happen to them?"

I'll forever be forced to prove my ability by skeptics and believers alike. Some will say I'm lying, other's will say I'm Satan's spawn for being able to see the future. Regardless of what happens to the people who did this to me, *I* will forever be an outcast.

"The same as you. But no one we've encountered so far is quite like you."

I narrow my eyes at him, intrigued with his statement. "What do you mean?"

"You're the strongest one we know of. The others aren't anywhere near able to do what you can. Their powers vary, but you, you're the holy grail in all of this."

"I am?" I look to Jude, then turn to see Frank's reaction, who's smiling.

I don't feel like smiling, I feel like hiding away forever.

"You are, and to them, you'd be their highest earner. But, because of Jude and Ronan, their plan is now foiled. They'll go to jail for a long time, murder being high up on the list of charges we're filing against them."

The room falls silent. My throat is parched, and my mind is filled with worry.

I'm stressing over what's going to happen to me once the media gets hold of this. My life will become a freak show. It's bad enough that I've lost my parents, and I'm infected with something for which I have no idea if there's a cure.

There really is only one thing I can do to make sure my life is as sane as it possibly can be.

Turning, I look to Jude who appears lost in his own thoughts. I wonder if he's thinking the same thing I am?

"Emmett," I say as I straighten my shoulders.

"What is it, Alexa?"

"I have a proposition for you. Something, I doubt you'll be able to refuse." Jude quickly places his hand on my thigh and squeezes. I look to him and notice his questioning gaze. He has no idea of what I'm about to offer, but this isn't about him. It's about me being able to live with myself.

Emmett's lips draw up in a smile. "I'm listening . . ."

EPILOGUE

"I DIDN'T THINK this was ever going to happen again," Dallas says as she picks at her lunch.

"Trust me, neither did I. It's only because of Jude's and Ronan's ability to think on the spot that saved me. And this is why we can sit out on the deck of this beautiful restaurant and eat lunch without the fear of anything happening."

"I have to thank you, Jude. You brought my best friend back," Dallas says as she holds her hand over her heart.

He smiles at her, and nods his head. "She's worth it."

I feel my body tingle with excitement as I grab his hand and link our fingers together.

"So . . . why did all this happen?" Dallas asks.

Both Jude and I blow out a deep breath. What a loaded question. "Well . . ." I start and look to Jude. "Basically, a doctor was trying to create a drug to suppress the memories of trauma patients. But, he ended up creating a drug that allowed people like me to be able to see snippets of the future or the past."

Dallas stares at me, her fork in midair, her mouth gaping open. She's totally invested. "And what was . . . I . . . what . . . man, I'm stumped. I don't even know what to ask."

I chuckle, and tell her what I can. "The intention was innocent to start, but when he figured out we could make him a lot of money, then it all became much more sinister. He was training the ones with the strongest power so he could hire us out to whomever had the most cash."

Dallas looks down at her plate, then back up at me. She's got a million questions to ask, but her blank expression says everything she can say. "But . . ."

"Money," I answer her unasked question.

"Ohh," she sighs.

"Problem is, his people lost track of me, and I caught the eye of people like Enzo." She visibly shudders, remembering our time together in the house of hell.

"You could've been hired out to anyone. Like terrorists, or . . ." she says, shocked by her own thought.

"That's exactly what would've happened. But, because of Jude and Ronan, it didn't get to that."

"How?" she asks.

"When we found Nick, we were suspicious," Jude answers. "Ronan is capable of a lot of things, and he found a paper trail of Nick's financials, and discovered Nick was working for them. He was a spotter. He'd move around to where they thought the rogues were, and he'd find them, gain their trust, and lure them in. If their ability was minimal, they'd kill them, because they couldn't risk being found out."

Dallas looks at Jude, then me, back to Jude and back to me. "And your ability?"

"Was one they wanted."

"Did you get rid of it?" Dallas asks. "Did they have a drug to reverse it, or did they operate to remove it?" She leans forward, captivated. Her lunch now forgotten.

"We tried, but it's integrated into my DNA. It molded itself around my chromosomes, making it impossible to get rid of without killing me."

"But, what happens if you ever want kids?" Dallas asks.

"Hey, no talk of that yet. I'm only eighteen, Dallas."

"Yeah, you might not want them now, but what if you do in

the future? What'll happen?"

I shrug my shoulders, "I don't know. But if it's in my DNA, there's a chance I'll pass it down to my kids. And I'm not sure I want to do that." Jude reassuringly squeezes my hand. It's something we've talked about, but being eighteen leaves us time to consider the options carefully.

"Wow, this is a lot to take in."

"Tell me about it." I chuckle and look down at my water, just staring at it.

"If you can't get rid of it, how are you coping?"

Ronan approaches the table and hands me his phone. "Alexa, you have a call."

"Excuse me," I say to Dallas and lift the phone to my ear. "Hello, this is Alexa."

"There'll be a jet waiting for you in half an hour. Ronan told me about your lunch, and I'm sorry, but we need you."

"Okay," I reply. I end the call and hand the phone back to Ronan. "I'm sorry, Dallas, but we have to go."

"Work?" Jude asks. I nod my head. Jude calls over the waiter and asks for our check.

"Work? Where are you working?" Dallas asks. "I feel like I don't even know you, Alexa. So much is happening with you. All I'm doing is going to college, *boring.*"

We both stand, and head out while Jude pays for our lunch. "So much has happened, but when I get back, I promise I'll fill you in with everything. I know today's been interrupted, and I'm so sorry, but we have to go."

"Promise me, the moment you can, call me or come see me. Promise," Dallas begs.

"I promise." She hugs me and I sneak in a quick vision. She's driving down the interstate staring out the window, not concentrating on the road. Suddenly, a deer runs out in front of her, and she slams on the brakes, but it's too late. She collides with the deer. I break contact with Dallas, and pull away from her. Turning to Ronan, I call him over.

"You okay?" he asks.

"Can you drive her back to the dorm? She's going to hit a deer on the interstate and have a car accident. Can you get her there?"

"I can," he smiles at me.

Jude joins us, having paid our bill. Ronan throws him the keys to our car. "Why am I driving?" he asks Ronan.

"Alexa asked me to drive Dallas home."

"I can drive myself," Dallas interjects. "Now that I know I'll have an accident, I'll be more careful."

I look to Jude, and say, "She's going to be distracted by everything we've told her, I asked Ronan to take her home."

Jude turns to Ronan. "Call Frank and have him come pick you up." Ronan's already on the phone as Jude gives him his instructions.

"I can drive myself," Dallas tries to protest again.

"I know, but I need you to trust me." I give her another hug. "Love you, Dallas. Promise not to give Ronan too much of a hard time, he's a good guy."

"I heard that," Ronan says.

"Okay, give him a hard time." I kiss Dallas on the cheek, and she hugs me tightly.

"I will." She sniggers. "Promise me, you'll call." She points at me as she walks backward to her car.

"Promise." I cross my heart.

Ronan opens the passenger door, and waits until Dallas is in, before he makes his way over to the driver's side.

When we're both in the car, Jude starts toward the hangar. "You okay? You didn't get a lot of time with Dallas and I know how much you were looking forward to seeing her."

"After this one, I need some time off. I need to regroup and get my head together."

"We can go for a vacation, anywhere you want."

I lean my head back against the headrest and look out the window. "Problem is, anywhere we go, they'll always want me.

I just need some time. Can we go to an island somewhere? Just us? No phones?" I'm hopeful, but I know what I'm asking is impossible.

"I'll arrange it." The silence in the car gives me a few moments to think. Closing my eyes, I center myself. I need to get into the right headspace.

But I can feel the turmoil coming from Jude. Placing my hand on his lap, I force myself into a vision. He's in his office, and Ronan is sitting opposite him. Both look concerned. "I'll always protect her," Ronan says.

"I know, but I hate that I told you to beat her. It kills me every time I look into her eyes. Knowing what we had to put her through." He's feeling guilty for the way Ronan treated me, just before the FBI arrested everyone at the Facility.

It's all I need to see to know this is a common theme with him and Ronan. They hated having to put me through that, but it had to be done. I take myself out of the vision, and come back to the present. "It's okay, I know why he did it. There's no need to feel guilty, Jude. He did what he had to in order for them to trust him. I don't hold it against either of you."

"I told him to put on a show for them."

"If he didn't, he would've been dead, and I'd be hired out to everyone on the black-market. I get it, and I appreciate everything you've both done for me."

"Can you get out of my head now?" He smirks as he says that.

"Maybe," I tease.

When we get to the hangar, the jet is already waiting for us.

Jude and I approach the stairs, where the first thing I see is Kimberley's flaming red hair. "Hello, Kimberley," I say to our regular flight attendant.

"Miss Murphy, Mr. Caley, welcome aboard." She smiles and directs us up the stairs.

We get into the plane, and Kimberley enters. "How far?" I ask.

"Short flight today, ma'am. We'll be there in under forty

minutes."

We buckle up, and before we know it, we're in the air. I need to be in the right frame of mind before I get to work. Concentrating now makes my job much easier when I get to it. I can focus better, and get into the subject's head with more accuracy and precision.

"Lexi." Jude brings me out of my intense concentration.

"What is it?" I turn to face him.

"You remember the nurse?"

"Hayley?" He nods his head. "Yeah, I do. How can I forget? Her murder was the first vision I saw." Her death still haunts me, and images of the guy with the scar still wake me at night sometimes.

"He's no longer a threat." I know it's wrong of me, but instant relief washes over me. I'm torn at my reaction. The police never found him, and declared the case cold a few months after her death. Jude stepped in and dealt with him in his own way, and even though I hate that he did, I'm also grateful to get scum like Hayley's murderer off our streets.

"Thank you," I say. Jude turns to look out the window, and I close my eyes, somewhat relieved to know I'll be able to sleep better at nights.

"We're here." Jude squeezes my thigh, bringing me back to reality.

"Thanks." I smile at him.

The jet comes to a stop, and Kimberley opens the door. "We'll be here when you return," she says offering us a kind and genuine smile.

"Thank you," Jude says as we head over to the town car waiting for us.

"Miss Murphy, Mr. Caley." The driver nods as he waits for us to slide into the back.

The ride is quick and I don't get to see too much of the scenery. I can't, I need to concentrate. The driver pulls the car up to an underground parking lot, and when we leave the car, we head to the elevator.

Jude and I have been here before, so we know where we're going. The elevator door opens, and I press the button for the nineteenth floor. The doors open, and there's a woman waiting for us by the door. "Alexa, I'm Sara, how was your flight?"

"Good, thanks. Where am I going?" I can't waste time on pleasantries, I need to stay focused so I can get the clearest picture possible.

"I'll take you to him." She leads me down a hall, and brings me to a room with a huge two-way mirror. She knocks once on the glass, and Emmett looks up.

He stands and comes to the door. Opening it, he leaves the room and catches me leaning on the wall opposite. "I'm glad you made it."

I walk over to Emmett and give him a hug. He's become such an integral part of my life since he rescued me. "So, what do we have?" I ask looking at the man sitting in the interrogation room. "Oh, I recognize him. He's a politician."

"He is, and he says he didn't kill his wife."

"Do you think he did?" I ask looking to Emmett.

"Alexa, truthfully in all my years of experience, everything tells me no. But, I never go against my gut, and my gut says yes."

I shake my head at him. "I suppose being an assistant director has its perks."

"The biggest perk is you. I've never had more job satisfaction than when we started working together. Now, can you help?"

Jude scoffs from behind me, and we both look over at him. "Can she help? Seriously? She'll solve your case in two minutes' flat."

"I think she'll solve it in one minute," Emmett arrogantly replies.

"Thirty seconds," I add.

"I'll take that bet," Jude says. I turn and give him a death stare. "Actually, no, I won't," he quickly retracts his words.

"Do you want me to arrest him, Alexa? I'll be happy to stick some cuffs on him and throw his ass in jail."

Looking at Jude, I wink at him. "Maybe next time." Emmett and Jude have an understanding. Jude's not above the law. And if Emmett needs to, he'll go after him. So far, Jude hasn't given him a reason. Taking a deep breath, I look to the man sitting in the room on the other side of the mirror. "What's the time frame?" I ask, turning to face Emmett.

"He called 911 four hours ago, but I think we're looking about five hours to when the murder took place."

"Okay." I shrug out of my jacket, and hand it to Jude.

"You ready?" Emmett asks. I give him a nod. He opens the door, and we head into the interrogation room. "Senator Wagner, I'd like to introduce you to a colleague of mine. This is Alexa."

The aging senator stands, and offers me his hand. His eyes roam my body, and instantly I get a dislike for him. He's sleazy, and disgusting. My stomach knots as my hands become clammy.

I reach for his hand, and the moment I touch it, I force my way into his visions. Standing in the present, I rewind his actions. Everything he's done for the last few hours. It's like I'm watching a movie in reverse. He walks backward, talks backward, does everything, *backward.*

I get to where he makes the 911 phone call, and rewind the vision further.

Stopping the vision at what I need to see, I watch as it unfolds in front of me.

She's in the kitchen, stacking the dishwasher and crying. Her tears fall from her cheeks, as she sobs. She stops stacking the dishwasher and looks over to the counter, where there's a photo of the senator with another woman. A woman who'd be at least thirty years his junior. They're in a compromising position. His wife's cries tear at me. She's heartbroken by the explicit image and her husband's betrayal.

I can feel the hurt in her heart, and how much shame it's bringing to her. The door closes, and his wife wipes at her cheeks with the back of her hand.

"I'm home; get me a drink," he barks at her.

She leaves the dishwasher, walks over to the bar, and pours him a drink. He's sitting at the head of the dining table, reading over something on his tablet. "Here you go," she places the drink down on a coaster on the rich mahogany table.

He blindly grabs for it, but instead he knocks it over. "Clean it up," he roars toward her. He looks up and sees her crying, he rolls his eyes and grumbles loudly. What an asshole. "Why are you crying?"

"Nothing," she automatically responds.

"I said, why are you crying?"

"It doesn't matter."

He stands and walks over to the kitchen, he notices the photo lying on the counter. "Where did you get this?" he asks.

She shrugs her shoulders slowly. "I don't know. It was delivered to me today."

"Have you been spying on me?" He storms over toward her and grabs her arms. She briskly shakes her head. "You lying bitch." He hits her across the face.

She grasps at her face and yelps out in pain. The sting echoes through to me.

"I promise, I haven't been spying."

He grabs her again, this time throwing her against the sofa. He charges after her, kneels over her body and wraps his hands around her throat. "You stupid bitch!" he yells in her face.

His hands tighten around her neck, I struggle to breathe, feeling everything she's feeling. His grip tightens. His eyes are filled with fury, his body shaking with rage.

"Please," she struggles to plead.

He tightens his grip.

"Can't . . . breathe," she begs for her life. "I . . ." Her eyes roll to the back of her head, and her body goes limp beneath his.

He continues to squeeze his hands around her neck, shaking her lifeless body.

He continues for a few more seconds, and I struggle to get my own breath.

When he lets go of her, he looks down at his dead wife. "Shit, what have I done?" he mumbles softly to himself. "Sweetheart?" He grabs her by the shoulders and shakes her limp body. "Sweetheart?" he says again.

He gets off the sofa, and paces nervously.

"Shit, shit, shit," he mumbles as he keeps pacing. Raking his hand through his thinning hair he looks around the room. Stopping his back and forth, he looks over to the kitchen counter. He grabs the incriminating photo and stuffs it in his pocket.

He's in panic mode now. I've seen it in other cases I've worked on. It's what they all do when they kill out of anger; they go into a panic and try to conceal their involvement.

I watch as the senator frantically tries to cover his act of violence by cleaning up the crime scene. When he finishes cleaning the spilled drink, he heads out to the backyard, where he lights the grill, takes the photo out of his pocket, and holds it over the fire.

He leaves the picture to burn, turns off the grill, and heads back inside. I stand over the picture, and watch as the flame dies out before the picture is fully destroyed. The top quarter is still intact. You can clearly make out faces, his and the other woman's in throes of passion. The breeze picks up the light paper and flies it away to lodge on one of the shrubs lining the fence.

I make my way back inside to find the senator cleaning everything again. He's finished stacking the dishwasher, and now he's stuffing the envelope the photo arrived in down the garbage disposal. He runs the water, making sure it's gone.

It's all I need to see.

He killed her, and he's trying to make it look like he didn't.

I take myself out of the past, and bring myself to the present.

"The pleasure is all mine, Senator," I say as I let go of his hand and head toward the door. Turning to Emmett I smile. "He killed her. He choked her on the sofa. He spilled his drink on the dining room table, and noticed she was crying. She was crying because someone sent her a photo of him and some young woman having sex. He tried to burn the photo out on the grill. Only, not all of it burned. You'll find part of it stuck in the shrubs in front of the fence."

The senator's face droops, his eyes wide, and his mouth gaping. "How . . . ?"

"He used to beat her too; she was frightened of him. He's a piece of shit. I'm sure he'll be welcomed in jail."

I walk out of the room and close the door behind me.

Jude smiles and casually drapes my jacket over my shoulders. Reaching for his hand, I choose to hold back on being in his vision.

I'm rapidly becoming an expert in my ability. I can see the future, and I now have the ability to see in the past. I once thought what I was given was a gift, then I hated it and thought it was a curse.

But now I know exactly what I am.

I *am* lethal.

THE END

ACKNOWLEDGEMENTS

When I finished my first book, *HiT 149,* I got an idea for a story about a seventeen-year-old girl who walks past a man and sees his future. That was the entire premise. I thought to myself, Margaret, you're delusional, because no one will want to read a book about a teenage girl.

Fast forward to today, four years after *HiT 149,* and I've completed a story about a seventeen-year-old girl who walks past a man and sees his future. This has been an amazing journey for me, because I've come to learn so much about myself and writing.

I love pushing boundaries, and I love how my readers can all be taken on a ride with me. These two books are no different. I've never written urban fantasy, and I had no idea if I *could* write it.

But what I do know is how much I love these characters.

Alexa is what I love about all my female leads. She's strong, she's sassy, she's brave, and she won't stop fighting for what she believes in.

As an author, I don't get much choice in what I write. I let my characters tell the story. I'm simply the medium they use to communicate. I've been asked why I don't stick to one genre when writing. The answer is simple. I can't. I want to allow my characters to tell me the story they want to tell. To open themselves and give me all of them, so I can share them with you.

I hope you've enjoyed The Gift and The Curse as much as I did creating them. To my readers, existing and new, thank you for being here with me. If it wasn't for you wanting to read my books, I doubt my characters would be as vocal as they are.

I also really want to say thank you to some important people who've made my voyage in the authoring world exceptionally fun and meaningful.

To my dear editor who's been a part of making these books read the best they can. Debi Orton, you put up with me and my Aussie terms, and help convert them into American terms everyone can understand. You're always there if I need to ask a question. You take my words, and make them beautiful without changing the voice of my characters.

To my sweet formatter, Tami Norman from Integrity Formatting. Boy, doesn't she do an amazing job to bring my words to life? She spends hours finding the right images to fit the stories, and always presents them in the most gorgeous of ways.

To my girls, my proofreaders. Terry, Cheryl, Sam and Mandy. Thank you for taking the time to read my books and send me any errors we may have missed. Having you on board has been wonderful.

To Kylie from Give Me Books. Kylie works tirelessly to help me promote my books for cover reveal and release day blitzes. Kylie always manages to fit me in whenever I ask her, and for that I'm so grateful.

To Kellie from Book Cover by Design. Just WOW. I sent her an image of what I wanted for The Gift and The Curse, and she told me it wasn't going to work. So, she came back with something else, and that something else was by far the best covers I've seen. She is amazing, and incredibly talented.

To Jodi. *Jodi, Jodi, Jodi.* She's my sounding board, and the one who reins me in when the sadistic part of me wants to make my characters bleed. She's there on the end of the phone, telling me off for putting my characters through hell. She's a pretty cool chick, she'll keep.

To my family. My mum, husband, and kids. You guys put up with all my craziness, and let me go off on my own tangents when my brain won't stop thinking and the voices keep talking.

Family is important, but most of all, *my* family is the most important thing to me. I write these books knowing my kids will read them, and I hope I can make them proud of the words on the paper.

To my good friends who are always there when I need something. Lyndal, Bek, Terry, Megan, and Tina. I love you girls. You always have my back. I'm truly blessed to have you in my life.

To two girls who always have my back, and are there when I need them. Anna and Kimmy.

But lastly, to you. You make the voices in my head happy. You make my heart sing. YOU are the reason I write.

'Til next time.

Margaret

Keep reading for a preview of
Dying Wish
Mistrust; and
Ugly

Dying WISH

Margaret McHeyzer
New York Times Bestseller

Prologue

As I lie in my bed, with only the persistent ticking of the wall clock to keep me company, memories of the night I fell in love flood every fiber of my being.

It could have been destiny, or fate, or perhaps it was my life path. Whatever it was, it was meant to be.

We were meant to be.

A smile slowly stretches my face and remembered happiness pushes the dull ache down deep inside.

That night my mind tried to reason with me, telling me soulmates didn't exist. That night, my heart spoke back to define what a soulmate truly is. Sometimes they come in the form of a partner, sometimes in the form of a friend.

I was one of the lucky ones to have two soulmates: my beautiful and incredibly spirited best friend, Becky, and my handsome boyfriend, Elijah.

Not only were they my soulmates, I was theirs.

And this is our story . . .

MISTRUST

NEW YORK TIMES BESTSELLER
MARGARET MCHEYZER

PROLOGUE

TRUST IS SOMETHING that has to be earned. It's not freely given.

There are some people in our lives we automatically trust. We believe everything our parents say and do. We know their actions and instincts are always to protect and teach us.

We learn to trust those with whom we develop a bond of friendship.

Strangers don't have our trust. We're wary of them; we keep them at arm's length until they prove themselves to us.

Trust, once earned, can also be ripped away. That can happen over a period of time or in an instant.

Tonight I'll discover how cruel the world can be when trust is brutally torn away…

UGLY

New York Times Bestseller

Margaret McHeyzer

PROLOGUE

IT'S DAYS LIKE TODAY I wish I was dead.

"Lily Anderson, you get your ugly ass out here right this minute. Don't make me come after you," Daddy screams.

He's so angry. I knew the moment I heard him come home from work I was in for it. I was in my bedroom, lying on the floor trying to do my math. He slammed the front door so hard the windows in my room shook.

And then I knew, I knew I was in for it.

"Lily Anderson!" he yells again.

As soon as I heard him yell I ran to my hiding spot. I'm inside the closet in the hallway, wedged as far into the corner as I can get. Mom's old coat hangs in front of me and I can still smell a faint waft of the perfume she used to wear.

"Lily Anderson!" he shouts. I can hear the anger in his voice and I can already feel the pain he's going to inflict on me when he opens the closet door. I know what's coming.

I close my eyes tight, scrunching them up so no light can seep through. I put my hands over my ears so I can't hear him.

"I swear to God; if I have to find you, you will not sit for a month."

My knees are folded into my chest. I'm trying to make myself small, invisible, so he forgets I'm here. I'm rocking myself, trying to block out what he's saying.

School is safe. School is safe. School is safe. I keep repeating the mantra because in a few short hours I'll be back at school. Maybe tomorrow I can go to the library after school, stay there until it closes and then sneak in after Dad's passed out, because he's had too much to drink.

It was never like this before.

I'm twelve years old and I can remember when Mom, Dad, and I were all happy. But that was years ago. It's been a long time since there's been any happiness in this house.

Well, before Mom died, and not a day since.

Mom died when I was nine. I don't remember much about her, except I remember her telling me how ugly I am. How life would be better if I were taken away from them. How I'll never be anything, because I'm stupid and ugly.

Sometimes I dream happy things. Like me, Mom, Dad and a little blond-haired boy all going for a picnic. The sun beamed down on us as we played outside and laughed. We'd eat yummy sandwiches Mom made for us, and we'd drink homemade lemonade. We'd spend hours outside, laughing and talking and just having fun. Mom would tell me how pretty I am, and how much she loved me. She would play with my hair, braid it, and then we'd go and pick bright flowers to take home and put in a vase. Dad would smile and call us "his girls", always kissing Mom and hugging me. Dad would put the little boy on his shoulders and run around the park, trying to catch the clouds.

I love those dreams, and I hold onto them; wishing they were real. But I've never had a mom like that, and my dad doesn't talk much unless it's with his fists, or to tell me how ugly and useless I am.

I feel him walking around the house. The floorboards creak and the vibrations from his footsteps come through the floor to where my bottom is. I close my eyes tighter and try and breathe as quietly as I can.

Please go away, Daddy. Please go away.

My heart is beating so fast. My hands are shaking and I'm trying really hard not to think about what's going to happen the minute he opens the closet door.

Shhh, it's so quiet. The only sound is my heart thrumming in my ears. Nothing else. Not a whisper, not a rattle…nothing.

Maybe Daddy's left. Maybe he's gone to the pub to have a few drinks. Maybe, just maybe, he's left...forever.

I take a deep breath and just relax for a moment. My shoulders drop and I finally stop rocking.

Slowly I take my hands down from my ears, and I'm so happy because I can't hear him yelling at me. I can't hear him at all.

Gradually, I begin to unscrunch my eyes from the way I've tightly closed them. But something's not right. There's light coming into the closet.

I don't even get a chance to open them fully before a rough hand reaches in, latches onto my ponytail and yanks.

"I told you it'd be worse for you if I had to find you," Dad says, as he drags me out of the closet by my hair.

I'm desperately trying to hold onto my head so he doesn't rip my hair out. My feet are trying to find traction on the dirty floorboards.

"Please, Daddy. Please. You're hurting me," I begin sobbing as I plead with him.

"Then your ugly ass should've come when I called you, you stupid bitch. You're fucking worthless, you ugly idiot," he says. But now his voice is calm as he continues to drag me toward the family room.

That's when he's most scary. When his voice is low and his eyes are filled with hate.

He throws me against the side of the sofa and takes a step back to look at me.

I look up and can see he's the angriest I've ever seen him. "You dumb, ugly piece of shit," he says, as he paces back and forth in front of me.

"Sorry, Daddy. Whatever I did, I'm so sorry." I cower into myself, trying to make myself as small as possible.

"You're just too fucking stupid, aren't you?" he spits toward me as he brings his hand up to scratch at his chin.

"I'm sorry," I say again. Tears are falling hot and fast down my cheeks. My head hurts from where he was pulling my hair, but I don't dare try to rub the spot.

"You ugly fuck." He kicks a boot into my leg.

The pain is instant and my leg feels like it's shattered. "Please, Daddy," I beg again, burying my face into my hands.

But 'please' never seems to work.

Nothing does.

I've just got to take the beatings, because that's what stupid, ugly girls do.

ALSO BY
Margaret McHeyzer

Dying Wish

I have three major loves in my life: my family, my best friend Becky, and ballet. Elijah Turner is quickly becoming the fourth.

He's been around as long as I can remember. But now he's much more than just the annoying guy at school.

My life was working out perfectly...until it got turned upside down.

Mistrust

I'm the popular girl at school.

The one everyone wants to be friends with.

I have the best boyfriend in the world, who's on the basketball team.

My parents adore me, and I absolutely love them. My sister and I have a great relationship too.

I'm a cheerleader, I have a high GPA and I'm liked even by the teachers.

It was a night which promised to be filled with love and fun until…something happened which changed everything.

Ugly

This is a dark YA/NA standalone, full-length novel. Contains violence and some explicit language

If I were dead, I wouldn't be able to see.
If I were dead, I wouldn't be able to feel.
If I were dead, he'd never raise his hand to me again.
If I were dead, his words wouldn't cut as deep as they do.
If I were dead, I'd be beautiful and I wouldn't be so...ugly.
I'm not dead...but I wish I was.

Chef Pierre

Holly Walker had everything she'd ever dreamed about – a happy marriage and being mum to beautiful brown-eyed Emma - until an accident nineteen months ago tore her world apart. Now she's a widow and single mother to a boisterous little 7-year-old girl, looking for a new start. Ready to take the next step, Holly has found herself a job as a maître d' at Table One, a once-acclaimed restaurant in the heart of Sydney. But one extremely arrogant Frenchman isn't going to be easy to work with...

Twenty years ago, Pierre LeRoux came to Australia, following the stunning Aussie girl he'd fallen in love with and married. He and his wife put their personal lives on hold, determined for Pierre to take Sydney's culinary society by storm. Just as his bright star was on the upswing, tragedy claimed the woman he was hopelessly in love with. He had been known as a Master Chef, but since his wife's death he has become known as a monster chef.

Can two broken people rebuild their lives and find happiness once more?

Smoke and Mirrors

Words can trick us.

Smoke obscures objects on the edge of our vision.

A mirror may reflect, but the eye sees what it wants.

A delicate scent can evoke another time and place, a memory from the past.

And a sentence can deceive you, even as you read it.

Grit

****Recommended for 18 years and over****

Alpha MC Prez Jaeger Dalton wants the land that was promised to him.

Sassy Phoenix Ward isn't about to let anyone take Freedom Run away from her.

He'll protect what's his.

She'll protect what's hers.

Jaeger is an arrogant ass, but he wants nothing more than Phoenix.

Phoenix is stubborn and headstrong, and she wants Jaeger out of her life.

Her father lost the family farm to gambling debts, but Jaeger isn't the only one who has a claim to the property.

Sometimes it's best to let things go.

But sometimes it's better to fight until the very end.

Yes, Master

***** THIS PROLOGUE CONTAINS DISTRESSING CONTENT. IT IS ONLY SUITED FOR READERS OVER 18. *****

ALSO CONTAINS M/M, M/M/F, M/F AND F/F SCENES.

My uncle abused me.

I was 10 years old when it started.

At 13 he told me I was no longer wanted because I had started to develop.

At 16 I was ready to kill him.

Today, I'm broken.

Today, I only breathe to survive.

My name's Sergeant Major Ryan Jenkins and today, I'm ready to tell you my story.

A Life Less Broken

****CONTAINS DISTRESSING CONTENT. 18+****

On a day like any other, Allyn Sommers went off to work, not knowing that her life was about to be irrevocably and horrifically altered.

Three years later, Allyn is still a prisoner in her own home, held captive by harrowing fear. Broken and damaged, Allyn seeks help from someone that fate put in her path.

Dr. Dominic Shriver is a psychiatrist who's drawn to difficult cases. He must push past his own personal battles to help Allyn fight her monsters and nightmares.

Is Dr. Shriver the answer to her healing?

Can Allyn overcome being broken?

My Life for Yours

He's lived a life of high society and privilege; he chose to follow in his father's footsteps and become a Senator.

She's lived a life surrounded with underworld activity; she had no choice but to follow in her father's footsteps and take on the role of Mob Boss.

He wants to stamp out organized crime and can't be bought off.

She's the ruthless and tough Mob Boss where in her world all lines are blurred.

Their lives are completely different, two walks of life on the opposite ends of the law.

Being together doesn't make sense.

But being apart isn't an option

HiT Series Box Set

HiT 149

Anna Brookes is not your typical teenager. Her walls are not adorned with posters of boy bands or movie stars. Instead posters from Glock, Ruger, and Smith & Wesson grace her bedroom. Anna's mother abandoned her at birth, and her father, St. Cloud Police Chief Henry Brookes, taught her how to shoot and coached her to excellence. On Anna's fifteenth birthday, unwelcome guests join the celebration, and Anna's world is never the same. You'll meet the world's top assassin, 15, and follow her as she discovers the one hit she's not sure she can complete - Ben Pearson, the current St. Cloud Police Chief and a man with whom Anna has explosive sexual chemistry. Enter a world of intrigue, power, and treachery as Anna takes on old and new enemies, while falling in love with the one man with whom she can't have a relationship.

Anna Brookes in Training

Find out what happened to transform the fifteen-year-old Anna Brookes, the Girl with the Golden Aim, into the deadly assassin 15. After her father is killed and her home destroyed, orphan Anna Brookes finds herself homeless in Gulf Breeze, Florida. After she saves Lukas from a deadly attack, he takes her in and begins to train her in the assassin's craft. Learn how Lukas's unconventional training hones Anna's innate skills until she is as deadly as her mentor.

HiT for Freedom

Anna has decided to break off her steamy affair with Ben Pearson and leave St. Cloud, when she suspects a new threat to him. Katsu Vang is rich, powerful, and very interested in Anna. He's also evil to his core. Join Anna as she plays a dangerous game, getting closer to Katsu to discover his real purpose, while trying to keep Ben safe. Secrets are exposed and the future Anna hoped for is snatched from her grasp. Will Ben be able to save her?

HiT to Live

In the conclusion to the Anna Brookes saga, Ben and his sister Emily, with the help of Agent rescue Anna. For Anna and Ben, it's time to settle scores…and a time for the truth between them. From Sydney to the Philippines and back to the States, they take care of business. But a helpful stranger enters Anna's life, revealing more secrets…and a plan that Anna wants no part of. Can Anna and Ben shed their old lives and start a new one together, or will Anna's new-found family ruin their chances at a happily-ever-after?

Binary Law (co-authored)

Ellie Andrews has been receiving tutoring from Blake McCarthy for three years to help her improve her grades so she can get into one of the top universities to study law. And she's had a huge crush on him since she can remember.

Blake McCarthy is the geek at school that's had a crush on Ellie since the day he met her.

In their final tutoring session, Blake and Ellie finally become brave enough to take the leap of faith.

But, life has other plans and rips them apart. Six years later Blake and his best friends Ben and Billy have built a successful internet platform company 3BCubed, while Ellie is a successful and hardworking lawyer specializing in Corporate Law.

3BCubed is being threatened with a devastatingly large plagiarism case and when it lands on their lawyers desk, it's handed to the new Corporate Lawyer to handle and win.

Coincidence or perhaps fate will see Blake and Ellie pushed back together.

Binary Law will have Blake and Ellie propelled into a life that's a whirl wind of catastrophic events and situations where every emotion will be touched. Hurt will be experienced, happiness will be presented and love will be evident. But is that enough for Blake and Ellie be able to live out their own happily ever after?

Printed in Great Britain
by Amazon

25178226R10141